ALSO BY
KIRSTY McKAY

The Assassin Game

Have You Seen My Sister?

PRAISE FOR
THE ASSASSIN GAME

"McKay keeps things ambiguous so that readers will continue guessing until the true culprit is revealed in the climactic scene. Her witty, self-deprecating voice captures the thrill of belonging and the complicated emotions that come with new money. Smart, edge-of-the-seat thrills."

—*Kirkus Reviews*

"Umfraville Hall, an exclusive boarding school on the windswept Welsh island of Skola, is an ideal setting for a mystery that takes a few cues from Agatha Christie's *And Then There Were None*... McKay (*Undead*) pokes a bit of fun at teen angst, using Cate's wry voice to tell this twisty whodunit."

—*Publishers Weekly*

"McKay's world-building is top notch, and the suspense palpable."

—*Booklist*

"Red herrings abound in this page-turner... The fast-moving plot will motivate readers to sort through the many characters, guess at their motives, and spot the real criminal."

—*VOYA Magazine*

"Perfect for readers looking for a good 'scary' novel... *The Assassin Game* has the perfect amount of romance, suspense, and action to make for a wonderful read."

—*TeenReads*

"An exhilarating thriller from start to finish, this action-packed book is full of betrayals, mystery, and heartbreak. Both the Game and Cate's love life kept us guessing until the end."

—*Justine Magazine*

PRAISE FOR
HAVE YOU SEEN MY SISTER?

"A packed-to-the-gills mystery laden with surprises."

—*Publishers Weekly*

"A fast-paced, twisty read that will keep readers guessing until the very end."

—*School Library Journal*

"Mystery with a lot of action and intrigue."

—*Youth Services Book Review*

"This fast-paced mystery will keep readers guessing until the very end."

—*Kirkus Reviews*

SEVEN ALL ALONE

SEVEN ALL ALONE

KIRSTY McKAY

sourcebooks
fire

Published by Sourcebooks Fire, an imprint of Sourcebooks
1935 Brookdale RD, Naperville, IL 60563-2773
(630) 961-3900
sourcebooks.com

Cataloging-in-Publication Data is on file with the Library of Congress.

Printed and bound in the United States of America.
PAH 10 9 8 7 6 5 4 3 2 1

For Ma,
because she's always
shown me the way home.

PROLOGUE

The sun was shining brightly the morning the bus driver kidnapped Maggie Atkins. As the bus door opened, she jumped up the steps happily, taking them both in one huge leap—the only six-year-old in her class tall enough to do so—and the driver was sitting there, staring at her. He didn't usually look directly at any of them, least of all her.

"Good morning, Margaret. I hope you are well."

He spoke with an accent unlike Maggie's and he said the words carefully, as if he had practiced them. Maggie felt her cheeks burn. This was odd. It was only the second time he had spoken in the few weeks that he'd been driving her. The "bus" was a small minivan, with nine seats, six of which were occupied with her classmates from the tiny village school.

"It is chilly, but it is going to be a beautiful day."

Maggie nodded, because her mother told her always to be nice.

The only other time she could remember the driver speaking was the very first day. She didn't fit into the booster seats, so the driver had suggested to her mother that she ride up front with him. It would be legal and perfectly safe, he explained, because of her unusual height and weight. She was big enough.

It was the only time that being bigger felt like a good thing.

Maggie loved being up front and on her own during the bus journeys. It was a twenty-minute ride past some of Scotland's most picturesque mountain vistas, but of course at six years old, she didn't care about any of that. She loved the calm, because things often got rowdy behind her.

There were Lawrence and Sebastian, the McTavish twins, always taking up the back row, throwing pencils and fighting with each other. Maggie's best friend, Ben, sat beside Nicholas in the middle, and swapped LEGO blocks and Pokémon, and the other girls, Stephanie and Antonia, were mismatched seat buddies in the front row—if and when Antonia could be persuaded to sit down and buckle up.

The driver mostly ignored them; he listened to jazz, or hymns, or nothing at all, and he chewed gum but without the gross noises, or he whistled, but quietly, concentrating hard on the winding country road. Maggie felt comfortable with that.

She felt comfortable on the sunlit, frosty October morning too, even when the bus took a different route, and the journey went on longer than it ever had before. Even when the driver parked halfway up a dirt road and gestured for them to get out. She trusted him.

All of the kids on the bus were the same. Sure, Nicholas whimpered for his stuffed elephant, and Stephanie asked a dozen times where they were going. Nevertheless, they all went along with the driver as he herded them up the long, steep mountain trail and, finally, into the dark and damp-smelling cave.

And although Maggie was a bright kid, she suspected nothing sinister, until she tentatively informed the driver that she had to pee, and he showed her the bucket. That's when she knew.

For three days and nights he held them captive in the cave, on the dark side of the mountain. He did not speak to them. He screamed when the others escaped and abandoned Maggie, but even then, it was noise, something guttural and terrifying, beyond language. It was only when the screams ended that he found his words.

He dragged Maggie out of the cave to the cliff face, showed her the bloodred moon, and told her that God wanted her dead, and that surprised her, because she'd always been taught that God loved her. It was then the driver sang to her, pulled her to the ledge, and told her what they were going to do. They were going to jump.

Oh when the moon
Oh when the moon
Oh when the moon turns red with blood
Oh Lord I want to be in that number

Oh when the saints go marching in

His breath was sour and sweet as he gripped her arms tight and sang on. The sun was low in the sky, the blood moon rising, and Maggie couldn't see the bottom of the cliff through the mist. What could she do? If God hated her, and her friends had deserted her, she knew she only had herself.

As the driver lifted her off her feet, Maggie sank her teeth into his hand and felt the loose skin move against muscle and bone. She bit as hard as she could, for longer than she wanted to, until something gave, and she tasted blood.

The driver yelled and tried to shake her off. Why did he care? He was about to throw them both off the cliff, what did it matter if he had to endure a moment's pain before they hit the ground together, hundreds of feet below? Maybe he couldn't help it, maybe it was just reflex.

Whatever the cause, his hesitation was enough. She broke free, and as he fell backward beyond the point of no return, they locked eyes again, just for a second, and his eyes spoke to her, of desperation, of fear, and of lost hope. His eyes were begging Maggie to save him.

But it was too late for that, of course.

CHAPTER 1

———

I have the worst luck.

When my mother told me *enjoy your trip*, she didn't mean the kind where you fall flat on your face. But being me, I did that anyway.

The café is an assault of bright lights and bacon smells after the frigid cold of the October morning. As I enter, my eyes still bleary with sleep, it happens. One of my dinner-plate feet catches on the trailing strap of a backpack stashed haphazardly by the door, and before I can help myself, I jerk forward, falling out of control.

Shit!

My hands slap the hard floor, and I die inside.

Get up, quick, Maggie! Before they notice!

I scramble upright, palms stinging, looking across to the half-dozen tables by the steamy windows. That's where my classmates are assembled. Did I get away with it?

A tentative yes. The air is thick with random shouted banter, and tinny, E-rated hip-hop blasts from someone's phone. Like I wasn't anxious enough already. A harassed, middle-aged waitress gruffly doles out breakfast sandwiches, which are duly examined and consumed, or, in one case, thrown across the room. The gang's all here—there'll be seven of us in total—and luckily zero of them have seen me wipe out. Everyone is the star of their own movie, and blissfully oblivious to me.

But as I turn toward the serving counter, I realize I'm wrong. Someone is watching. We lock eyes.

Ben.

How could I have missed him? My former best friend, my ex, the one person I really didn't want to see me do anything dumb. He's only a few feet away, ketchup in hand, staring at me like he had no idea I was even going to be here. *Faker.* Of course he knew. A hint of emotion flickers across his face, and it freezes my heart. He could have picked snide, gotcha amusement, or disdain, or terrible indifference, but it's way worse than any of those: he looks *guilty.* Like he's responsible, like he actually pushed me to the floor himself. But that's ridiculous. I did this to me, didn't I, Ben? Like I always do.

"Help me with these bags, Maggie!"

My dad, shouting from outside. I break from Ben's gaze, and experience the rare sensation of being genuinely pleased to hear my father barking orders. *Okay, let it go; there's work to be done.* I exit, grab more backpacks, and haul them inside. I can do this. I can zombie through the motions for the next four days like I don't care about Ben, and don't care that he doesn't care about me. But am I convincing anyone? Nope. Not even myself.

Woman up, Maggie. You've had over a year to get used to being around these kids again. You'll always be the homeschooled kid, you'll always be the teacher's daughter. Suck it up. Nobody cares about your little non-rom-com psychodrama anyway.

"That's the last of it."

My dad, aka Mr. Atkins, math teacher and designated group leader for this hell hike, drops yet another pack on the floor, smiling tightly and vaguely at the assembled teens. *God.* It's so important to him this trip goes well, it's excruciating. Redemption, personal and professional. Sad that his enthusiasm is not shared by the rest of us. A hiking trip in the Scottish Highland mountains? Pick me, said absolutely no one currently present. But it's a school-mandated "Enrichment Week," and frankly we all need something to put on our not-so-distant college applications.

I dump my bag for someone else to fall over, and shuffle farther into the room, studiously avoiding Ben's eyeline as he sits at a table, eating his bacon sandwich. It would be great if there was a cozy hole in the ground to swallow me up, but no luck. I stand, swaying a little, trying to look like I'm taking in the atmosphere or something, whereas in reality, my mind is whirring with unhelpful thoughts. *Just breathe.* I need a moment to regroup before we set out into the wilds for four whole days and three freezing cold nights. Why the actual hell did I agree to this? Why did any of us? Coming here, of all places?

"Oh, you didn't find barbecue sauce?"

A girl's voice, disappointed, behind me. I turn before I engage my brain—because of course she's not talking to me—to face Stephanie, breezy as this early mountain morning. Ben's new girlfriend. She's returning from the bathrooms where she probably just splashed her fresh face with ice cold water. That's her wholesome, beautiful aesthetic right there.

"You wanted barbecue?" Ben tuts at himself, dorkily, crest truly fallen. "Wait, I'll look for some! I didn't realize there was a choice!" He springs to his feet again. *There's always a choice, Ben.*

"It doesn't matter." Stephanie swishes past me, smelling of baby soap and chiding disappointment; god, doesn't she feel the awkward going on here too, the three of us thrown together like this? Nope. She doesn't even notice me—or maybe she does, but I'm so not relevant. That might be worse.

Yes, it's premium-rate cringe when your best friend becomes your boyfriend, and a few months in, falls for another girl, especially a girl like Stephanie. Not that it's her fault. She doesn't have those.

None of it was my fault either. Like I said, I'm unlucky. My parents split up in spring, Ben and I were over by summer. But it's not the end of the world when a relationship dies, as my mother tells me—and she should know.

"Got it!" Ben gushes, delivering the barbecue sauce with a flourish, like he found the Holy Grail. But Steph barely glances at him as she sits at the table with her sidekick, Cass.

"Ooh, Benny. You certainly know what a girl wants," Cass trills, lightly mocking, but throwing him a killer grin to soften the blow. He smirks back at her, and even Steph deigns to crack a smile. Ugh, they make the grimmest of throuples.

Okay, maybe I'm being unfair. Cass isn't grim. In fact, I think we'd get on just fine if things were different. The two of us were fresh meat at Strother High last year. She's from London, so she has that city kid cool, but we were both floundering. In theory there was potential for bonding, but it didn't happen. Stephanie co-opted her pretty damn quick as BFF. She's always liked a rescue case. See also: Ben.

Stop looking at them, Maggie! Find a seat already!

I edge toward the tables, but there are no safe seats. Lawrence and Sebastian McTavish are manspreading their expansive selves over two tables, hurling salt and insults, and exuding that special kind of lazy viciousness exclusive to siblings.

"Did you remember to shower this morning, you slob?" Lawrence drawls at his twin.

"Did you remember to bring your mirror so you can fix your goldilocks?" Sebastian counters, but it doesn't hit. It rarely does. I'm not getting caught in their cross fire if I can help it. Maybe I'll hang out in the bathrooms until it's time to leave—

A shadow flies toward me.

"Watch your back, Maggie!"

"Hey!" I flinch, but of course I'm too slow, and my punishment is being kicked on the shoulder by a booted foot.

"Told ya, move!"

The final member of our party—Ant—is doing some kind of café parkour, a bite of sandwich flopping out of one side of their mouth as they jump from the window ledge to the counter. It's Ant's phone that's giving us the music, although Ant's the kind of kid who moves like they've got a constant soundtrack in their head anyway. As Ant leaps onto a table, the waitress swats at them with a towel and throws out some ancient Gaelic curse that we're all bilingual enough to appreciate. I can tell the waitress thinks Ant's a boy—wiry and vital and bloody annoying—but Ant's just Ant.

"Wake up, Mags! I need you on your game!"

Ant's impersonation of my dad's gruff voice is shockingly on point. They bop me over the head with a spoon as they pass again, jumping out of the way before I can retaliate. Ant's the hyperactive shadow I can never shake, and thank god for having someone in my corner. Especially on this trip.

"Hey, Stephanie, don't forget to tip your waiter if he gives you good service, know what I'm sayin'!"

Ant coos from across the room, eyeing Ben, ever-zesty, and making me low-level giggle in spite of myself. Yep, I'll never escape the Ant-love. Least of all this early in the morning, before their drugs have kicked in.

"Settle down!" Dad enters, yelling at everyone, but meaning Ant. I think all the teachers are directed to do that. *Don't single them out!* Like we don't know they mean Ant. Like Ant doesn't know they mean Ant.

"Here's your tea, Mr. Atkins." Cass tucks a strand of glossy black hair behind her ear and hands my dad a mug, giving a wink that's only just on the right side of appropriate. "Big, strong, and hot, with lots of sugar."

Och, save us from the English! I can almost read my dad's mind; he blusters out a thanks and takes a swig of tea.

"We mobilize in five minutes!" Dad's doing sergeant major now. "We're on the clock. I want us to reach the shepherd's hut before afternoon, there's a chance of a storm. So, look sharp!"

Sebastian stands up and salutes.

"Yessir!" He kicks out a leg in a goose step, upending the table Lawrence is sitting at.

"Asshole!" Lawrence lashes out, punching his twin on the arm.

"Language, Lawrence!" Dad glances at the waitress. "Get yourselves together and clear up this mess."

"Listen to the man, you idiot!" Lawrence berates his twin like he's personally offended by the dad-mocking. He idolizes my father. Especially since Dad cheated with the sexy supply teacher and became the talk of Strother High. Oh yes. My return to conventional education has been one big, fun party.

"Boys, huh?" Dad mutters as he passes, raising eyebrows at me, and anger curdles in my stomach. *Don't try and bond with me on this trip. Don't make it about us and them, I'm not on your side. Let's keep our relationship to every third weekend, and, you know, every damn day at school when I pretend we're not related.*

But that's a lie, isn't it? It's why I'm here, after all. Because I want Dad back. That's the only reason I'd ever consent to coming on this trip, facing Ben, and risking the dark side of the mountain.

"Tea, hen?" The waitress hands me a scalding hot mug without me asking, and I instantly want to beg her to come with us, be my friend. Or maybe I could stay here and clean toilets?

"Roll call!" Dad looks at a clipboard. He clears his throat, overly formal. "Margaret Atkins?"

"Yes, Daddy!" Ant squeaks. I reach out to whack them, but of course they dodge.

"Present." Dad chooses not to engage; he knows it's wise to pick your battles with Ant. "Lawrence McTavish, Sebastian McTavish."

"Yes, sir! Here, sir!" Seb calls out before his brother can, seals the deal with a puckering of the lips.

"Thank you, Sebastian." Dad doesn't make eye contact. If ignoring bad behavior fails, he'll turn on the hard stare, but that's a last resort. He doesn't like confrontation. Why he chose to be a teacher, god knows.

"Cass Prentiss, bringer of tea, you're here. Stephanie Wang, here." Dad's motoring through the list now. "Ben Young." Dad hurries past my ex's name so quickly he almost chokes on it. "And Ant Zito."

"Present and correct, Mungo!" Ant crows, as my dad tries very hard not to react to them calling him by his first name. We may not be in school right now, but there are boundaries. Even if Ant makes a habit of ignoring them.

"Actually, you know what, Ant? Everybody?" Dad smiles

with an idea. "Forget 'Mr. Atkins.' Go ahead and call me Mungo. This is a weekend-only deal. Because for the next four days, we work together as equals."

"Ooh, equals?" Seb snorts and leans over to Stephanie, out of my dad's earshot. "What is this, *Communist China*?"

"Racist loser." She rolls her eyes at him.

"Learn to take a joke." Seb guffaws.

"Yeah, you're not funny tho'." Steph sighs. "Let me know if that ever happens."

Seb blows her a kiss.

"Ignore him," Ben tells Steph, like it's all her fault.

"I see you guys took my note about not bringing phones *totally* seriously." Dad has retrieved an old tea box that used to live on the dresser in our kitchen. He holds it out. "Time to hand over all your devices. Only real-world interactions from here on."

"Ugh. Real world." Cass chuckles. "What's that?"

"Gear up and move out, everyone," Dad says. "If you're not at the trailhead in five minutes, I'm leaving you behind."

"Sounds like a plan," Ant whispers to me with a wink, but I know this kid is itching to move.

Chairs scrape, plates clatter, people disappear to the bathroom, and one by one we hand over our devices, our lives, to my father. I'm last. He gives me a look as I place my phone in the box.

"Chin up, Maggie. It won't kill you."

Huh. What does he know?

The trailhead is situated a couple minutes' unpleasant stroll through the mud outside the café. *Here we go.* I wrench my curls back into a no-nonsense bun, zip up my too-tight jacket, and five minutes later, we're a ragtag band of reluctant warriors set against the *dreich* murk of the Scottish morning, headlamps bobbing as we go, bent against the wind and rain and heading toward whatever the mountain has waiting for us.

CHAPTER 2

———

Cairn Gealach—the mountain, our destination—hunches menacingly in the distance. After a couple of hours of joyless trudging over the moors, under a weak and barely rising sun, battered by wind and stinging rain, we have reached the point of no return: the river.

My legs are jelly, and it's not with the exercise. Thanks to Dad dragging me on endless hikes as a kid, I can handle the outdoors, bad weather, maximum effort, even pain. The endorphins kick in, and at the end there's that nice dopamine hit like you achieved something. But I've never been a fan of being in mortal danger. The prospect of crossing this river feels a lot like that. Not everyone's a scaredy-cat like me. Ant is balancing precariously on a log at the water's edge.

"Oh my, that's some heavy flow to be dealing with. Am I right, ladies?" they cry, as they lean into the wind.

Sebastian makes a retching sound. "You're such a freak."

"Loud and proud." Ant grins, giving major golden retriever energy, like they live for wild adventure. The river is full, fast and furious—and Ant is taunting it like they taunt everyone, dangling a foot over the tumbling torrents. It's very tempting to push them into the water, but I'll resist, because they're triggering Seb, and that makes me feel oh-so-warm and fluffy. And there are bigger issues at stake.

"So, Mungo!" Ant shouts. "We're supposed to row, row, row our boat gently down the rapids?"

Dad frowns back, says nothing. He's probably thinking that if Ant's got doubts of their own invincibility, we're all in trouble. Nobody speaks, we only stare, fixated, reverent, as the water thrums past.

"The river has certainly doubled in width." Dad does understated like it's an art form. He wades into the shallows tentatively, but even ankle deep he's struggling to keep upright, the current so fast I'm getting motion sickness standing on dry land.

"No lie, it's kind of terrifying." Cass snickers nervously. "Was white water rafting in the risk assessment, sir?"

"We've trained for this, remember?" Dad's casual. Too damn casual. "With care, we should be fine."

"*Should* be?" Sebastian is bent double over a rock, dripping and sullen.

"Man up, bro," Lawrence growls at him. "We're doing it."

"You in charge, suddenly?" Seb snaps back. Out of all of us, he's least suited to any of this, and that's saying something.

He likes to act as if he's Loki to Lawrence's Thor, but all those hours lost to the virtual world are clearly taking their toll; he has the limp physicality and stamina of a middle-aged basement dweller. I almost feel sorry for him.

"Quit squabbling, McTavishes," Dad says evenly. "It's nothing we can't handle, or we wouldn't have come."

"Loving that confidence, Mungo!" Ant jumps down from the log and thumps the bag with the inflatable dinghy inside. "Is she big enough for all of us, or do we take it in turns to ride her?" They grin juicily. "Shotgun."

My dad doesn't answer immediately; he's been lugging the dinghy with Lawrence's muscly help for the last stretch, and I think he's a little more tired than he wants anyone to realize. At least I'm hoping it's that, because the alternative is, he's doubting the wisdom of putting seven teens in a boat I'm planning on naming *Imminent Peril. Maybe we just don't go, eh, Dad?* And this was supposed to be the easy part.

"Is it really safe, Mr. Atkins, er, Mungo?" Stephanie's raincoat is pulled tight around her face. It would look deeply dumb on most people, but the hood frames her delicate features perfectly. Raindrops hang off her long, black lashes, and the hike has made her cheeks flush a flattering, tawny apricot.

Dad ignores her, wades in a little deeper, flashlight scanning the water. Finally, he straightens up, decision made, and heads back to the grass.

"All good. We'll set the dinghy up here. Hope you've got the energy to pump her, Ant."

Oh god, Dad.

"Abso-frickin-lutely, Mungo!" Ant cackles, bouncing through the sludge and dragging the boat bag to the spot.

"But isn't it too rough?" Stephanie persists. "How can we even row when it's like this?"

"We're steering, not rowing, and it'll be perfectly safe if you remember your training and do exactly as I say," Dad says. "This kind of rig is used for these situations, trust me, Stephanie." He gives a half-assed smile. "We'll land downriver a little farther than I'd planned, but it's not a big deal."

"Seriously?"

It's the first time I've heard Ben speak since we left the café. I've been spending quite a lot of energy making sure we didn't walk together, and a couple of times we almost fell into step on the trail, but I sped up.

"Oh, don't be such a loser, Ben," Sebastian moans, suddenly massively into Plan Death Launch, purely because Ben's not. At least I can relate with him on that. "What, are you scared?"

"Thar she blows!" Ant cries as they unbuckle the dinghy bag. The boat bursts out, and it's a done deal, because we're never getting it back inside. Dad produces a foot pump and we take turns until the boat is inflated, huge and proud and startlingly orange. We drag it to the water's edge.

"Life jackets and helmets on, everyone. Get these backpacks stowed!"

I'm sure I can hear my blood thudding in my ears, and if it gets too loud, I'm done. *Keep moving, don't think about it.* We form a line and pass the cumbersome packs. There's a covered compartment under the back seat of the boat which is quickly filled, and the rest of our stuff is lashed together on the floor with carabiners and bungee cords.

"Lawrence! This is for you!" Dad hands Cass a flimsy plastic paddle. "Pass it down the line." Cass nods, but as she turns to me, I reach out and the wind whips it out of her hand. The paddle spins around in midair like some kind of martial arts fighting stick and almost spirals away into the river before Lawrence shoots out a long arm and snags it.

"Nice catch!" Dad laughs, relief in his voice. *Was that my fault?* Too close for comfort. "Lawrence, grab the tether at the front of the boat; when everyone is on board, you and I'll lead us out." Lawrence gives Dad the OK sign, and Dad shouts at the rest of us. "Listen carefully, I want you all to sit exactly where I say, just as we practiced. I'm at the back, Sebastian, Ben, and Stephanie in front of me, Maggie and Cass next. Ant, you'll be up front with Lawrence, help him get in quickly when I say."

"Like I'll need help!" Lawrence shouts back, as Ant salutes at him.

"No messing, you hear me?" Dad gives his tether a pull and the boat swings close.

Oh god, we're doing this. I step into the water and feel the grip of the icy drench as it surrounds, and then invades, my hiking boots. Damn, soaked-through feet for the rest of the trip. But that was a given, might as well commit to the blisters now. I cling to a handle on the side of the boat and Ben splashes over to the deeper side, taking one for the team to impress Stephanie, no doubt. One by one, we clamber in, squeakily; I sit where I'm told, and shoot a look at my neighbor, Cass, whose face is blanched, her black brows knitted together as she finds her own handle to hold. Lawrence and Dad take us in deeper. This is it, no going back, and my stomach is turning inside out. I feel so helpless, like when you're at the waterpark and you've stood in line forever, and you sit in the slippery rubber tube while some bored, sunburned kid hauls you to the top of the chute, and you feel that mixture of awkward and scared. All that. But likely without the post-ride ice cream.

"Lawrence, hop in!" Dad yells. "We're deep enough."

He waits until Lawrence has nearly sunk us by jumping in with too much enthusiasm before giving the boat a shove and launching himself onboard too. The inflatable does a random wobble and a sway, the current takes it, and holy moly, we're off.

Shiiiiiit… Around me there are whoops, and I'm white-knuckled to the handle, barely looking. Dad's shouting something inaudible. I whip my head around and see his face, deadly serious, like he's moving this vessel by sheer force of calm, considered will, but oh lordy, he's loving it, plunging his paddle into the water. Behind me, Seb has chosen to squat on the floor, and Ben and Stephanie are clinging to each other—*unnecessary*—half screaming, half laughing.

"We're going too fast," Steph cries, and Ben holds her a little closer. I look away and distract myself with fear, which I find works really well. "How do we stop?"

Jeez, we are going fast, so frighteningly fast, but Lawrence totally looks the part, long blond hair flying, full Viking mode, kneeling up front with teeth bared, stabbing the pathetic plastic paddle hither and thither, and—look!—Ant is flinging themself from port to starboard as if we're traversing the Colorado River, and *it's working*. We're getting closer to the other side. *Please let this end soon.*

Ugh!

The boat barrels diagonally, hitting a wave and slapping down on the other side, my whole body lurching—*whoa!*—then we're riding another, and I grip the handle tighter and rise with it, but this wave is huge, and before I can react, I see the boat move out from under me, like I'm stuck in the previous frame, and I fall backward, hitting something solid, landing legs up and helpless on the bottom of the boat like a dead beetle...

Oh, thank goddess! There's the scrape of land beneath us, the splash of someone leaping out, and *tug, tug,* we're hauled toward dry land.

I sit up, slowly sinking forward onto my hands. *Not going to puke, not going to puke. Just breathe.* Dad and Lawrence are out, Ant and Cass quick to follow, and I've never seen Seb move so fast.

"Great work!" Dad is panting hard, exhilarated, and I feel a surge of love and pride that he's delivered us. But then, he ruins everything. "Get up, Maggie, for goodness' sake!"

With shaking legs, I stand, wobbling, and Dad, annoyed, gestures for me to hurry.

"Secure the boat! Drag it all the way up the bank. Make a chain, get everything off!"

I heft myself over the side; Ant glances at me, offers a hand. *Thank you.* I splash through the shallows, get gravel underfoot and crouch for a minute, blessing the dry land, catching my breath. We did it.

This side of the bank is steep, but there's a small beach, with black, gnarled trees and slick, jagged rocks. I'll take it over water any day. Slowly, the bile that was rising in my throat dissipates, my fingers tingle with feeling again. Wow, that wasn't great. Even Seb is doing better than me, willingly getting back into the boat, handing packs to Ant and Lawrence, who brave the shallows, while Cass holds the tether.

I can see the disappointment on Dad's face. I was merely a passenger, maybe worse, maybe dead weight. That's all I do, I weigh him down. *Ha.* I feel a spike of anger replacing any good stuff I was feeling. Like I was ever going to be okay with coming here, with doing all of this. What did he expect?

"Count the packs!" Dad is shouting at everyone, but mainly me. "Cass, pull the boat all the way onto dry land; don't just stand there, help her, Sebastian! The rest of you, check tents, sleeping bags, all your kits, see that nothing has come loose. Double-check."

"Mungo!" Ben shouts from somewhere farther up the beach. "Can you come here, please? Steph needs—"

"Hold your horses." Dad chases after a rogue life jacket that is cartwheeling over the gravel in the wind. "We need to pull that boat *completely* out of the water, do it now! Cass! Seb! Everyone!"

I walk back into the water, half-heartedly grab the tether that Cass is holding, and prepare to haul.

"Heads up, my pack's not here." Ant is on the beach, re-counting.

"No?" I'm watching-trying-not-to-watch Ben and Stephanie out of the corner of my eye. Looks like he's holding Steph's face in his hands, they're having a moment. *Can you not leave each other alone for a second?*

"Someone left bags on the boat!" Ant yells. "Don't worry, I'll get 'em."

And then it happens.

Ant sprints past Cass and me, takes a flying leap into the boat, and as they land, the bounce pushes the boat a few feet away, wrenching the rope from our hands and launching boat, bags, and Ant back into the river.

"Whoa!" Cass stumbles against me and lurches after the boat, losing her footing and falling waist-deep into the water.

"Cass!"

Dad is there before anyone else has a chance to react, somehow managing to snag the tether and scoop Cass out of the water at the same time, wrangling her like a struggling sheep weighed down with wet, lifting her clear of the water and getting her to the shallows, where Lawrence wades in to help.

"Gotcha, Cass."

"Ant's getting away, Dad!" I yell, and before he can react and pull on the boat's tether, it pulls on him, toppling him over backward. "Dad!" I scream as he's completely submerged in the torrent.

Ant's face is stretched in horror and a kind of crazed excitement as the boat speeds downriver, but I only glance—where's Dad? Where's Dad? I realize I'm screaming the words as someone—Ben—grabs my shoulder, my arms, and it's only then I find I've run into the water blindly.

"It's okay, Maggie! He's gotten hold of the boat."

Dad looks far from okay. He reels himself in with the tether, hooks an arm over the side of the fast-moving dinghy, and tries to pull himself up, but it's too fat and slippery. I see his upper body jerk and I know he's kicking his legs to bump himself up like he taught us, but the water's too rough, they're moving too fast. Meanwhile, Ant is at the front—prow? God, what does it matter?—trying to steer the boat to the bank by paddling furiously, cartoon-like, and it's doing nothing. Dad's yelling, we're all yelling, and finally I see Ant look back at Dad, make a decision, abandon the paddle, and go to help him. Thank god. *Now pull him in, pull him in…*

But I don't see it. Because there's a bend in the river, not even a huge one, just a turn with overhanging trees and rocks, and as they round the corner, the boat swings achingly close to the bank, but nobody on board or on land is in a position to do anything about it—and then they're gone.

24

"Dad!"

I run, skidding on gravel and leaping onto the steep downstream slope, my feet raking tracks of mud as I power up the riverbank, but hardly making any ground as I ascend, like I'm on a treadmill. *Got to catch that boat.* It's impossible to follow the path of the river right by the water's edge, I can't even see the water from where I am now, but *must keep going, we need to reach them, can't let them get away.* Someone overtakes me, pulls on my arm—it's Cass, and almost immediately we've got Lawrence in front of us, Seb is somewhere behind, shouting. And suddenly there's a gap in the trees; I reach the top of a hill and can see the river again.

Where…?

No sign of the boat, how can it have moved so fast? Maybe it hasn't come around this corner yet? Can't get down to the water here, the bank is a cliff. I run on farther and up another hill, my lungs shocked and stinging, outraged at this sudden burst of activity.

Lawrence, ahead, shouts; he's seen the boat. I careen downhill, trying to watch my feet and scan the river at the same time.

"Be careful, Maggie!"

I think it's Cass, but I don't care if I fall, whatever gets me down there fastest. I draw level with Lawrence, standing where a steep gulley cuts in front of us, blocking any further travel along the riverbank.

"There!" He shoots out a hand. In the distance, in the foaming rapids, is a glimpse of orange.

"Dad! Ant!" I scream.

The boat whips around another corner and is swept from reach and out of sight, forever.

CHAPTER 3

Ben and I are sitting in my bedroom. We're on the floor, side by side; his legs stretched out in front of him, whereas mine are bent at the knee, my arms wrapped around them in a hug.

It's February, and our backs are pressed to the cast-iron radiator for blessed warmth. Ever since we were little kids, we have always sat in my room like this during the colder months, which in Scotland is most of them. It's a damp cold here. The damp seeps into your bones, slows you, making you feel dull and heavy. It creeps on your skin like death's caress, shivers down your spine to your very core, and freezes you from the inside out.

And worse of all, it reminds me of the cave. The damp was suffocating there.

"We're no closer to choosing an activity and the deadline's in thirty minutes." Ben flops the brochure on the floor with an overdramatic sigh. The brochure looks impressive; glossy, even.

The words on the cover read STROTHER HIGH ENRICHMENT WEEK, written in blood red, against a sky-gray background. "We have to select two options online: first choice and backup. Tell me what you're thinking."

Enrichment my ass, is what I'm thinking. What, lessons are not enough? Now I have to endure school-out-of-school, and pretend to be happy about it?

I bury my head in my sweater. It stinks of secondhand vape. I don't smell like myself anymore. On my first day back at school after nine years, that was what my mother asked me about as I walked through the door: *Have you been vaping, Maggie Atkins?* It was Dad who came to my rescue. He told my mother that he's always chasing the vaping kids out of the bathrooms, or yelling at them walking down the road to the bus depot after school, enveloped in candy-smelling clouds.

Ben's still waiting for my answer; I can tell by the way he's breathing.

"I don't want to do any of this forced fun." I groan from the depths of my sweater. "Is that a valid choice?"

The ridges of the hot radiator fit nicely between my shoulder blades; the heat feels so good, but at the same time, almost too much to bear.

"If we don't pick something, they'll assign us randomly," Ben states flatly. "Don't you want some control?"

Stupid question, Ben. I never feel in control. Maybe sometimes on the basketball court, when I'm driving to the basket and I know I've got the jump on the defender, and the size, strength, and sheer bloody mindedness to deliver. But not in real life.

"Obviously, we're not climbing friggin' Cairn Gealach with your dad."

"Obviously."

"And London's ruled out, too expensive; that goes double for the Paris trip." Ben holds up a thumb and two fingers, counting off the choices on his hand. "I cannot see you enduring the cooking course, and neither of us plays an instrument, so the music option is a nonstarter. Golf?"

I make a face at him.

"I think I'd rather do the Yarn Bombing, whatever the hell that means."

Ben laughs softly, but I know him too well not to hear the hint of irritation in his voice. He picks up his phone, scrolls. Checks his watch, which he didn't even need to, because he had his phone right there. That's his way of telling me he's going to go soon if I keep this up.

Before, this reaction wouldn't have bothered me. Before, I would have thought *whatever* and let him get on with it. But now we're together, that's changed. I don't want to irritate him anymore. I don't want any tiny thing to be wrong between us, ever.

"Okay, so there's an animation course." I pick up the brochure. "Drawing, storyboarding, editing. Might be bearable." I sniff, find the page, and shove it under his nose. "Enriching, even."

"Says here there're only ten spots available." He looks at me. "We won't get a place."

"How do you know?" I give him a half smile. "Maybe we'll get lucky."

His face flushes slightly, his pupils widen, and with all the confidence I never knew he possessed until three glorious weeks ago, he leans in for the kiss. I let myself go blank, lose myself just for a moment as his hand snakes under the bottom of my sweater, and we break apart, giggling like idiots. This is all still very new territory.

"I didn't mean get that kind of lucky." I snort, covering my face with my sweater again, and Ben falls on top of me, laughing.

Downstairs, the front door slams.

Ben sits up so quickly he smacks his head on the radiator. He gives an exaggerated but silent *ow*, jumps to his feet, and grabs his bag. "I'd better go. So we're choosing Animation?"

I nod. "No second choice. That way they'll have to give it to us."

I hear Ben and Dad cross on the stairs. *Just breathe.* I straighten my sweater, like Ben left a handprint, and hope I don't look too guilty.

Dad appears in the doorway.

"He left in a hurry."

"Yeah." I can't meet his eyes. "We have to select our Enrichment Week options online by five."

Dad grunts. "Hope you're coming with me into the hills." My heart clenches. "It would be really good for you. Ben too. Physical, new skills, teamwork. And, you know. Slay a few demons."

I'll never go near that cave again, my mind screams, but I shrug. "I guess we'll see what we get assigned."

He nods, turns to leave.

"Oh, Mags? Your mother was saying, maybe leave this door open when Ben comes around from now on?" His face crinkles with discomfort. "You guys are older, and, well, stuff can happen…"

Oh god, he knows about us.

"Actually…" He smiles at me. "Strike that. You make good decisions. I trust you."

"Oh, okay," I practically choke.

"And I trust you to make the right decision for Enrichment Week!" He walks out the door and shouts back at me. "I'll be right there with you, Maggie! Every step of the way."

A couple weeks later, we find out what activity we've been assigned. Ben, Ant, and I go to check the noticeboard together, and our jaws hit the floor when we see our names on the sheet headed CAIRN GEALACH HIKING TRIP.

"I didn't select that. Did either of you?" I croak, feeling like the air just drained from the room.

Ant shakes their head, Ben thumps the noticeboard with his fist, and we stare with mounting disbelief at the other names on the list. This can't be happening. Our classmates from the bus, the cave, all those years ago. Did Dad put all of our names down? Ben thumps the wall again, and I put my hand on his arm to get him to stop, because someone will notice, and I don't want anyone looking at us, making the connection—but it doesn't matter.

A few feet away, there's commotion, screaming, and laughing. The crowd who came to look at the Enrichment Week assignments has found something way more interesting to look at.

Down the hall, someone has drawn a huge arrow on the wall and scrawled words with red lipstick.

Mr. Atkins banged Ms. Fawcett in this closet!!!!

The ground drops away from me, and I'm falling.

My mother and I moved out of our home two weeks later.

CHAPTER 4

"Was my dad in the boat? Did he make it?"

I scream at Lawrence, but he stands there, transfixed, staring at the spot where the river turns.

"Could you see him? Was he in the water, or did Ant pull him in? Lawrence?!"

Forget you. God, maybe Ant's in the water too. They're super strong but half Dad's size, maybe the boat tipped when they tried to get him back onboard! I turn away from the river and run along the side of the gulch that has stopped us in our tracks. Below, there's a furious-flowing stream that leads into the river, and a waterfall. No obvious place to get across. Either side of the gulch is a slick rock face. I look around, desperately, for a route, but there's no way I can climb down without a rope.

"It's too dangerous!" Lawrence shouts, but he's barely glanced, how does he know? Okay, the only way across is to follow this stream past the waterfall. I keep running until I'm scrambling upward, but it feels all wrong to be heading in the opposite direction from the river. I stop. *Shite.*

"Please, Lawrence. We have to hurry!" I yell back, but he's not budging. I roll the dice. "What, are you actually scared?"

"Don't be pathetic." He stomps up the slope toward me. "You wearing your invisible wings, Maggie? Because that's the only way across this gap."

"All we need to do is climb up the side of the waterfall," I beg him. "Somewhere we'll find a place we can cross and come back down to the river on the other side."

"Yeah, and by that time they'll be in the North Sea." He grinds his teeth, and I feel pinpricks of hope as I watch the cogs turn. Lawrence hates to lose. There is pacing, swearing, but when he kicks a bunch of small rocks down into the gulch, I know he's given up.

"Wait!"

Cass is running over the brow of the hill, with Seb lumbering behind. Nope, I don't like my chances of getting either of them to help. This is on me. I run back down toward the river, back to the steeply sloping bank. It's not as bad as the gulch; yes, there are rocks at the bottom but there are lots of trees and little bushes growing out of the side. *Let's go.* I can use them to lower myself down to the water's edge.

One last glance at Lawrence, but he's a lost cause, heading back toward Seb and Cass. Whatever. I'm better solo. Scooting on my butt, I maneuver my legs down over the edge, grasping the trunk of the first tree, slide down and twist onto my belly, find a foothold. I can do this. Suddenly, the drizzle is back. *Great, because we needed to make this even more difficult.* Okay, focus, slowly now, got a face full of brambles but I'm strong, just need to hold tight, lower myself, move feet, find a place to balance my weight...*no!* There's a crack of a branch, my foot slips, hands too, stomach jumps as the rest of me slides. I cry out, in panic—*shit!*

Something catches me; a slipknot cinches sharply around my hand.

Ow.

I crane my neck, look up. The wrist loop of my jacket has snagged on a bush, holding me in place. *Just breathe, don't move.* I'm flat against the slope, chest crushed, legs dangling into the abyss while my snared hand throbs with hot pain. Slowly, I wiggle my other arm up, *carefully, carefully,* and thank all the mountain gods as my hand finds a firm hold, and I pull. I'm strong. Rain or shine, Dad had me outside every day when I was homeschooled, shooting practice. *You're tall, but you're slow, so if nothing else, you've got to be able to shoot with strength, even with your left hand.* Practice pays off. I haul myself up, unsnag my wrist, and hook my arm around a prickly trunk.

"Maggie!" Cass shouts, from somewhere above. "What the hell? You wanna kill yourself?" I squint upward to see her shock of black hair fly as she flings herself flat. "I've got you!" She shuffles forward, reaching down for me.

"It's okay, I can do it!"

Stupidest statement ever, and I'm glad she completely

ignores me, her fingers clasping around my wrists, surprisingly strong, tight as a vice.

"You're not going to fall, Maggie." Her voice is low, deliberate, steady. I blink rain away. Her dark eyes are glowering; she might sound calm, but she looks frickin' furious with me. "Lawrence, get over here!" she yells. It's obvious to both of us she can't haul me up by herself. "Maggie, just hang on." Not much else I can do, although my arms are burning and I'll bet Cass can't stay like this forever.

Miraculously, Lawrence has decided that he won't leave me to die, at least not this time, and after some scuffling beside Cass and a good amount of earth and undergrowth crap falling on my face, he reaches down and grasps me by the scruff of my jacket. We huff and puff, I cycle my legs, and they heave me up the slope until we're all lying on the ground, annihilated.

"Thank...thank you."

Never felt so glad to feel the mud seeping cold through my back. I blink away rain, it's getting heavier, the sky slate gray, but off in the distance, there's a rip in the cloud cover, sunlight breaking through. Somewhere, there'll be a rainbow.

Sebastian looms over, blocking out my view.

"Maggie, have you got a death wish, you stupid cow?"

I swear at him, but it sounds weak and breathless, and only encourages more onslaught.

"Think you're Wonder Woman? You could have pulled both of them over with you!"

"Yeah, right," grunts Lawrence.

"Yeah, back off, Seb," Cass snaps, as we stagger to our feet. "She's only trying to go after her dad." She looks around. "This rain is the storm coming. We should get back to the others."

"But Dad and Ant—"

"It's too late to do anything, Maggie." Lawrence is matter of fact. "Your old man's not stupid. Ant *is* stupid, but at least she can paddle."

"They," I say automatically.

Lawrence rolls his eyes. "Whatever. The two of 'em will steer the boat into the bank farther down and walk back, simple."

"Yes." Cass nods vigorously. "We should go back to the landing place and stick together, that's what we're supposed to do. They'll make their way there."

"What if they can't reach us?" I gesture to the gulch. "And what if they're hurt?"

"Look, your dad is better at this than we are," Lawrence says, clapping me on the back like he's trying to move a particularly reluctant cart horse. "He'll find a way. Bet he's got ropes and gear in his pack."

Yeah, I'd put money on it. I want to believe Lawrence about the rest too. I'm beaten up, there's the rain, and no one will come with me. More than any of that, I know what my dad would say. *Be clever. Know your limits. You're stronger as a team.* There's a beat where I wait for the decision to resolve in my mind, the relief to descend. But nothing comes.

"What if they're still in the water?" The thoughts are like

bugs biting under my skin. I know exactly what I'm doing. I need someone to give me permission to quit.

"They'll easily land. The river straightens out after this last bend," Sebastian says. "Gets wider, slower." He nods, confident. I stare at him.

"How the hell would you know?"

"Huh?"

"That the river runs straight after this bend. How come you would know something like that?"

Seb swears at me, his mouth twisted in disgust. "Your problem is, you always think you're the smartest in the room." He starts to walk away, back in the direction of the landing. "Exactly like your deluded dad. I happen to know the shape of the river, because I actually looked at a map before we set off." He taps his temple. "Photographic memory, babe."

"But…I can't…" I mutter, staring at my feet. Cass is making moves to follow Seb, and in the weirdest way I feel like I owe it to her to follow; she saved my life after all. "I don't think I can leave."

Lawrence squares up to me. It's subtle, he's not in my face, but he draws himself to his full height, and there's that McTavish glare.

"You're coming with us, Maggie, end of story. Mungo would kill me if I left you here." He looks at me, and I know he's meaning, if I left you *again*.

Because ten years ago, back in the cave, they all left me. The memory is a jag, searing cold into my veins.

"Oh, stand down. She's thinking about how she's going to bitch-slap your pretty face!" Sebastian shouts back at us. "Daddy and the freak are fine, Maggie, I told you." He groans. "They both had paddles, your dad even gave me the thumbs-up."

"What?" That gets me moving toward him. "You never said that before."

"I only just remembered."

"When was this exactly?"

"When he was on the bloody boat, obviously." Seb sniffs. "You were ahead, but I had a good view up there. He knew we were running after them, and he was telling us not to worry."

It does sound like something he would do. Give a dorky-dad thumbs-up to tell the kids everything is going to be okay. I shift on the spot, uncertain.

"Look, this weather is getting wild," Cass says. "We need to go back to Steph and Ben." She puts a hand on my arm, pulls me with her, just a little. "Collect our stuff and make a plan?"

So I let myself be led. Let their voices join with my dad's imagined voice in my head, telling me to give him and Ant up... for now, at least. And with every step of the way back, I hate myself for it.

We reach the landing to find Ben and Stephanie sheltering behind a bush. He has an arm around her, their heads bent close. *Oh, stop.* This is not the time.

"Are they okay?" Ben stands when he spots us, his expression concerned, and when he clocks our faces, there's a flicker of fear.

I soften slightly. The fact he chose to stay with *her* instead of coming after my dad—when he's done so much for Ben—will not stop hurting. But maybe Ben does care a little.

"They'll be fine." Lawrence retrieves his pack.

"We couldn't catch them, couldn't get any farther downriver," Cass mutters. "But at last glance, they were okay. No doubt they'll land someplace and hike back to us."

Ben nods, glances at me. I'm careful not to meet his eyes. Don't want to justify why I've given up on my only remaining friend and my father. But he doesn't question me.

"Steph and I have been thinking, we should shelter in the shepherd's hut. That was in the original plan, after all." Ben looks at the sky. "It's only a three-mile hike, we need to go before the weather gets worse."

"What? No." I feel my throat tightening. "I'm not walking even further away from the boat."

"I'm with Ben, the shepherd's hut is the smartest idea," Cass says, picking up her pack and fastening the clips decisively. "I'm soaked. We can light a fire, dry off, eat something."

"No!" *You want me to get comfy and feel even more guilty?*

"Yes!" Ben shouts back, and his fervor shocks me. "We need to rest. I have to get Steph somewhere she can lie down."

"What the hell? Why?"

"Because you broke her nose, Maggie."

He steps aside, and Steph raises her head. I gasp as I see the blood-smeared nose, mouth, and chin, the mottled, swollen cheeks, and the tear-filled eyes.

"On the boat." Her voice is small, muffled. "You fell back onto me, Maggie, remember?"

The way she says it, almost apologetically, the delicate hand hovering in front of her face as if she doesn't want to make a fuss. Makes it all ten times worse.

Seb whistles. "Wow, Mega Mags. You smashed Steph's face in."

"Oh god. I didn't realize. I'm so sorry." Shame washes over me, way more than it even should, but I'm already like a bottle waiting to pop. The big, bulky mammoth crashes into the delicate flower. That triggers so many of my worst anxieties. And damn, I hope Steph doesn't think I did it on purpose. *Did I do it on purpose?* Of course not. It was the boat. I feel like I should go to her, hug her? But I'm stuck fast. "Are you okay? Are you sure your nose is actually broken?"

"I mean, I haven't had an X-ray, but..."

She says it like I'm the dumbest person in the world. I don't think she even means it to cut so deep, but it does, more than Seb's digs or Ben's pissiness. And Ben truly looks furious, he's glaring at the sky again, and I'm sure it's because he can't actually bring himself to look at me.

"I already plotted the way to the shepherd's hut," Steph says, holding out a floppy weatherproof map with a compass attached. "First part is an easy hike. We head over this bank behind us"—she points to the map—"there's a long, low hill, then we skirt around the wood, here, and climb Devil's Chute."

"My, that sounds fun." Cass shivers.

Steph nods, a drop of blood flies off, and she winces. "It's only a foothill. Looks like a steep slope, a scramble—but the hut's immediately at the top."

"Where?" Lawrence leans in to see. The drop of blood from Steph's nose has fallen on the laminate, and she tuts and wipes it away to reveal the hut.

"Sixty minutes, tops."

"Let's make it forty-five." Ben's really taken over from my dad at frowning at the sky. Bang on cue, there's a roll of thunder off in the distance, and we all look at each other. "Yeah, thought so. Grab your stuff!" Ben shouts, but my feet feel fixed to the spot. He turns as he climbs up the bank. "Stay here if you want, Maggie, but your dad won't thank you for it."

Oh, screw you, Ben Young. How the hell would you even know what my dad would think?

The sky shudders with sheet lightning. Crap. Ben's right. God, why does he have to be right?

I glance down the river again, like the orange dinghy is going to magically appear, motoring upriver; Ant perched at the front, a grinning figurehead, Dad waving lazily.

The thunder rolls again. *Get moving, Maggie!* My legs are seizing up, my stomach churning. The wind blows an abandoned life jacket against my legs. Okay, I'll take these, they're bright yellow, I can leave a breadcrumb trail for Dad. Worst case scenario, we reach the shepherd's hut, and if Dad and Ant aren't there in the next couple of hours, the storm will have passed and we'll search for them. I need to think positive.

We have the map, so I can work out a route directly from the hut to wherever they might have landed.

I shoulder my sodden pack, gather as many of the life jackets as I can carry, and carabiner them to one of the D rings on my bag. As I turn to go, a flash of yellow catches my eye in the trees on the bank farther downstream.

Another jacket?

I hurry, wobbly on the stones underfoot, toward the trees. But it's not a life jacket. A plastic paddle is wedged between the trunk of a tree and a rock. But...Seb said that Dad and Ant both had paddles. Did we have three? No, of course not. So, could this be a random paddle from some other hapless dinghy? Stupid. Like there's anyone else out here doing what we're doing.

They didn't have a paddle each, Seb was wrong, or he lied to make me feel better, or more likely, to shut me up.

And there's something that bothers me way more. If Seb lied about that, he could have lied about Dad's thumbs-up. That thumbs-up is doing all the heavy lifting of my conscience right now. That thumbs-up is my justification for abandoning Dad.

I glance at the others, climbing the grassy bank. I'm going to lose them if I don't go now. I tie the first life jacket breadcrumb to a tree halfway up the slope and hurry to catch up.

———

"You're going to die!"

Stephanie is crouching low in the mud, yelling at us. We've spent the last half an hour following her, with her map, her plan, and her bleeding nose, plodding uphill, the rain clobbering us, the wind blowing so hard, at times I felt like I could lean my entire weight into it.

And then the thunder roared, directly overhead, and we all made a break for the woods. All except Stephanie.

"Lightning will strike the highest point! Get out of the trees!"

"She's right," Ben says. "We're almost at the hut, come on!"

Feels all kind of wrong to come out from cover, but we follow him as he runs out to Steph and helps her up. I try not to look as I see her smile at him, his arm briefly go around her shoulders to hug her, whispering something in her ear, their cheeks touching. But then her gaze wanders and her face changes, distracted. She stiffens, pulls away from Ben, holds up a hand.

"Hey, you! Over here!" She waves into the woods behind us. "Hello?"

"What is it?" I whip around. There's nothing but trees and the darkness between trees. "Is someone there? Is it Dad and Ant?"

We stand, frozen in place, scanning the woods.

"There's nobody." Seb groans. "You're seeing things."

"I think…" Steph blinks, wiggles out of her pack, and ventures a few paces into the trees. "Hello!" She stops and cups her hands around her mouth. "Who's there?" She runs farther in, awkwardly, nearly falling, but not stopping.

"Wait up!" Lawrence bounds after her.

"Seriously, Stephanie, what's going on? You said we shouldn't be under the trees!" Ben shouts, but he follows her in, and you can bet I'm on his heels. We reach her, and she's standing perfectly still, a frown on her face.

"I thought I saw…" She shakes her head. "That was so weird. There was definitely someone."

"Where?" I do a three-sixty, but there's no sign of life.

"Right here, where I'm standing," Steph breathes. "A figure. A man, I think. He was tall."

"Get lost." Sebastian snorts. "You're trying to freak us out."

"It must be Dad. Dad!" I bellow at the top of my voice. "Dad, we're here! Ant!"

"Is it them?" Cass reaches us, and I shush her.

"Listen!"

We stand stock still. The wood is thick here, insulated and velvety with moss. The pine-infused air is calm and cool on my wind-slapped cheeks and somewhere out there the thunder rolls again, moving away. The white noise of rain on evergreen treetops fills my ears, but I hear no human voices, no rustle of bracken or crack of broken sticks underfoot. If Dad and Ant were near, they'd shout, of course they would. Lawrence runs off farther into the woods. Stephanie hugs herself.

"I'm sure of it. There was someone standing right here, leaning against this tree."

"But why would they disappear?" Cass says. "I mean, if it's not Mr. Atkins and Ant, it must be some other hiker."

"They were watching us?" Seb says.

"Who'd do that, especially in this weather? No." Ben puts

his arm around Steph. "You're shaking, you're freezing. We have to get you to the hut."

"But we can't just leave when there's someone here!" I say. "They could help us."

"Maybe we should leave." Seb makes a face. "Maybe, whoever it is, they don't want to be found." He inhales dramatically. "Maybe, it's a *bodach*."

Cass frowns. "A what now?"

"A bodach, it's like, a Scottish bogeyman." Ben snorts. "Seriously, shut up, Seb. It would be a deer. The reindeer can get pretty big—"

"They have four legs!" Steph says. "This was person-shaped."

"Bodach!" Seb's eyes are wide.

"You probably just saw a shadow, movement, out of the corner of your eye," Ben says. "A squirrel darting up the tree, a badger—"

"It was not a friggin' badger." Steph scowls at him. "I might have a broken nose, but I'm not hallucinating."

"Steph, you could be concussed." Ben's eyes dart to me and I feel heat rising in my chest.

"No sign of anyone." Lawrence arrives back just in time to avert the lovers' tiff, bulldozing his way through the undergrowth. "Unless they ducked down a foxhole or flew up into the treetops, there's nobody close by."

"Flew up into the treetops?" Seb gulps. "I was wrong, not a bodach." He looks up slowly. "A *vampire*."

There's a thunder roll bang on cue. Cass swears, Stephanie shudders, and Ben gives Seb a withering look.

"We're leaving, now."

We don't need to be told twice. Everyone runs so damn fast out of that wood—who gives a crap about the lightning now?—and slips and slides and doesn't slow down until the trees are a safe distance behind. I tie my last life jacket breadcrumb to a bush, hopefully pointing to our trail upward, and the only obstacle that remains between us and a roof over our heads is the final hill.

And what a hill.

"This is the way?" Lawrence stares at the steep slope that rises up in front of us, rubbing rain from his face.

"Devil's Chute," Steph says. "Mr. Atkins marked it as the friendlier route."

Far to our left, the hillside is all rocks, a series of crags that look like they might require more climbing skills than we possess. But the closer, "friendlier" route is a sheer, concave slope of muddy grass, dotted with the occasional cluster of ferns and spiky, gravity-defying gorse bushes.

Without discussion, we clamber on all fours, clutching at clumps of anything to propel ourselves upward, frightened to stop in case the weight of our packs drags us over backward, prey for the devil. My breath is painful, acid rising from my stomach, sweat making my hot scalp itch under my waterproof hood. *Keep going.* There's shelter ahead. Safety. From lightning strikes, and…whatever else. Steph probably just saw a shadow, but I really, really like the idea of being inside four walls.

Lawrence beats me to the top of course. He's standing at the crest of the hill, looking around, eyes narrowed with confusion. And as I join him, I see why.

CHAPTER 5

I think I was expecting a little log cabin. A rustic but picturesquely moss-fringed, AI-perfect image of some small but super cozy folklorish hobbit hole. Sure, it would be basic, we'd need to fire up the wood-burning stove and batten down the hatches, but we'd soon be warm and hearty and full of smug, outdoorsy authenticity.

The hut that squats above us looks like a giant golem's turd. It's made of ancient-looking, dull-gray stone and it's the weirdest rounded shape. One end perches on the top of the slope, as if waiting to launch itself into oblivion, behind it a field of mud leading up into the mountains proper. Is this where we were expected to sleep? I mean, I wasn't expecting a hot tub, but maybe a window. Wait, there is one, a slit. Must be where they used to fire arrows from.

The others arrive, wet, wild, and breathless. Ben and Cass are helping Steph; Seb is complaining, bringing up the rear. Ben straightens painfully, taking in the grandeur.

"Jesus Christ."

"Yeah, I reckon this predates him," I say. "We might have to roll back a stone."

"Open sesame." He shoots me a smile, but thinks better of it as quickly as it arrives on his lips. There's a gust of wind while thunder grumbles overhead, and he shrinks into his rain jacket. "Come on, Steph. Let's get inside."

Lawrence stands at the door and slowly turns a cast-iron ring that lifts a latch. The rest of us gather nervously a few feet away, as if something within is going to reach out and grab us.

"Anyone got a headlamp?"

"Here." I throw him mine, because hell no, I'm not going in first.

Lawrence takes two steps inside, and when he doesn't scream or immediately exit pursued by a bear, the rest of us follow into the gloomy portal, one by one, our beams of light darting around the interior.

"This is great," says Steph, entirely without sarcasm. "Walls, and a roof. And there's a bolt to lock the door. I like it even more, five stars."

She's being kind. The hut is dank, dark, and tiny. I was hoping it was somehow bigger on the inside, like the Tardis, but nope. The ground is covered with flagstones, and on either side of the hut there are wide, low wooden platforms... That's where we're supposed to sleep.

"Urgh, what's the smell?" Seb covers his nose with his arm.

"You," Lawrence huffs. But the hut smells even worse than

Seb, of mold, sheep, and something else…curry powder? Weird. Remnants of hapless hikers gone before, or their meals, at least. "Now you know what the rest of us have to put up with, smelling your funky junk."

Seb flops down on one of the platforms, too exhausted and dejected to bite back at his brother.

"Hey, I'll get the fire lit," Cass says, winking at Steph. "Soon be toasty in here."

There's a wood-burning stove in the middle—at least I was right about that—with a huge pile of logs scattered higgledy-piggledy behind it. In the corner stands a metal sink, shelves on one side, and on the other, a small table. Cass kneels at the stove and gets busy with kindling, and we dump our packs, shake off the rain. Okay, deep breaths. This is going to work. For now, sanctuary.

Ben grabs the only chair and steers Stephanie toward it.

"Let's take a proper look at your face. God, it's so dark in here."

He flicks on a hurricane lamp that is dangling from the ceiling on a bit of twine. I spot another lamp on the table and turn it on. Still dark and dingy in here. I'll unshutter the window. I go outside and brave the lashing rain once more, all the while questioning why it's so important to me to be helpful to Ben and Steph. The window is on the side of the hut that hangs over the steepest part of the hill, so I have to shuffle carefully along the edge of the slope until I reach it. One slip and I'll tumble to my death, and then how will you feel, huh, Ben? I unhook the latch with freezing fingers. Now I can watch for Dad and Ant through the window. A way to assuage my guilt at being inside while they are out.

When I reenter the hut, Cass is still coaxing the fire, and there's a McTavish brother splayed out dramatically on either sleeping platform, like they just scaled Mount Everest. Ben is cleaning Steph's face with water from his bottle, and she's sitting with her head tilted back and her eyes closed while he leans in. The swelling looks so much worse. I move my backpack to a spot by the window, pretending I'm looking for something, all the time watching them and hating myself for it. Ben's gentle, careful. It's really…intimate. So gross. He looks up, suddenly eyeballing me, and I look away, caught for the *second time today*, hoping that the sadness and weird rage that is going on inside doesn't show on my face.

"Her nose is definitely broken," Ben says pointedly. Oh god, this is so bloody typical. Why did I have to fall on Steph? Why couldn't I have broken *his* nose instead? That would be the universe doling out some justice.

"I'm fine," Steph says, except that it comes out more like "Ibe fibe." Seb whoops with laughter on his platform, and grabs my leg, and Steph, Ben, and Cass look at us like we're *both* loling about her poor nose. I shake Sebastian off.

"Honestly, Steph, I'm so, so sorry if it was me."

"It *was* you." Ben's staring at the floor.

"Well, yes, but obviously, it was an accident." That comes out way more snappily than intended. "I slipped. The boat moved unexpectedly."

Ben's eyebrows shoot up. "Unexpectedly?"

"That's what I said!" I shouldn't shout, but I'm absolutely shouting. "I couldn't help it!"

"You're like…a wrecking ball." He still won't actually look at me, he's staring down, shaking his head like he's severely disappointed with one of the flagstones. "Your problem is, you don't know your own…"

He struggles to complete the sentence. We all wait for it.

My own what, Ben? Not *strength*, no, not that, but do you mean *size*? That's my *problem*? Yes, I'm ridiculously tall for a girl, taller than you, full-bodied and strong, and wasn't it wild how you suddenly hated that when we were together? And yes, I'm *way more massive* than pint-sized princess, here.

"Mags, I'm sorry, but…" Ben falters, and I can't actually believe he's still talking. "You just don't know your own…"

"Velocity?!" Seb jumps to his feet behind me. "Mags got magnitude!"

Ten years ago, I would have thumped Seb. Hell, five years ago. But right now, I'm not going to give them any more *wrecking ball* ammunition. That's personal development, I'd say. I take a breath, turn to Steph.

"We have painkillers, let me—oh no." I facepalm. "They're in Dad's backpack."

"Here, I've got you." Cass produces a bag containing several small bottles of pills and pulls one out. "Kill that pain, my friend."

"Prescription," whistles Seb. "Where's your permission note, pusher?"

"Period cramps," she claps back. "Happy to give you all the grisly details."

"I'd rather die." Seb snorts.

"That can be arranged." Cass's face is placid; I really envy her skills.

"Thanks." Steph reaches over, takes the bottle of pills, and shoots me a sympathetic look. At least I think that's what the look is, it's hard to tell in this light, and with the bent nose and the swelling and everything. Urgh. I did do a number on her. She reads my mind. "Please don't worry, Maggie. I'll be fine with the pills, maybe something to eat."

"Yeah, I'm starving!" Seb moans, collapsing across the platform again. "What's for lunch?"

"Whatever you've got in your pack, obviously." Cass turns back to the stove, the flames flaring up in the draft from the wind. Impressive; she clearly did her homework. And god, that glow feels good.

"But Mungo promised there'd be real food in the hut!" Seb moans. "We were supposed to restock for the rest of the trip! Are you telling me I've got to survive on protein bars?"

"That's all you have?" Cass raises an eyebrow.

"There is definitely food here somewhere, Dad brought it."

I glance around the hut. Not that I want to be of any kind of assistance to Sebastian, but I'm glad of the focus shift.

And there it is, our bounty: a large, black, plastic crate beneath the table. Nice one, Dad. He prepped the hut by hiking here a week ago with some helpful friends. Must have been a bitch to carry this stuff, bet he cherished every minute.

"Yay, success." I crouch down and pull at the crate. It's heavy. Good for us, I guess. Oh, hello. There's a combination lock built into the lid.

"So what have we got?" Seb's expecting table service, no doubt. Cass comes up to look, sees the lock.

"You know the code?"

"No."

She turns around to the room. "Anyone? Three-digit code to unlock lunch. Was it in the expedition notes?"

Deafening silence. I mean, why would Dad bother to tell anyone? He would have been expecting to be here to open it himself. And of course, he *will* be. But that doesn't help us now.

"Why the hell lock it in the first place?" Seb whines. "Must be some hungry, thieving shepherds around here."

Cass kneels at the crate, spinning the tumblers, trying all the obvious combos. 123, 000, 007.

"Today's date?" She sighs. "Too many digits."

"Try September tenth." My birthday. I have this stupid hope it will be correct, and feel a stab of sorrow when it's not.

"999, what is your emergency?" Lawrence intones, from the other side of the room.

"More like 666, knowing Mungo!" Seb guffaws. "Or would he go for a little 420? No, I've got it: ooooooh-69!"

I bite my cheek.

"All yours, Sebastian." Cass abandons the crate and goes digging in her pack, bringing out an apple.

Seb fiddles with the lock. Then Lawrence. Ben. We all try our luck. But no dice. One by one, we give up and eat what snacks we brought from home. Seb hasn't got protein bars. Instead, he produces a tub of evil-smelling mackerel, because of course Seb would bring the most antisocial food imaginable. Everyone abandons him on his own platform by the stubborn crate, and we sit on the other one, looking out the rain-streaked window as the sky occasionally flashes. There is no sign of the storm abating; if anything, the wind is worse, whistling through the rafters, rattling the shutter. And there is no sign of Dad and Ant. After my trail mix, I chew on a dirty thumbnail and wonder how long it will be before dark. In truth, the day never really got properly light. My hand automatically reaches for my phone, before I remember that it's currently in the Lyons Tea box inside my dad's van.

"Anyone got the time?"

"There's a clock on the GPS navigator." Steph frowns, then winces at the frown. "Oh—your dad has the GPS."

Lawrence punches a meaty fist into the air and pulls his fleece sleeve down to reveal a chunky and ridiculously expensive-looking silver watch.

"Breitling."

Ben mutters something and shakes his head.

"You complaining that someone actually came prepared, Benny?" Lawrence smirks at him. "It's twelve thirty-nine p.m. precisely, Maggie."

"Why does it feel like bedtime already?" groans Cass. "The wind is getting worse; we should close the shutter, it'll keep us warmer."

"I want it open." I lean into the window protectively, looking down the hill, even though I can hardly see a thing, my breath steaming up the glass.

"Speaking of being prepared, what is everyone carrying and what got left on the boat?" Lawrence says. "We have sleeping bags?" Nods all round. "Thank god, 'cos I'm not sharing. How about tents?"

"Duh. We have a hut." Seb gestures.

"In case we need it for the trek out of here, because I'm not staying any longer than we have to." Lawrence kicks out a long leg, and Seb returns and misses.

"I have a tent," I offer.

"Me too," Ben says.

"Awesome, that means you two won't have to shack up." Lawrence chuckles, and I stare at the floor, willing myself not to burn red. "I've got mine, so looks like you're sleeping in a ditch, bro." He pulls a face at his twin, who shrugs. "Mungo had the camping stove."

"We can use the wood burner," Cass says. "There are cooking pots by the sink."

"Pointless, if we don't know the combo for this." Seb thumps the crate.

"Calm down," Lawrence says. "We can smash it open, it's only plastic."

"Nuh-uh," Seb says. "Looks built."

"Yeah, and I'm built." Lawrence smirks, stretching out lazily and flexing a bicep. Seb hauls the crate off the floor with a grunt and makes as if to throw it at him.

"Stop." I stand up, my hands out. Don't want a crate smashing into me, or even worse, into Steph. "My dad will be here with the code."

"What if he isn't?" Seb says.

My teeth clench. Seb does that to me on a good day, and this is definitely not one of those. I try to think calm thoughts.

"Sebastian, you told me he gave you the thumbs-up."

"Oh yeah, Margaret. I did."

I can't read him, beyond the usual McTavish curl of the lip set against an otherwise expressionless face, eyes that have just a hint of interest in waiting to see if you'll buy what they're selling.

"My dad *will* be here." I plant myself firmly in front of the window, my back to the rest of them. "Wait and see."

———

We wait. Wait for the storm to die down, wait for night, wait for the stomp of feet and the relieved laughter of Ant and Dad at the door. My neck and shoulders are stiff from my vigil by the window, but I'm long past the point of caring about that. I earned the pain. The rain is lashing the glass, the wind threatening to free the wooden shutter, and the stone wall is cold as death under my shoulder. Our waterproof jackets hang in a line from the rafters, dripping and wrinkled, like dismembered people, their innards sucked out. I feel just like that: immobile, empty. There is no one climbing up Devil's Chute, but I have to keep watch, as if by being here, I'm holding an invisible thread, reeling them in.

Seb falls asleep and snores, loudly. Cass flicks through some magazines from a box on the shelf. Lawrence's obsessive-neatness thing kicks in and he stacks the firewood logs beautifully, perfectly, against the back wall.

"I left toilet paper in there, if anyone needs it."

The door suddenly opening makes me jump, even though I know full well that Ben had gone out, because of course I'm always hyperaware of where he is at any given time. He shuts the door, shakes like a sheepdog, and peels off his jacket.

"How was it?" Steph's brow crinkles.

"Better than a hole in the ground. I mean, it *is* a hole in the ground, but at least I didn't have to dig my own."

"Glad to hear my poop trowel can stay in the bag for now." Cass chuckles.

Urgh. I'm holding in all bodily excretions for as long as I can, saving them up until bedtime for a group one-and-done visit, because I sure as hell don't love the idea of a solo excursion to the outdoor toilet in the early hours. We were massively relieved to discover that the hut had an "outhouse," but not so thrilled to find that it's a full five-second danger dash across the muddy field to reach it.

If I stay absolutely still, and don't drink anything, I should be golden.

Ben resumes his spot beside Steph and Cass, sitting as close to the wood stove as possible, playing some kind of card game that Stephanie was mindful enough to bring along. They're soon laughing, in hushed tones. Damn, they're even having a good time. How can they relax like that? Maybe I should be comforted by their mood. They're obviously sure that Dad and Ant will be back, otherwise why would they be so unbothered? I feel needles of anxiety and irritation pricking me. I want to scream.

"And...I own you!" Steph's laughing at Ben, because apparently she's won the game. I don't look directly, of course, but in my peripheral vision I see her push him playfully. He grabs her hands and they do that annoying, loved-up wrestling that couples probably only engage in when there are other people around to see it.

"Careful of your little nose!" he chides her quietly, and we all want to puke. Steph giggles at him and pushes him off, clearly not so beaten up by me that she can't get physical with my ex.

"What time is it now?" Cass gets up, stretches, catlike, and comes to the window. As she looks out, I see the twitch in her jaw, the tiny wrinkle between those neat, arched eyebrows. Interesting. She doesn't like the performance either.

"Three fifteen," Lawrence answers.

"Alright, that's it." My legs have gone to sleep, but I pull myself up. "I'm going out to look for Dad and Ant."

"You can't," Cass says, gesturing at the sky. "Massive ol' storm."

"I haven't heard the thunder for half an hour. 'Scuse me." I resist the urge to kick Ben and Steph into the stove as I shuffle past them and reach up for my jacket. "It'll be dark soon."

"You can't go out there." Ben's not even looking at me.

"Don't tell me what to do," I mutter, before I can help myself.

"It's plain stupid. The weather's even worse than before."

"I'm surprised you even noticed." I make a mock-shocked face, not able to prevent my bitterness from showing. "Don't worry, I can go alone."

"I'll come," Lawrence says. He never took his jacket off, which figures. I'm secretly pleased, and it would be pointless to argue with him anyway.

"There!" Cass whips around to the window.

"What?" I hurry back to her side. "Dad and Ant?"

"No," she mouths the word like I'm absolutely basic. "Lightning. There was a colossal flash, it must have struck a tree down there."

"But I didn't hear any thunder—"

There's an almighty crack and a deafening roar, directly above us.

"Shit!"

We hit the deck like the sky has been broken in half, and I'm belly down, hugging the floor, feeling the thunder rumbling through the earth, my cheek raw against the coldness of the stone. The cacophony rolls away down the hill, and I peek up through my fingers, fully expecting the roof to be in pieces, but remarkably, our hut is still in place.

"Oh my god," Cass splutters, cool gone. "Was that a direct hit?"

I drag myself to my feet and stagger to the door.

"Whass happenin'?" Seb says, groggy from sleep. "Is Maggie going for pizza?" He giggles, which sets off the others—because how the hell did he sleep through that?—and they all look at me, laughing, and my heart is in my stomach knowing I can't go out. I'm stuck here, useless.

And something else comes to me, a flash of memory. The way they're lying on the rough, stone floor in the half-light—Seb to my right, with Lawrence; Ben's big, sad eyes; Steph peeking up at me through her hair. It takes me right back there, to the cave. Back when my legs were sticky with the pee I couldn't hold any longer, my lungs full of dust, and they're all looking at me, blaming me for making *him* angry. I'm on my own in this group, knowing that no one is coming in to bat for me. I'm the weakest link, the biggest liability, one they'll have to leave behind.

I do what I couldn't do then. I run outside.

CHAPTER 6

It's hard to be sure what is pure memory, and what has been planted there. In my mind, our time in the cave is like a parade of half-remembered snippets, warped by snatches of overheard conversations, a TV special I wasn't supposed to watch, illicit internet searches. Ant and Ben and I don't talk about it. Not really. All we want to do is forget. But you can only train your brain so much. Years pass, and my dreams come thick and fast, of versions of events, layered with whatever visions the anxiety of the day whips up.

The clearest memory I have is of the time I tried to save us.

"He's asleep!" Stephanie hisses. "We should do it now! Push him off the ledge!"

The driver always sat in an archway, at the opposite side of the cave from us. To the left, there's the tunnel where we entered the cave, but none of us ever dare go down it, because it is inky black. We rarely move at all, huddling together for warmth and protection, like scared baby animals, crushed into a corner. Beyond the driver and the archway is light, and cold, and the ledge. That's where the toilet bucket is. We're allowed out in twos, to hug the wall and squat, and he never peeks. I weep hot tears every time. The mountains look beautiful from the ledge, home and hugs lie somewhere beyond, but we are trapped. It feels like we're on the very edge of the earth, and if we fall, we will just keep on falling forever.

"I'm not going to go anywhere near him," Nicholas whispers, shivering. "He'll wake up and punch us in the teeth."

"Don't say that!" Stephanie, ever positive, because she has a plan. "We can be quiet as mice, and if we're quick and we all push at the same time, he'll fall off."

"You do it, then!" Sebastian gives her a little shove, and she squeals in protest. We all freeze, waiting for the driver to move. But he doesn't.

I think Steph's plan is flawed. The ledge is too wide. He'll wake up before we get him to the edge.

"Maybe he's dead already." Ant's head is on my shoulder. "He looks old enough."

"I'll kill him if wakes up. I'll smash his bones," Lawrence growls.

"With what?" Seb scoffs.

"With my fists, stupid!" Lawrence curls his fingers tight, his teeth gritted hard.

"Don't do anything," Ben says. "The army will rescue us. They have sniffer dogs, and there's X-rays on the helicopters."

"Pah! X-rays!" Seb snorts.

"Be quiet!" Lawrence thumps him, he cries out, and this time the driver does move, and we all gasp, but he just shifts, turning toward us. He's sitting up, but leaning against the wall, snoring gently.

A flash of silver. Something tumbles out of his pants pocket and clatters onto the dirty floor.

"Look!" Steph claps hands to her mouth.

"A phone," Nicholas rasps.

We can all see it. It's the old-fashioned kind, the type that flips open. There's a little green light on the end of it, flashing. My gran has a phone exactly the same. The light means it's on, and I feel excitement bubble in my belly, tears prick the corners of my eyes. The phone is the sort where you don't need to put in a passcode or a fingerprint to work it. It unlocks when you press *menu* and *. I know that, my gran gets me to do it for her all the time because she can't see the buttons very well without her glasses. Sometimes I press the numbers for her too.

I could do that now.

"999," I breathe. "That's how you get the police to come. And the ambulance, and the fire engine."

"We don't need the fire engine, stupid!" Seb hisses.

"Yes we do. They have a ladder," Steph says.

"We need the army." Ben shakes his head nervously. "They can fight him. We need to wait until they come."

And that panics me, because I can't wait any longer.

"I'm going to get the phone." I drop forward onto all fours, and crawl toward the driver.

"No!" Ben gasps.

"Me too, Mags!" I turn to see Ant's eager face, before Lawrence and Nicholas pull them back into the shadows.

"It's okay!" I mouth.

Sometimes, it's good to be slow. *One hand followed by another, rock is cold on my palms, keep low, steady as you go.* My heart is beating so hard in my chest, I'm afraid he will hear it. I feel every pore on my skin, every hair tingling. I glance at him, but only for a second, because otherwise I will lose my nerve. His face is turned to us, his chin up, head against the wall, eyes closed, breathing softly. Still asleep. *I need to pee so bad.* Only a few feet away now, I stretch an arm out, my fingertips reaching for the phone, almost touching it... I glance at the driver again.

His eyes are open.

For a moment, time stops.

I lunge for the phone, the driver roars, kids are screaming behind me. The phone skids off somewhere across the floor as he staggers to his feet. I roll away from the looming shadow above me, arms up over my head, waiting for the blow. All around me, feet are running, the others have scrambled off in all directions, even down the dark and scary tunnel, and that saves me, because the driver pauses, not knowing which of us to catch.

Where did the phone go?

I see Lawrence bend down by the far wall, pick it up. But

the driver has seen him too. Before he can move, I hurl myself at his ankles, tackling him. I'm big and strong for my age, but I am only six. He kicks me off easily, but it's enough time for Lawrence to run, to disappear into the darkness of the tunnel.

The driver sighs, flicks on a flashlight, and jogs after him.

When he emerges from the tunnel, he has the phone in his teeth, and a McTavish twin in each hand; wriggling puppies carried by the scruff of their necks.

The rest of us are back in our corner. The driver throws the boys at us, pockets his phone without a word.

He stands there, breathing heavily, watching us. And then he leans in and punches the side of Seb's head with a sickening thud, and Sebastian cries out, curling up in a ball of indignant sobs.

Did he mean to punish Lawrence, and hit the wrong twin? In those days, everyone got the wrong twin. Maybe that's why they grew up looking so different. They evolved so no one would ever make that mistake again. Perhaps the driver just needed to hit one of us, any of us, so we would know the consequences. Whatever the reason, it was my fault.

The driver put plastic bracelets on my wrists after that, to tie my hands together. It marked me out as different, the one he was most worried about escaping, perhaps. But he shouldn't have worried. I was already different. Too large to fit through the gap in the wall at the end of the dark tunnel when it came to it. No matter how much I wriggled, and cried, and kicked my legs, the rocks pressing down on me, dust falling in my eyes, I could not follow my friends through that hole into the outside world. No matter how much Ben and Ant pulled my tied hands and begged me to move. I was stuck.

And then…I draw a blank. I can't remember exactly *how* they left me. What they said. Who held out longest. My memory has failed me on this, or maybe it has saved me.

I only remember them gone.

CHAPTER 7

I lean back hard, pressing against the outside wall of the shepherd's hut, gasping for air; the stone is so very cold, but it is the only thing keeping me upright. How stupid was I to come back to the mountains? *Too close.* I wish I could melt into the cracks, hide there, because I have no other option.

One hundred eighty degrees around me, the sky judders with light, like a time-lapse of a storm, but this is playing out in the here and now. I can still feel the vibration of the thunder, swear I can smell something sharp, acidic, singed. It would be madness to try to venture further. I'm trapped here, between the inside and the outside. *Trapped.* That old, familiar panic creeps up my body, threatening to paralyze me, the scream rising fast, too fast to control.

You can't scream. You'll be heard. You mustn't be heard.

I open my mouth, screw my eyes tight shut, and scream silently into the sky, arms rigid, fists clenched, head back, just like all those years ago. Letting all the tension out of my body, except it doesn't go, because there's no sound, no scream, no release.

The door latch clatters, my eyes open, and a hooded figure steps outside, looking down the hill. Ben turns, and his face crumples with relief. I feel a rush of something good—*he was coming after me*—but that brief flush of joy is immediately overlayed with anger. *Took you this long, pal?*

"Jesus, Maggie." There's the frown. How dare he be angry with me? *Right back at you. If you're pissed off, I'll double it.* He hooks a thumb at me. "Seriously, get back inside." It's almost like he wants me to hate him. "You cannot go anywhere in this. Your dad would tell you so himself."

"I know!"

I feel like I'm shouting, but the sound is muffled, as if my ears are blocked. *Don't cry, don't cry, don't cry.* I shut my eyes again, and after a second, Ben's there, beside me, leaning on the wall too, his shoulder pushing up against mine in a closeness we haven't had for weeks. There is no hug, no clasp of the hand, but it's enough.

"I'm so sorry, Maggie."

I risk opening my eyes and he shakes his head, raindrops flying off his hood, and for a moment I feel shocked, a punch to the gut. Like he's sorry about *us*, or worse, he's talking about the cave. I flush hot because *of course* he doesn't mean either of those things. "This is so hard on you. But your dad will be okay, and Ant's tough. You have to believe that."

I find myself nodding too, because it's easier, and because yes, I do believe it. I can't think anything else right now, because that would be too much to bear.

"Your dad knows what he's doing, and they have food and a tent, right? The camping stove, the GPS." Ben's eyes are so dark. I look for the boy I know, but it's like the shutters are closed. "By morning, the storm will have passed. We'll find them, if they don't find us first."

Now comes the arm squeeze. I dare to hold his gaze, and for a few seconds, it's like we're still okay, we're still us. But all too soon he drops away from me, turns, and goes back inside without another word, as if I'm nothing, as if he really doesn't care what I do after all.

I close my eyes, exhale deeply, and count to ten. And then one hundred.

And when I'm done, I round the hut to the downhill side, carefully sticking close so as not to slip down Devil's Chute. With clumsy fingers, I unlatch the shutter, close it. Forget watching for them. It'll be too dark to see soon anyway.

Operation Open Crate is in full flow as I reenter the hut. They've already moved on from my drama. Looks like nobody else was particularly bothered about my fate. A fact that is made all too clear to me by Seb. He taps the crate.

"Feel like taking this outside and playing hunt the lightning bolt, Maggie?"

I pretend I don't hear.

"What's even in there, anyway?" Steph asks. "Anything we desperately need?"

"Eggs for breakfast," Cass says. "And ramen and space meals for the trail."

"Space meals?"

"Just add water, you know?"

"Appetizing." Steph rolls her eyes. "But I'd take it."

"Don't get excited. Nothing is getting this open. It's military grade," Lawrence growls, shooting out a foot.

"Eggs! Don't kick it!" Cass says. "All we need is the right tool."

"Take your pick." He holds up his penknife. There're a couple of dinner knives on the floor, too, and a long, thin metal rod, which given our luck has probably been snapped off some part of the hut that is integral to the structure. More usefully, there's also a very dinky hand axe, no doubt responsible for the new gouges in the side of the crate. But clearly nothing has worked.

"Hundred percent, you're a tool, Law. Just not the right tool." Seb smirks, and his brother kicks him this time. Seb chucks the metal rod, and before we know where we are, Lawrence is on top of his brother, brandishing the axe.

"I'll clobber an' eat *you*, you bampot! See if I don't!" We watch, as we've seen this play out many times before—though, perhaps not with an axe. But after a few seconds of entertainment, Steph elbows Ben and he reluctantly wades in and separates the two. Not by force of muscle, but by producing two tins of baked beans he was apparently carrying with him this whole time and waving them in front of Lawrence's face.

"You don't have to kill him. These'll taste better."

Steph has half a squashed loaf of bread. We use the metal rod to string up slices in front of the fire and make toast, the beans warming in a pot on top of the stove. Ben produces canned mystery meat, someone else has a handful of those little cheese rounds in red wax, and everything is pooled. There are camping plates on the shelves, and some bowls and spoons. We share them and eat.

Every time I feel any echo of memory of the cave, I push it down. Because this is nothing like that. Steph is generous with her bar of chocolate, and we wrap ourselves in our sleeping bags. It's almost cozy. That makes me feel terrible, because Dad and Ant are lost in the dark and cold. Dad, who I have shut out of my life. Ant, who I all but dropped when Ben and I got together. But what can I do about any of my sins right now? I have to hope they'll find us.

"Och, do you think we should ration food for the rest of the trip?" Steph says, as she tucks away the remnants of her chocolate.

"My dad will be here—" I begin.

"What rest of the trip?" Ben interrupts. "It's over. We never should have set out in the first place with this weather." He shakes his head. "Yet another bad decision from the king of bad decisions." I feel a rush of blood to the head, but I bite my cheek. Ben won't even look at me, coward. "Tomorrow, whatever happens, we're going home."

Nobody has the strength to discuss it further, and I don't trust myself to speak. We finish our food. Lawrence washes the dishes.

I glance at Steph, lying there on her sleeping bag. Ben is propped up on his side in a way that can't be comfortable, hanging over her. Thank god Steph's chilled out after her woodland visions. Maybe she is a little concussed, maybe she did hallucinate.

We go about the reassuringly normal process of settling down for the night. Teeth are brushed in the sink, boots taken off and lined up hopefully in front of the fire to dry. But, god, I'm way too wired to sleep. No phone, obviously. Wish I'd brought a book.

There's a box on the shelf with a few magazines that Cass was looking at earlier, and I leaf through them. *Visit Scotland*, *Mountain Living*, and something called *Highlands Larder*, with a picture of a reindeer on the cover. Wow. If Lawrence gets too hungry tomorrow, it could be bye-bye Rudolph. There's a ski trail map, a pamphlet about wildlife, and, *ooh*, a couple of well-thumbed books. That'll kill a few hours.

I check out the first one, a novel. It has powdery, yellowed pages and *Hungry Hearts Series* printed on the spine. Hey, whatever, I could do with a laugh. It has the kind of cover that looks like a retro painting. There's a woman rocking a glossy, black 1960s beehive hairdo, and she's deep in an embrace with a man with an open shirt and wandering hands. Behind them, just visible through a gap in the door, another woman glares from the shadows. Maybe the illustrator messed up the perspective, but the woman in the doorway looks like a giant. I gulp. And the title is…*Love Triangle*. Below, the tagline reads:

Two's company, three is...murder! Oh, hell no. Seb would roast me for hours. Call me paranoid, but this book needs to disappear before anyone else sees it.

"Anything I missed?"

I jump, caught in the act, as Cass kneels down beside me and picks up the magazines again.

"Dunno." I lean in and wedge the novel behind the shelf, grabbing the other book and flicking through it quickly, like I'm super interested, but not taking anything in.

"Done with these." She throws the magazines back. "What you got there?"

"Um." I look at the cover for the first time. It has pictures of stained-glass windows and people with shiny, golden halos. "*The Book of Saints.* It's, er, an encyclopedia, I suppose."

"Sounds like a laugh a minute," Cass says. "Is it too much to ask for sudoku? I'd settle for a sodding word hunt." She groans as she abandons the box. "So hit me with the holy highlights. Can we pray to the saints to stop the rain? Maybe get us raptured away from here? Or at least stop Sebastian's noxious fish farts?"

"You love them like your own!" Seb shouts from the sleeping platform.

"I don't fart," Cass says. "Or if I do, they smell like perfume."

"What, cuz you're such an angel?" Seb snarks.

"Nope, actually, I'm a saint." Cass grabs the book from me. "Here." She searches the index. "If this really is an encyclopedia of saints, I can prove it." She leafs through the book and finds a page, holding it up to us. "Yaaas! Jackpot." There's a medieval-style picture of a man, hands pressed together in prayer. "Saint Cassian, see? My namesake."

"You make one ugly dude, Cass." Seb bundles over to us and looks over my shoulder. "Hey, find Saint Anthony. Isn't he the saint of missing things? How come our dumb Saint Ant got lost?"

"You need to stop." Cass sighs.

"Why? You don't want Ant back?" He waggles his tongue at her. "If *it* ever shows up again, you should get to know each other better. Seeing as you both have dude names." He grabs for the book, but she's too quick, turning her back on him.

"My grandparents named me. Saint Cassian's the patron saint of a town called Imola in Italy, that's where they're from." Cass hands me the book. "Saint Cassian was a teacher, killed by his students. He was martyred because he died for his beliefs."

"Och, I can think of a few teachers I'd be happy murdering!" Seb chortles. "So what would you be prepared to die for, Saint Cass?" He tries again. "Maybe…a chance to get into Stephanie's knickers?"

"Stop!" Steph cries out in protest.

"Would that make you wet yourself, Sebastian?" Cass turns and leans toward him, provocatively, her voice low and rasping, her head on one side, teeth biting her lower lip. "Tell everybody, we could do with some entertainment. You've obviously imagined it."

"Oh my god, no!" Ben claps a hand over his face overdramatically. "Behave, both of you."

"I wouldn't waste my time!" Seb blusters back at Cass. He cannot deal, and we all can see it. Lawrence laughs heartily.

"Busted, bro."

"You're so wrong, because you know what? I'm a saint too." Seb whisks the book out of my hands, swishing through the pages like it's going to save him. "Saint Sebastian sounds like it's a thing, let me see—yep! I was right, here I am." He beams at us. "And check out my abs." He turns the book around. The illustration is an oil painting of a beautiful man, naked but for a white loin cloth, his arms raised above him, hands tied to a tree. The abs are great, true. What's more noticeable is the arrows sticking out of them. "Daaamn, I'm so pretty. Says here they strung me up and shot me down, but they couldn't kill Sebastian!" He lifts his arms up, like in the picture. "Can't touch this."

"Yeah, didn't you know? That painting's a famous work of art." Stephanie chimes in. "And, get this, Saint Sebastian. You're a bona fide gay icon."

Seb swears at her.

"Check that pic. You are fire! You ate." Lawrence chuckles. "Lovin' the man-diaper. You wearing it now?" He snags the waistband of Seb's pants, like he's trying to see, and the two fall to the sleeping platform, tussling. Cass rescues the book.

"Saint Sebastian did indeed survive the arrows, sadly." She shakes her head. "Ooh—says here he was 'full of pricks'!"

"Truth!" Lawrence yells, sitting on top of his brother, who he has successfully pinned to the floor.

"Oh, but wait; when that didn't work, they clubbed him

to death in the end." Cass pulls a sad face. "Another martyr. Persecuted for his faith."

"Nope," Lawrence says, covering his brother's mouth with a large paw. "Mercy killing. They tired of his foolish ways."

"What about you, Maggie?" Cass says brightly. "You in here?"

I blink. Like I'd know. I've never felt particularly saintly. But Steph has beaten me to it, she swipes the book from Cass.

"There's a Saint Stephanie, I'm sure of it." She flicks through. "Huh. No. Only Saint Stephen. Typical, the girls got edited out."

"Because they nagged everyone to death!" Seb shouts from somewhere underneath his brother. "Female saints sound boring as hell, unless they were like, pole-dancing nuns or something."

"That is a wee bit too specific for you not to have thought of it before, you sick puppy." Lawrence strangles his brother.

"I guess I'll take Saint Stephen," Steph reads the page anyway. "Oh! Saint Stephen was a martyr too. *Stoned* to death."

"Sounds like fun." Ben grins at her.

"I don't think that means what you think it means." Steph smiles coyly back.

Seb has finally freed himself from his brother's grip. "Look up and check if there's a Saint Lawrence. See how that guy died, because I'm going to make sure it comes true."

"Nuh-uh. I need to look up Ben first." Steph pirouettes away from Seb and searches the index. "Ben, Ben, Ben... Oh! So, remind me, are you a Benjamin or a Benedict?" She frowns at him. "How wild is it I don't know that?"

Yeah, wild, Steph. He's Ben, just Ben. It's not short for anything, *you don't know him like I do.*

"Whichever you prefer." Ben shrugs, and Steph laughs.

"Och, dangerous, leaving it in my hands." She finds the page and scans it. "Hmm...okay, well, Saint Benedict was a celibate monk, that would *not* be accurate." She bats her lashes at him, and I pray that I'll randomly self-combust and escape this hell. "Whereas, Saint Benjamin, let's see..." She turns the page, reads, and winces. "Whoops. Oh no."

"What is it?" Cass leans in, eyes wide, grinning broadly. Steph cringes.

"Saint Benjamin was tortured to death with, and I quote, 'reeds, pushed under his fingernails and toenails, and into his tender, fleshy parts.'"

"Oof?!" Ben grabs at his groin, Seb whoops, everyone falls about laughing.

Suddenly the door swings open and crashes against the wall.

"What the—?"

"Oh my god!"

We scuttle back, Steph clinging to Ben, and Ben clinging to the wall. The wind blows in, the door open, nothing but darkness outside.

"How did that—?" Ben whispers.

Nobody moves.

We wait, watch the doorway, petrified to the spot, cornered

and helpless, until Lawrence swears heartily, takes a brave step forward.

"Don't!" I hiss, hardly recognizing my own voice. Lawrence swears at me this time, but he doesn't move any closer to the door.

"Hello?" Cass calls out.

"What do you mean, 'hello?'" Lawrence growls at her. "There's no one there."

"Like there was no one in the woods? Go and look!" Steph shoos him, but he doesn't move, so she stumbles forward a couple of steps and throws the saints book through the doorway, as if casting out a banshee. "Get away, whoever you are!"

The book lies on the stone step, pages fluttering.

"You sure told them, Steph." Seb giggles nervously.

We watch the darkness. After what seems like an age, Lawrence takes a step forward.

"This is pathetic." He moves to the door. And that's my cue to wake the hell up.

"Oh my god, it could be Dad and Ant!"

I barge past Lawrence onto the step, kicking the book out of the way. "What was I thinking?" I find my headlamp in my pocket and fumble it on, strafing the darkness. "Dad! Are you there? Dad! Ant?" I take a tentative step forward, the wet mud seeping into my socks, but I don't care. I scan the shadows, but the only voices I hear are those in the hut.

"Is it them?"

"No way."

"They wouldn't fling the door open and run off!"

"Come back in!" Ben shouts to me.

"Dad!" I take another step into the night. "Are you there?"

"It's not your dad, Maggie," Steph calls from somewhere behind me.

"It must be, who else could it be?" I turn around to the faces in the hut.

They're all too scared to come out, even Lawrence. They're just lingering inside the threshold, because that way nothing evil can touch them. A chill goes up my backbone and I swing around.

"Who's there?" I say, more quietly. The wind rushes me, and I step back. The night doesn't want me out here.

It wasn't Dad.

My foot finds something hard, something sharp under the mud, and I flinch.

Ow.

There's something shiny on the ground, glinting in the light of the headlamp. A huge knife. I pick it up, carefully, limping back into the hut. Behind me, Lawrence swipes the saints book and throws it inside, slamming the door shut and bolting it.

"This was in the mud." I hold up the knife, and there's a second where everyone gasps and it's kind of scary, kind of satisfying. "I...stepped on it."

"Oh god, are you okay?" Cass clutches her sweater.

"Jeez, is that blood on it?" Seb's so excited, he's practically salivating.

"Yes, it must be my blood." I turn the knife around, looking at it. "This was buried right in front of the door." I look up at their rapt faces. "How did it get there? Lawrence, is it yours?"

"No way."

Ben zeros in on Seb. "You didn't bring it, did you?"

Seb pulls a *maybe* clown face, and Lawrence answers for him. "Of course he didn't."

"It's a hunting knife. Hardcore," Steph says. She takes it from me, turns it over in her hands, and swears. "This means someone's definitely out there."

"Like who?" Ben's eyes dart to the door. We *all* look at the door.

"Did you use the dead bolt just now, Lawrence?" Steph's voice is so low I can hardly hear her above the wind.

He nods. "We're locked in tight."

"I'm sure it was bolted before," Cass says. "How the hell did it swing open like that?"

"It was only on the latch." Lawrence takes a step forward, studying the door. "The wind caught it."

"Still doesn't explain who's standing outside our hut with a hunting knife!" Steph's voice has a tinge of panic. Lawrence snatches up the small chair, strides to the door, and wedges it. When we don't look that impressed, he hauls the crate and hefts it up on top of the chair.

"There ye go." He rubs his face. "If there's a PCP-fueled knifeman out there, that will do sod all to stop him, but at least we'll get fair warning."

"What if Dad and Ant arrive and can't get in?"

Lawrence gives me a look, and makes as if to move the crate and chair.

"No!" Steph says. "We'll hear them if they come." She walks over to the table and carefully places the knife on it. "This knife stays here. Agreed, everyone?" She grabs the axe by the woodpile, the random crappy cutlery, and the metal rod. "These too. All our weapons together, in plain sight."

"Easy to grab when the bodach comes to kill us all." Seb's jokes aren't landing, and he knows it.

"It was the wind," Lawrence says determinedly. "If anyone was coming for us, they wouldn't leave us the knife, would they?"

This kind of makes sense. We're grasping at straws here, but it feels ridiculous that anyone would be out there screwing with us in this storm. For all we know, the knife has been there for days, even weeks, hidden in the mud.

"We should look at your foot." Ben's suddenly at my side. "Does it hurt?"

"No!" I blurt. "I mean, a bit, but it's not going to fall off or anything." I feel heat flush my cheeks as I sit and peel off my sock. There's a long, red slice along the ball of my big toe joint, but it doesn't look deep, and whatever is in this Highland dirt has stanched the bleeding.

"Hmm, you should wash it out." Ben crouches down, taking my foot in his hand. I jump at his touch, covering it up by acting like I'm ticklish, which in itself feels dumb as hell.

"I can do it myself!" I'm half laughing, but I still manage to sound like Prime Bitch, and his face reads hurt for the tiniest second before he's on his feet, backing off.

"Course you can." He chucks his first aid kit at me; I fumble it and it falls, but I'm grateful to bend down and hide. *Stupid, stupid. Why can't you be normal with him?*

I patch myself up. My foot's throbbing, and it's going to sting like a bastard to walk on tomorrow, but it's not like I've damaged anything major. By the time I'm done, everyone is yawning exaggeratedly, as if that will make us all nod off. Cass stands by the sink, holding up one of the cooking pans.

"Say hello to your piss pot, people. Because I'm betting no one's going to be taking any trips to the outhouse during the night."

I wriggle into my sleeping bag by the window. I'm never peeing into a pot again. I'll make a bet that none of us from the cave will. We'd rather face a storm, and all Seb's bodachs, and go outside. But Cass doesn't know that. She must wonder why nobody responds. Seb doesn't even crack a joke.

The hurricane lights go off, and I hold the sleeping bag up to my chin and watch the shadows from the fire dance on the opposite wall, on the door, making it look like it's moving. The wind rattles the hut, and I press myself into the floor. This is tense. I'm never going to sleep.

CHAPTER 8

———

After the bus driver took us, my parents needed me to be a million miles away from school, but they also needed me *socialized*. It's not like they wanted to hide me from the world completely. Someone had tried that already, and it hadn't turned out well for him at all.

To solve this dilemma, my folks enrolled me in clubs. So many clubs. Sports first, because Dad said I was strong, and that was a win, because he was right. Saturday was my happy day, when I was sweating, scoring, and getting bloodied knees. But when it was the off-season, we had to find other stuff, and one summer that other stuff was drama class.

And drama class was the best thing ever, because Ant came too.

Creative Release was the name of the program. It was some kind of worthy, government-funded outreach initiative to bring "the arts" to the Highlands, and it consisted of three chaotic hours every Saturday at Strother's community center. Actual professional actors taught the sessions. A youngish, beaming guy called Karl who we recognized with starry-eyed glee from a yogurt commercial, and Cynthia, who swore constantly, and had the longest glossy mane of hair I'd ever seen in real life. She was like a potty-mouthed Disney princess, and Karl her prince, and they let us dress up and run around the room swearing too. It was beautiful. Ant and I were most impressed. We were, like, twelve years old at this point, so naturally it took a lot to impress us.

Some days we did improv, or voice work, or songs from terrible musicals. And we'd warm up by doing group icebreakers and trust exercises. The latter was definitely not approved by any safety regulation body. There was something called the human knot, and this other thing with eggs that Cynthia had forgotten to boil. That situation wound up quickly as full-scale floor omelet.

But the trust exercises that I enjoyed most were just me and Ant in a pair. I'd wear a blindfold and they'd lead me around the room, over obstacles and under barriers. It was kind of scary, but funny as hell, because Ant would get bored and speed up, or dance around me and cackle in my ear like a naughty angel on my shoulder.

One Saturday, Cynthia and Karl took it further. We had to catch each other. First in the group, falling backward off a chair into everyone's arms, with a thick gym mat to stop ourselves from ending up like the eggs if the catchers chickened out at the last second. Needless to say, I didn't volunteer to fall. But then we went into our pairs, and we were great. Ant was a natural at falling. They stood on the floor, perfectly straight but relaxed, arms out and head tilted back slightly, eyes closed. And they would breathe, fall back, and allow me to catch them. We did it again and again, like it was a dance. Ant executed their part perfectly, I didn't drop them once.

But of course, it was never going to happen the other way around.

"I'm too heavy," I hissed at Ant when they clapped their hands and told me to swap places.

"Trust me, silly," Ant giggled back. "You won't squish me. And if you do, I'll bounce right back."

I shook my head. "Not going to happen." I looked around the room. Everyone else was doing it, with yells and squeals of laughter, but no one else was as mismatched as us. "Let's go back to you falling and me catching."

"Nope." Ant pouted. "You've got to trust me too, or this does not work out."

"I do trust you!" I bent down and got in their face. "But it's common sense. I'll hurt you."

Ant frowned and looked up at me through their thick mop of a fringe. "I don't care if you do. It's worth the risk."

I stamped my foot in frustration, and oopsy, before you can say Low Fat GoGURT with Summer Berries, Karl had spotted us and was moving in, telling me I could do the exercise with him. I clammed up and shook my head, and then Cynthia was there, pulling out all her best-worst words, telling me to be brave, to sock it to her, but I couldn't, because she was even shorter than Ant. I was sweating through the pits of my favorite tee, knowing any second I was going to cry. There was literally no one in the room big enough to catch me.

The rest of the morning I watched the clock, and for the first time, willed the class to end. When it finally did, my dad messaged me to say he'd be late picking Ant and me up, so we walked through town to the bakery, in silence. I had my allowance, and a massive urge to make things up to Ant, so I bought us two jam donuts in a paper bag. We took them back to the wall where we usually waited for Dad and sat down—or at least I did, while Ant found a dozen ways to get on the wall and get off it again—and finally, they spoke.

"So, you know about the trust exercise…?"

I felt my chest go tight. "Don't want to talk about it."

"Guessed as much." Ant just nodded slowly. "Doesn't matter. I've got a better trust exercise. Will you do it? To prove we really trust each other?"

"Okay." I rolled my eyes. "As long as it's not jumping off the roof or something."

"Nope!" Ant grabbed the bag of donuts out of my hand. The perfect steal. "Too slow, Mags!" The bag ripped, but Ant deftly grabbed the first donut as it fell. "This"—they held it up to my face—"is the Donut of Trust. We have one each. In order to earn the right to eat your Donut of Trust, you have to tell me a deep, dark secret."

"That's so sus!" I groaned at them. "Like, what?"

"Something *huge*," Ant said. "And I promise never to tell a soul, or judge you on it. But it has to be deep and dark."

You don't want my deep and dark. You don't want to know about how I dream about the driver, constantly, about pushing him over the edge, about how sometimes I jump too, only I can fly, and I laugh all the way down with him, watching his terror as he falls, seeing him smash as he hits the ground—splat—like those eggs.

"I promise you, I'll never let you down." Ant bobbed up and down on the spot, the Donut of Trust held aloft between their finger and thumb, the sugar glistening. "Trust me, Maggie." They squeezed my donut, and the hole where the jam goes in oozed like blood.

"Okay, okay." I held a hand up to stop the donut murder. "I've got one. It's…gross, I'm warning you."

"Bring it!"

I nodded, serious, doing my very best acting. "You know last month when we found that dirty magazine behind the wall here?" Ant's eyes widened. "Well, I kept it." I flushed hot at the thought, no faking needed, and Ant whooped.

"What the hell, dude?" They hugged themselves, delighted. "Why?"

"I have no idea." I really didn't, because it never happened. My whole body itched with the lie. "I hid it in my nightstand and I want to get rid of it, but I'm paranoid because I think one of my parents is going to catch me." I exhaled. Wow, give me the Oscar, that was some *Creative Release*, right there.

"Thank you for trusting me," Ant said formally, but their eyes sparkled with joy, and I felt like the worst friend ever. "Your reward." They handed me the donut. I ate it, even though I wanted to puke.

"Now me, do me," Ant panted, shoving the donut bag into my hands.

"'Kay…" I coughed, sugar sticking in my throat, and held up the bag. "This is the Donut of Trust. Tell me a deep, dark secret."

"And show me you trust me," whispered Ant.

"And show me you trust me," I muttered. "And I'll keep your secret forever, no judgment, blah, blah, blah."

Ant nodded, vigorously drumming their thumbs against their thighs. "Get ready."

"Hit me."

They inhaled loudly, hands clasped together in front of their chest as if they were about to break into song.

"I'm…emby."

I waited for more. None came. Ant grinned at me. "There! I said it! I'm emby."

"You're…*envy*? Envious? Of what?"

"No, enby!" They laughed like a drain. "It's the letters. *N. B.* Non-binary."

I nodded, like they'd just said they were Sagittarius or vegetarian, and my brain was spinning because although I *kind of* knew what non-binary meant, I didn't exactly know what it meant, and I wasn't sure if Ant was having a laugh with me or if they were serious, whereas at the same time I absolutely knew in my bones what they were trying to say and that they were deadly serious.

"You understand?" Ant was so eager, my stomach twisted. "Neither gender, just something…different. I'm not female, I'm not male. Or I'm both, I'm not sure about that part yet. But in the meantime, I'll just be all and nothing." They looked up at me underneath their messy hair. "Mags, this is probably not really news to you, is it?"

I shook my head, not knowing what else to say. I knew I loved Ant, and I believed them, wanted to be there for them, but all those words felt awkward in my head…

"This is, like, me making it official. It's important to say it. I needed to tell you properly," Ant said, twirling around on the spot. "We can tell Ben too. Together, yeah?"

"Totally." God, I hoped so much I was reacting like I should. "Um, what do I call you? I don't want say the wrong thing and upset you or anything."

"Don't sweat the pronouns!" Ant cocked a finger at me. It sounded like something that they'd read somewhere. "I dunno? We'll work it out together. It's not like I'm an expert, yet." They stared at me. "Now, come on! Gimme my bloody donut."

Ant trusted me. And that made me feel so good. But it didn't cancel out the bad I felt, knowing I couldn't trust them back. Something inside of me was broken. Something I couldn't mend, not with a stupid donut or a drama exercise. It would never be fixed.

CHAPTER 9

My eyes open, fear shooting through my veins before I even
know why.

I'm waking up—no, being woken—by someone shaking my
bed violently. What the hell? It's dark, but there's no blissful
microsecond of kidding myself that I'm safe at home.

I instantly know the full, horrible truth: I'm in a hut, my
dad and my best friend are missing, and, wait—there's no bed.
Someone must be shaking the heavy sleeping platform...?
Huh? How could they even do that...?

Voices, panicked:

"What's going on?"

"Holy crap!"

A flurry of movement. Flashlights dance around the
inside of the hut. I see shadowy figures around me, but no
one's doing any shaking. Why am I moving? A hurricane
lamp flicks on to show faces wearing versions of the same

shocked, confused, and all-around terrified expression I must be pulling.

"Is this an earthquake?"

Steph is standing in the doorway, hands braced on walls at either side. My first, ridiculous thought is that she looks amazing, like a thermal-clad goddess holding the rocks apart. "The whole place is shaking!"

"Scotland doesn't get earthquakes!" Ben looks dazed, personally affronted by the idea.

"D'ye want to tell that to Scotland!" Lawrence shouts back, stuffing his pack and flinging it over his shoulder. "We need to get out of here before the roof collapses!" He rushes toward the door, followed by the others. I find myself on my feet, pulling on boots—*go!* I grab my coat, sprint outside, flashlight in hand, to find everyone huddled and shivering a few feet from the hut.

"It's stopped." Steph breathes hard, glued to Ben—like he's ever going to be man enough to save her.

"The storm too," I whisper, more to myself than anyone else. The wind has gone and there's no suggestion of thunder or lightning. The night is eerily still, as if it, like us, is waiting for the aftershock.

"That was frickin' psychotic!" Seb says, leaping into the air and skidding on the mud as he lands. "Total head rush! Felt like someone spiked the baked beans!" He howls with laughter. Lawrence thumps him on the shoulder but he's grinning too, and they're slipping around in the muck and laughing, because that's what they do when they don't want everyone to know how shook they really are.

"Is it really over?" Steph shudders, and frankly, I'm right there with her. "Because they say there's never just one tremor."

"It can't have been an earthquake." Ben is insistent.

"Yes, it totally can." So easy to snap at him. "We have them here. Just not very often, and not very big ones." Jeez, it's so cold, we need to get back inside. I shine my flashlight on the hut.

"Well, it's still the same old pile o' rocks."

Steph nods. "Probably seen its share of random Scottish seismic disturbances. Safe enough."

"Safer than out here…" Cass shudders, and then we all remember the knife and get the hell back inside the giant turd.

Cass revives the fire. We crowd around it, shivering, as much from shock as cold. There's no more talk of earthquakes, but funny how we're stalling, dragging our heels to return to sleeping bags, waiting for the aftershock, ready to run out again but dreading the thought. The aftershock doesn't come, and one by one, our tiredness wins over fear. The twins fall asleep first. Cass chucks a last log in the burner before turning in beside me by the window, and Ben and Steph curl up together.

But I can't sleep. I wriggle way down into my sleeping bag until it is over my head and read the saints book with my headlamp on, my mind trying to take in the words, concentrate on anything rather than letting stupid thoughts run wild through my brain. Hmm, Seb was right; Saint Anthony is the patron saint of lost things, lost people. Find your way back with Dad, Ant.

Suddenly, I hear movement to my left, and peep over the top of my bag. Steph sits up, her back to me, and butt-scoots over the platform to her pack. She retrieves something—is that the map?—and pores over it by the light of the fire. She plotting an escape? She hasn't noticed I'm awake. I put my book down quietly, watch her concentrating on the map. Funny how you can know someone from years back and barely know them at all. I don't know Steph, not really. Only the version from when we were six.

I ease out of my sleeping bag, onto all fours, just to see if I can do it without Steph spotting me. It feels like something I did a long time ago, and I want to see if I've still got the skill. She doesn't move. She's engrossed, not paying me any attention, perhaps because I'm barely relevant to her existence, like she was to me until so recently. Why would she notice me? So, I pad over to her, big-cat-like, curious to see how far I can get. I get all the way.

"What time is it?"

"God!" She swings around, putting her hand to her chest. "Didn't hear you move, stealth queen. Can't sleep?" I shake my head. "I have no idea what time it is, but it's too early for you to play search party." The stern look she's giving me doesn't quite hit, because I'm way too busy feeling guilty about her face and the evolution of that bruised, swollen nose, which is only getting worse. Shit. I wonder if her parents will sue me for plastic surgery? I mean, Steph's not a bad person, she wouldn't want to hurt me, but she's strong, with definite opinions.

That's why she works with Ben, because he's…not weak, but… willing to be led. It was the same when we were together. I was the driver, Ben the happy passenger. And someone's got to be, haven't they? But with me, he grew to resent it, and perhaps he'll begin to resent Steph too.

Steph's expression has turned expectant, and I realize that she's waiting for a response, reassurance.

"Not going anywhere yet. Dad'll find us." The words are too easy, and that shocks me. Does it sound like admitting defeat? But Steph seems comforted.

"Sensible. The life jackets you left behind, that was clever." She blinks, those huge brown eyes boring into mine. "Maggie. Stop looking at my nose." I think it comes out a little harsher than she means, because her full lips turn up into a smile. "What I mean is, don't sweat about bashing my face in. It wasn't your fault. Ben was being a dick about it."

My heart beats double time. *Ben was being a dick.* He *is* a dick. And Steph knows it. I glance at him, checking he's still sleeping. Not that Steph seems to care if he hears. Maybe she's going to dump him. Or maybe, better yet, he'll dump her and want me back. And then I'll lead him on and hang him out to dry, because like it says in the song, I want sweet revenge.

Steph's giving me the expectant look again, because she's done me a solid, she's bestowed her forgiveness. I half smile, nod, mutter thanks.

"Look, I'm sorry how everything has been so…tricky." She's nodding back, and oh god, she's actually clasping my arm with her bony hand and this is cringe beyond all cringes. I glance again at Ben, hoping he'll turn over and fart in his sleep so that Steph and I can laugh and move on from this hideous *moment* we're apparently having. But once again, Ben disappoints. "This hasn't been easy for any of us." Steph's whispering, but I feel the itch of red heat crawling up my neck because it will be just my luck if Seb overhears and never lets me live it down. "You've been a trooper." *Argh, don't know where to look. Who even says stuff like that?* "No." She nods at the book on my sleeping bag. "A saint. You've been a saint, Maggie."

Hardly. Oh, if she only knew the thoughts I've been thinking. What to say?

It's actually Seb who saves us with a fart. A long, low, trumpeting triumph. Something that most people would have to work on and practice, but that comes so naturally to Seb. We crack up; Steph's giggling and I'm pretending it's hysterical too, so we can forget everything else.

"They're hard work, these boys." She sighs, tucking the map away in her backpack. "Tomorrow, whatever happens, I'm out of here." She reaches over for the bottle of pills Cass gave her, taps out two, and pushes them into my sweaty palm. "Take, eat. You need sleep. Oblivion makes everything better."

With that, she slinks back across the platform and into her sleeping bag. Ben snoozily spoons her and she gives me a resigned smile like it's some major hardship. I'm left there, on the edge, in the dark, not knowing what to do next.

I swallow the pills, that's what I do.

I wake like someone's shouted my name, but the room is still, quiet. *Urgh, brightness and freezing cold.* Someone opened the shutter.

Daylight? How long have I slept in? I sit bolt upright, so suddenly my head spins. The fire is dead, but, wait—where is everyone? Panic grips my chest, and I am pinned, unable to move. They left me here? How could they? I fight for breath as tears flood my eyes, the hut feels like it's collapsing in on me. *You're not trapped, just breathe, you can do this.* How the hell did I sleep through everyone getting up? My stomach flips. The pills Steph gave me.

Why would they leave me?

No, calm down, look...backpacks, sleeping bags in disarray—some of the jackets are gone, but they wouldn't abandon all of their stuff.

The crate's missing.

That's it. They must have taken the crate outside to break it open. Or—my heart leaps and I flash hot—Dad and Ant have arrived? That's it! Damn, can't see anything out this window, it's so fogged with condensation. Got to hurry, got to get dressed...

When I run out of the hut, I don't spot the others immediately. The storm has passed, at least the worst of it has. A fine drizzle of rain wets my face, there's a cold, brisk breeze, and the light is finest, fragile, weak-as-piss sunshine.

Where are they? Voices come from the other side of the hut. *Thank god.* The mud sucks at my boots as I traverse, my injured foot throbbing, and there they are, standing at the rocky outcrop at the top of the crag. Lawrence has binoculars, Seb is looking bored, and Steph, Ben, and Cass are holding corners of the map, splayed and blowing slightly in the wind.

No Dad, no Ant. What time is it, anyway? Shouldn't they be here by now?

I hurry over.

"If we head due west once we're at the bottom of Devil's Chute, we'll cut a corner, get to the river quicker. It's only about four miles upstream to this footbridge." Steph is animated, tapping the map with a pencil. "Once we're on the other side of the river, yes, it's a few hours' hike across a boggy moor, but we're basically home."

"How do you figure that?" Seb asks. "Because home for you is a paddy field, Steph?"

"Don't start, Seb!" Ben snaps.

"And you're leading us right off the edge of the map! We won't even know where we are!"

"See here?" Steph's stabbing the map with the pencil now, maybe pretending it's Seb's face. "That's a road, or at least some kind of marked track, for vehicles. There might be other hikers, or a farmer."

"Hey." I break into the circle. "What's happening?"

Steph ignores me. "And then we head southeast. Because logic dictates that track will eventually join up with the road that runs up to the café."

"Sooner we leave, the better." Ben nods. "It's the best plan."

"You what?" I splutter. "Leaving? We can't leave. We have to wait for Dad and Ant." I look over to Lawrence, who's a few feet away, gazing down the valley through the expensive-looking binoculars. There's a thick mist rising off the valley floor, obscuring everything below us, so god knows what he's seeing. Makes me feel dizzy, like we're up above the clouds. "What time is it, Lawrence? They'll be here soon."

"Maybe." He shrugs at me. "Or maybe not. For all we know, they're counting on us to raise the alarm and get them rescued. Either way, don't know if Stephanie's right about the bridge, but I'm not sitting on my ass all day." He walks past me.

"Amazing vacay, guys," Seb snarks. "Just time to order room service before our lil' safari."

"Wait!"

The brothers ignore me and walk off in the direction of the hut.

"Look, for what it's worth, I agree with Maggie." Cass sighs, hands on hips. "The rules of the trip are, you get separated, you shelter in place."

"But for how long?" Steph turns to me. "I'm sorry, Maggie, but for all we know, your dad couldn't land the boat anywhere nearby and they're miles away by now. He's smart enough to realize that if they get so far downriver, they might as well float all the way to civilization and raise the alarm so they can send a proper search party. The storm has passed, hasn't it? They'll have people out looking for us already."

My chest feels tight. "But even if that's right, they'll look here, at the hut!"

"I don't want to hang around waiting for something to happen." She hugs herself, her voice almost a whisper. "We're all spooked. I definitely saw something in the woods, and there's the whole...knife weirdness."

"If someone is messing with us"—I'm lowering my voice too and I'm not even sure why—"isn't it better to be inside the hut, where we can lock the door?"

She shakes her head vehemently. "It's bad vibes. And I don't want to play the broken nose card, Mags, but I need a doctor. This is our chance to leave. Who knows when the weather will turn again?"

Ah, the broken nose. Can't argue with that. Last night she said it didn't matter, but suddenly this morning it's everything. I glance at Cass on the off chance she'll be on my side, but she shrugs. She won't go against Steph.

"Anyway." Steph smiles, as best she can. "If there are rescuers coming for us, we'll be walking right toward them. There're only two ways out of here on foot. Down, or up." She glances behind us, over the mountain. "And it would be madness to choose up."

Back at the hut, they're packing. And I will too. Because if we're leaving, then fine, but when we reach the river, I'm not heading west to find some footbridge. If the others make it back and raise the alarm, that's great, but I can't rely on that. I need to head downriver and go after Dad and Ant myself. I have a sleeping bag and a tent. Maybe I'll take the knife. Yes, definitely the knife. For reasons. Let me find it, it was on the table.

Hmm. Not there.

"Who's moved the knife?"

"Huh? The knife's gone?" Lawrence, by the door, is immediately on high alert, because clearly, he'd had similar ideas of swiping it for himself. "What are you talking about?" He stomps over, stares at the tabletop like that's going to make the knife materialize, and when it doesn't, he grabs the little table and pushes it across the floor. "One of you has taken it? I want to eat something before we go, and we need that knife to get into the crate."

"Er, where's the crate?" Ben says.

"What the actual hell?" Lawrence doesn't do hungry, that much I know. We all search, but it's not like it takes long for them to see what I already know: the crate isn't here.

"Whoever moved stuff, you better stop playing." Lawrence's face contracts into a snarl and he turns on his brother. "Is this you?"

"Try again, you loser," Seb barks back at him. "Haven't touched anything." He points to me. "She took the crate outside yesterday, remember?"

I gape at him. "I did not. That was your lame joke, to take it out into the lightning storm. I didn't actually do it."

"Okay, this is ridiculous. It can't be far away." Cass steps in. "It was under the table last night. Did anyone notice it after the earthquake, or this morning?" No one speaks.

"Come on, did someone take it outside?" Steph shrugs. "And maybe...forgot they did?"

Lawrence spits out a laugh. "Like someone would forget! If this is a prank, fess up, because it's not funny."

Nobody says anything. We all look at each other, until Seb bursts out laughing. Lawrence kicks out at the table, shattering the leg.

"Calm down, let's think this through," Ben says. "We've all been in here, all of the time, except for after the so-called earthquake." God, he still won't give in on that. "So, someone moved the crate and the knife this morning."

"Maggie was in here on her own." Seb pulls a face at me. "Where'dya hide everything, Mags? In yer big girl panties?"

Don't rise to it, don't give him the satisfaction.

"The crate was definitely gone from under the table when I woke up and came outside; I thought that's what you were doing, opening it."

"The bodach came back for his blade and took our crate too!" Seb laughs ghoulishly.

"We're wasting time," Cass says, marching to the door. "I'm looking outside." She stabs a finger at Seb. "This reeks of you, and I'll find the stupid crate because you won't have even bothered to lug it far away."

"If I had hidden it, you'd never find it." Seb smiles at her sweetly. "But I haven't."

Lawrence looks like he's going to punch his brother, for once thinks better of it, and follows Cass. Seb blows a raspberry and marches after them, slamming the door behind him. Outside, we hear them all shouting at each other.

"I don't think Seb took it." Steph crosses her arms, and a slow tear makes its way down her cheek. "I really, really wish he had, but I think there's someone trying to scare us. And it's working." She bites her lip, more tears come, and Ben's straight in, arm around her shoulder, comforting.

"There's no one out there." He strokes her face, gently, like I'm invisible. "Seb probably hid the friggin' crate to wind Lawrence up, and now it's gone too far and he can't come clean. We're all stressed. It's got us paranoid. Anyway, we're out of here now, aren't we? Forget the crate, let's focus on you leading us home."

"You're right. I'm sorry." She nods, wiping away her tears efficiently. "I'll get it together. But you really, truly promise me you don't think there's anyone out there doing this to us?"

"Cross my heart and hope to die." His face creases with a smile.

Steph smiles back, bravely, and gathers up the rest of her stuff, sufficiently reassured.

But I'm not. Because unlike Steph, I can tell when Ben is lying.

CHAPTER 10

Hi Dad and Ant—we stayed here last night. We're all fine.

"Fine" is a stretch. So, what do I put in this pathetic note?

I lean on *The Book of Saints'* back page, grip the pen I borrowed from Cass so tightly it hurts, and cross the last sentence out. Got to hurry. Ben and Steph left at least a minute ago; I can't hear them outside and I have zero confidence that anyone will wait for me.

Hi Dad and Ant—we stayed here last night. Steph's got a broken nose but apart from that we're OK. It's morning and we are heading back to the river. Everyone is walking west upstream to a footbridge and then south toward the road, but I will be looking for you downstream, following the river east—

Shite. Reading that, I'm already hearing what Dad's reaction will be. *What are you thinking, Maggie! Stick together, have you not seen this mist?*

I bite the pen, which is a mistake because now I have ink in my mouth. Quickly, make a decision! Urgh, my head hurts. Is it smarter to go with the others after all? Get to safety, and call in the professionals? What can I do to help Ant and Dad that they couldn't already do for themselves? And it serves no one if I get lost myself.

Chicken…

No, be logical! Dad would know about the footbridge—he likely crossed it when he brought the crate up here a week ago. What's more, he'd realize we couldn't access the food in the crate without the code. So, would he guess we'd make for the bridge, and head that way himself? *Just roll the dice…* I cross the last line out.

Hi Dad and Ant—we stayed here last night. Steph's got a broken nose but apart from that we're OK. It's morning and we are heading back to the river. Everyone is walking west upstream to a footbridge and then south toward the road.

Done. For what it's worth. But…should I tell him about the crate going missing, and the knife? About a shadow in the woods, and a dodgy door flinging open, and how we're freaked and barely holding it together?

"Maggie, you still in there?"

Cass, from outside. Thank goodness someone actually gives a damn where I am. The note will have to do. At least they'll know which direction we're going. And somewhere in the middle of all of that, I've made a decision to stick with the group. Cowardly, or smart? I scribble my name on the bottom, tear the page out of *The Book of Saints*, and leave it on top of the wood stove.

Outside, there are foreboding, slate-gray clouds scudding across the sky, but the sun is still gamely putting in the effort to make the best of things, filtering through the gloom, holding back the darkness. I'm going to do the same. Time to make a positive move before either of us gives up the fight.

Cass is leaning against the wall, breathing heavily.

"Thanks for the pen." I hand it back to her. "Sorry, I kind of chewed it at the top."

She frowns and puts it in her pack. "Only, it was my dad's. I don't have much that belonged to my folks. I guess I shouldn't have brought it on a stupid hike, anyway."

Oh god. Yeah, she lives with her grandparents. Someone at school told me she lost her parents in a car crash or something? When she was little.

"I'm so, so sorry!" I grimace. "I didn't realize."

"Hey, no big deal." She pats my arm. "It was a smart idea to write that note."

I nod. Awkward. "So, any sign of the crate?"

"Nope." She lowers her voice. "And I don't think it's Seb, he doesn't look any more shifty than usual. It's a total mystery. But I found the answer to something else. Guys! Come over here!" She shouts across to where Ben and Steph are standing, and waves to Lawrence who is emerging from the outhouse, for some reason, carrying an armful of black plastic sacks.

"See up there?" Cass points east, to a rise on the hillside. "I climbed it, looking for the crate. Ben was right. It wasn't an earthquake last night, it was a frickin' landslide. The other side of the hill has totally gone."

"What do you mean, gone?" Steph frowns.

"There's just rubble at the bottom, you know, loose rocks, scree," Cass says. "The whole slope has completely disintegrated."

Lawrence whistles. "The rain must have triggered a collapse."

"Oh my god, that's what we felt?" Steph says, swaying slightly, as if the ground is trembling again. "Are we safe here?"

"Wouldn't bet on it." Ben looks grim. "Another reason to leave, like we needed one."

We gather our things and head to the top of Devil's Chute. Maybe the landslide explains why Dad and Ant haven't made it up here. Would it block their way? But surely they could still cut through the woods we were in yesterday, and climb Devil's Chute?

Or maybe not. When we reach the top of the slope, I stare down the hill in despair. Where there was once grass to grab, now there is little but mud, mud, glorious mud. So many hours of hammering rain has left a steep slide of the finest thick Scottish clarts, tricking with water.

"How do we even…?" Cass groans.

"Remember Slip 'N Slide?" Lawrence drops the black plastic sacks he was carrying. "Found these in the outhouse. Our transport." He picks one up and hops into it to demonstrate.

"Och yaasss, mama!" Seb cries, grabs a bag too.

"You can't be serious," Steph says. "We're supposed to slide down here? What about the mist? I can't see the bottom."

"One way or another, we're leaving on our butts." Ben shrugs. "Might as well be in a bag."

"Body bag, more like. It's too steep, how do we stop?" Steph says. "And what if it triggers another landslide?"

"Spoilsport." Lawrence looks her up and down. "Die young, leave a beautiful corpse."

"I'd rather live ugly," I deadpan, shoving my face in the sack, taking a breath and almost gagging. It smells of dead things and dung, and—*why?*—a hint of curry powder. What's with all the goddamn incongruent spice? "Urgh, this reeks."

"Yeah, right?" Steph nods. "God knows what these sacks have had in them."

They're going to have us in them now.

We sack up. It quickly becomes apparent that this is never going to work with backpacks on, so more sacks are found and Lawrence tosses his, Seb's, and Cass's packs into the first one, bunny-ears the ends, and ties them. With the rest of us sitting in our sacks, lined up like we're back at the waterpark again and waiting to get the green light, he yells, "Geronimo!" and hurls the sack down the slope. It bounces a couple of times, filth flying, and rolls chaotically, before coming to a stop on a mud mogul.

"Daaamn," Cass coos. "Hope there was nothing breakable in there."

Lawrence wastes no time with the second batch, sandwiching my pack between Ben's and Steph's—oh, how ironic—and yeets it down the slope, end on, torpedo style. It slides an impressively long way, suddenly hits something and the back end flies up, making it cartwheel until it is enveloped in mist and out of sight.

"Yep, that will be me in a minute," Steph whimpers.

"Hey girl, might fix your nose." Seb gives her a shove.

"No, you bastard!" she screams, rolling sideways and over the edge. Ben tries to save her, but he can't save himself, and the two of them set off at speed, yelling and clinging to one another, until they bash into the first sack, and Ben, Steph, and sack ricochet in three different directions, disappearing into the mist.

"Are you okay?" I shout, at the same time bumping myself along the bank so I'm out of bloody Sebastian's way. There's no answer, just the mist swirling below, an ominous soup.

"So long, suckers!"

Like I should be worried Seb would stick around long enough to push me—he's off, like it's a race, followed by Lawrence, because it *is* a race, and both of them have to win. Cass and I sit and watch, until the mist has swallowed them whole and Seb's manic laughter is no more.

"Do you think it's okay at the bottom? I mean, they'd warn us if it wasn't," I babble, as I grip the edge of the sack. "I can't remember what was down there. Does it flatten out gradually, so we'll slow down? What if we get stuck? All end up in totally different places? Will we even be able to find each other in this mist?"

"You can go first," Cass says. "That way if you get stuck, I'll bash into you and get you moving."

"Sounds great."

It doesn't. It sounds shit. But I'm sitting in the equivalent of a giant doggy-poop bag, waiting to bobsled down a death slide, so let's not quibble. Ugh, glad there's nothing much in my stomach, or I'd be losing it about now. I edge myself forward, hands sinking into the freezing mud, but this is no time to be squeamish. I inch over the top of the hill, leaning back and digging my heels into the mud to slow my roll. There's nothing to say I have to go quickly, is there? I can just ease on down the road. Take my time, enjoy the ride. Gently, gently…

Oh, f—

The earth slips out from under me and I and smack backward, breath knocked out of my lungs, bag flying up over my face— *what the hell?*—as I shoot downhill, out of control, who knows in what direction. Instinctively, I spread my arms, desperate to stop, feeling every lump in the ground rattle my rear as I fly down the slope, over a bump, actually leaving the earth for a second, before crashing to the ground and barreling on. *Sit up, slow yourself!* My abs scream and my legs jackknife and I swivel and *no!* Now I'm headfirst, so I curl around and then I'm rolling like a hotdog without a bun, my head feeling like it's going to bobble off and *don't fight the roll just go with it because you*—oof!

Eyes tight closed. *Breathe. Remember breathing?* Ground is solid beneath me. I wipe muck from my eyes and open them to see faces staring down at me.

"Bloody hell, Maggie." Seb crouches tentatively beside me. "Did ye not fancy the bag much, or what? You didn't have to bodysurf down."

I lost the poop bag somewhere. Probably when I did the three-sixty. Do I not get extra points for style and difficulty? I made air.

I stand on oh-so-shaky legs, and I'm heavy with soil, a wedge of mud under my chin, so much it's kind of working for me as a mud turtleneck. I'm brown, and reeking of muck, like I've emerged from the bowels of the earth, or maybe just bowels.

"You're okay...?" Ben doesn't want to touch me. How nice. Concern, but with a side of disgust. Oh, I recognize that face, seen it more than once. I push down the impulse to tackle him to the ground, rub that pretty face in dirt, hurt him, generally.

"Yeah. I'm okay." I blink at them all.

"Cass? Cass!" Steph shouts. "God, can't see anything in this mist. We should clear the deck before she takes our legs out."

We move back into the fog, but Cass doesn't show. There's time to find the backpacks, shake off some of the mud and think about the futility of getting anywhere in this weird, swirling miasma, and still Cass doesn't turn up. Steph shouts again, and Ben joins in this time. We're just beginning to have worried thoughts when, suddenly, a shape looms through the whiteness.

"Woo-hoo! That was actually fun." Cass's eyes are shining. "Once I accepted my inevitable death."

"You dodged it, though. Shame." Seb pulls a face. "So where the hell now, Stephanie? Because I couldn't find my own nob in this mist, let alone the river."

Steph's on it, of course. We follow—or more like, Lawrence forges ahead, having to be constantly called back by everyone else, because Steph has the good map, the compass, and the skills. Maybe Lawrence's watch does something to help him navigate? But aren't you supposed to need the sun? None to be had. Looks like we've had our hour's ration of rays today.

We eventually reach the river, can't see it through the mist, but we can certainly hear it, a roar even more deafening than yesterday. As we turn west and troop upstream through the wet, at times, we dip below the mist. It's the weirdest thing, perfectly flat above us, like a painted, swirling ceiling. Only then do we have eyes on the torrents; not even identifiable as a river anymore, but a wide, wild stretch of gray-brown water, viscous and tumbling. I hang back at times, scanning the banks for any sign of my dad and Ant, and notice Ben glancing back too, surreptitiously, to check if I'm still following the group.

After about an hour, the mist has closed in around us again, and Steph signals for us to stop.

"The bridge is close, keep eyes peeled."

"Maybe it's hiding with the crate and the knife." Cass groans.

We're trudging through a boggy plain, following the water's edge as best we can.

"Keep walking, slowly, and we'll spot it," Steph urges. "It should be any minute now."

But ten minutes later, nothing.

"This isn't right." Steph unfolds the map again. "See the meander in the river? That's where we are now. The bridge is a third of a mile downstream from here. We definitely should have passed it."

"Maybe it collapsed?" Cass says. "Bang on trend."

"Unlikely." Steph tuts. "This isn't some small, wooden thing. It's marked on the map so it must be a proper bridge, stone foundations. We'd see something." She twists the compass around and strides off again, splashing through the water. The mist is thickening, stroking our faces with dampness. It feels so close, so claustrophobic. A few minutes later, Steph stops. "Here. This is exactly where it should be." She sighs. "We'll have to wade in a bit."

"*Wade in a bit*?" Seb's voice is mocking. "Better yet, let's go for a nice swim, the water's lovely!"

Steph's chin goes up, she takes another step. Oh god, exactly how deep is she expecting us to wade?

"How's your foot, Maggie?" Cass takes me by surprise. "You look like you're limping."

"I do?" I frown at her. "It's fine, I can barely feel it."

"That might be a sign it's worse than you think." She frowns right back. "Steph, let's take a moment. Mags needs to sit."

"But we're so close to finding the bridge!"

"Hey, it's not going anywhere." Cass smiles at Steph, and like so often, the boys have already made the decision for us and sloped off to drier ground.

I shrug, move to find somewhere to sit, trying my hardest not to limp, my foot immediately way more painful than it was before anyone mentioned it. I twist off my boot. The sock is sodden and the bandage comes off with it. The skin around the cut is pale and puckered, and it stings like hell when I attempt to pull my foot closer to my face to see, but it's not bleeding.

"How's it looking?" Ben calls over.

"Fine, I knew it would be." What does he care? Is he trying to make me feel uncomfortable?

"Better to check though," Cass says.

I nod, because it's easier to agree, to shut them up. I delve into my pack to find a bandage to redress the wound. No dry sock left, but it doesn't matter; at this rate it will be wet again in a tiny second.

"Oh jeez!" Sebastian bursts out laughing. "It was there all along!"

I look up. The mist has cleared a little, and the bridge is right in front of us, both ends submerged, but very much still standing. Cass curses.

Because the bridge is not a few feet away. There's half a football field of churning water between us and our salvation.

"Still fancy wading in, tho'?" chirps Sebastian. "How the hell do we get to that?"

"We don't." Lawrence shakes his head. Suddenly, the heavens open, and rain stair-rods down onto us. Stinging rain, ferocious and icy.

"Awesome, more water!" Seb laughs. "Just what we need. Might as well dive right in, bruh?" He jumps on Lawrence, who staggers but somehow keeps upright, and they tussle, predictably, irritatingly. The weight of disappointment and despair descends, smacking me over the head like the downpour, as I watch the brothers play out yet another tiresome battle.

It's Steph who stops them. Her eyes screw up, she flings back her head and lets loose a full-on, heart-wrenching wail, snot and tears flying. It is the primal scream of someone who has put up with all of the crap for way too long and has held it together, but now their way out is denied. We stand in awe. Steph does not lose it, ever. This is new ground. We are in the Upside Down.

After she has cried and cried and still not cried it out, we all turn to Ben, one by one, because if anyone's going to tackle this, we want it to be him. He's mesmerized. Only when he feels our eyes on him does he leap into action. And by "leap" and "action," I mean he stays exactly where he is and mutters: "Steph, don't worry. We'll find a way. Don't get upset."

"Bitch has finally flipped, no surprise," Seb grunts.

"Shut your mouth." Ah, finally Ben gets a little fire in his belly.

"Or what?" Seb laughs. "Hey Benny-boy, does she scream like that for you when you—"

"You heard what he said, shut the hell up!" I swivel, shoot

an arm out, and push Seb on the chest. He folds easy and goes down hard, landing on his soft bum in the shallows with a deliciously satisfying splash.

"You…fat, stupid, cow—" He's winded. I jump on him, grasping the neck of his jacket with both hands and shaking hard, *so easy to slam dunk the funk out of you right here and everyone would thank me for it—*

"Stand down, Mags." Lawrence gets between us. "He's embarrassed himself enough. Get away."

I drop Sebastian in the freezing water again, reverse out of there in shock, all *why did I do that* and *how come my heart is beating out of my chest*? Lawrence is following, blocking me, what's more, Ben is too, while Cass stares, aghast. I hold my hands up, quite literally back off, because their reaction feels way too much. Jeez. I only pushed the loser. Did they think I was going to finish him?

"Steph!" Ben calls out, and we turn. She's snapped back to normal, walking away purposefully downstream, backpack on. We didn't even notice it. "Are you okay? Wait!"

He runs after her, Cass follows, and I do too, because I've got to release this adrenaline somehow, pound it into the ground, so I'm shouldering my wretched pack and striding away from the mess of McTavishes, hauling their asses and pride out of the water.

Steph has the good map and skills, and a head start. Cass is shouting, "What's the plan?" and "Which way now?" but Steph doesn't answer. Perhaps she can't hear us over the rain, but as we jog after her, packs feeling heavier with every footfall, I can guess the answer. We're heading east, downstream, like we always should have. We'll find a way around that waterfall, around the landslide, and we'll follow the river out of here, because no matter how long it takes, all rivers lead somewhere.

Steph keeps on, not speaking to anyone, even when Ben catches her. My jog slows to a walk, and after a sweaty, silent toil, where Lawrence passes me without a word, and Seb bores holes into the back of my head, the mist dissipates and a few feet away, a yellow life jacket hangs on a tree. Yes! The first breadcrumb I left Dad and Ant; we're back to the place where we landed the boat. Finally. I'm getting my wish: we're going after them.

But as we draw near to the tree line, there's a deep, rumbling noise.

CHAPTER 11

——

"Run!"

Someone ahead of me yells, don't know who. The rain is pelting my face, the rumbling too loud. Thunder?

What's happening? I rub my eyes.

"Turn back!"

Huh? Why? Faces, Ben's and Steph's, mouths open in horror; they're running toward me, and beyond them I see movement, trees toppling like dominoes.

Oh shit.

"Landslide! Move it!"

I turn tail, someone—Lawrence?—grabs me, pulls me up the bank. The air fills with yells and screams until that terrible rumble drowns out everything.

God, it's loud, never thought it'd be so loud, so fast. I'm running back over the flat, slipping on sodden grass and looking behind and I can't believe it but the dark is closing in on me. *Don't look back, keep going forward*, a voice says. The grass gives way to something thicker, clumpier, harder to run on, and I'm bent over, using my red-raw hands, clambering over huge tufts as the deluge of black mud roars behind, threatening to catch and consume me.

"This way, Maggie!"

Where—? It's Ben, up the slope, but why is he beckoning? It's quicker to run back here—oh. In front of me, the earth is moving too, sliding down toward the river, cutting off my exit. I scramble up the slope, looking up for Ben, for anyone—but he's gone, so I keep going, terra firma shrinking rapidly like I'm some stupid little NPC fleeing hopelessly in a battle royale, and it's dangerously close to game over.

What's that?

There's a backpack in a ditch to my left, bright red. It's Ben's! Has he fallen? No, just his pack—*just keep moving, have to keep moving whatever else*, and I dig in and run for my life.

"Maggie! Up here! Head for the rocks!"

Cass, yes, rocks, I think I see them, *just keep moving* in the direction of the voice. You can't outrun a landslide, or maybe that's an avalanche, or tsunami, or probably all three, it doesn't really matter, *Maggie, keep moving!* Get to high ground. My legs are crying, but I'm doing it. I can see the shape of the rocks in my peripheral vision. Please, please let everyone have the same idea, god, let everyone be okay.

The ground is rising with me. I'm almost there. I hit the rocks, straps of my backpack cutting into my shoulders, my chest burning, but can't stop now, scurrying up as fast as I can, feet slick and heavy with mud, the weight of my pack almost pulling me backward as I climb. There are shouts above me. I haul myself up onto a ledge. Stephanie, Cass, and Ben bend and there are hands that yank me to my feet, and together we cling to each other and fall flat against the rock wall, panting, crying, sliding to our butts.

"It's okay," Cass says, breathless, in my ear. "We're safe here."

I lean forward slightly, dare to look. She's right. We're high enough. We dodged death. Only rocks above and a slurry of mud and broken mountain below.

"Where are the boys?" I gasp. Ben shakes his head.

"They were ahead of me, I think—I hope. At least Lawrence was. Probably higher up these rocks." He pants. "I didn't see Seb."

"Any chance he's still down there?" My stomach lurches at the thought. I didn't realize how much I cared, but I do. Sometimes I hate his guts, but I wouldn't wish that on anyone.

"Want to go look?" Cass breathes.

"Maybe pick up my backpack while you're there?" Ben shakes his head. "Stupid. I don't know what I was thinking. It was slowing me down so I ditched it and ran. Maybe Lawrence did the same with Seb."

"Lawrence wouldn't leave his brother," Steph says, and Cass gives her a look. "Oh, come on. They hate each other, but Lawrence would have his brother's back, and vice versa."

"Well, maybe not vice versa." Ben chuckles, and for some

reason, it makes us all laugh in that sharp, sudden, fake, nervous energy way that is too much. He does a little Seb move, sitting there on the wet rock, running his legs and pumping his arms in slo-mo, with a sus expression on his face. We laugh even more, until I stop, because none of this is funny and if I don't get myself in control, I'm going to pull a Steph and start wailing. Steph checks herself too, I think, because she shakes, exhales deeply, and stands up.

"Come on. This is the bottom of the same crags that lead around to the rock face west of Devil's Chute. If we climb all the way up and walk across the top, we'll reach the hut. Shouldn't take more than half an hour."

"Do you think the hut is still there?"

"Only one way to find out."

Damn straight. I stagger upright onto jelly legs, leaning back slightly, and check out the rock face. Long way up. I mean, there was a very good reason we originally chose to slog across a boggy field and tackle Devil's Chute over this, but it's not exactly K2. And it's our only choice now.

"Let's go." Ben gestures for Steph to give him her backpack, and with a little light protestation, she hands it over. Cass is already picking out a way up the rocks, and Ben follows. Steph gives me a look.

"Slow and steady wins the race for us two. How's your foot?"

"Yeah, not bad," I mumble, like I'm even thinking of that right now.

I let her go after Ben, ease my gloves over stiff, frozen fingers, and begin the climb. It's not too difficult, once my legs remember they have muscles, although heaven knows I'll be happy when it's done. Climbing was my other favorite sport, until puberty and nerves kicked in. But the indoor kind. Dad would take me, Ben, and Ant every weekend. I had great reach, and I was strong, but I never did super well with the heights. When I got curves, I was self-conscious up there, always feeling like I was too heavy, too cumbersome for a girl, and now there were these extra fleshy parts that squeezed out of the side of my harness, or prevented me from hugging the wall like I used to. Dad was disappointed when I quit. Such a lame reason to stop, I know, but all the while I was having those sessions, I was panic-stricken he was going to take me to the mountains. Never wanted to get too close to the cave. And yet here we are.

I'm hot and shaky, but I focus on the rock ahead, concentrate on not falling or freaking out, keeping in reach of Steph. After a few minutes we meet Ben and Cass, paused and panting on another ledge.

"Any sign of the boys?" Please don't let them be porridge. I wouldn't want that, not even for Seb.

Ben shakes his head. "They'll be fine. Can't see Lawrence letting a little landslide win. Bet they're already at the hut."

"Hope he puts the kettle on." Cass pulls herself up the next rock. "We should keep moving before the adrenaline crash hits." She disappears, and after a few seconds, with permission from Steph, so does Ben.

"I think I'm crashing already." Steph gives me a rueful smile.

"Want to go in front of me?" I do. I want to speed up this hill, because suddenly I'm picturing my dad and Ant at the hut, wondering if by some magical chance they could be waiting for us there—but it feels right to let Steph go ahead. In case Ben thinks I'm being a bitch by leaving her behind.

"It's okay, you first. I'll catch you if you fall." I do the smile back, even though I'm definitely not feeling it.

"Yeah, I think you would." She nods and looks down. For a horrible moment I could swear she's going to start crying again, and I'm not even sure why, or that I want to know why. "You know, this whole trip is beginning to feel like karma."

Oh god, *not* the time or the place. Not that I want to have this conversation, ever, anywhere.

"Don't you think? As if the Fates are getting their revenge on us? For something we did wrong?" Steph's so overly earnest I can't tell if it's real or if she's being sarcastic.

"Nope. It's bad luck and Scottish weather, Steph, nothing more," I say, making light, joining in with her joke, even if it wasn't supposed to be one. "We're tough, we won't let it get the better of us. Come on! I'll even make you a tea when we get back to the hut—"

"Maggie, you know we've already had our fair share of bad luck. Enough for a lifetime."

Oh no, please don't go there. I try the vague smile again and move toward where the others disappeared up the rocks, hoping she'll drop this, but she doesn't. She stares at me, her eyes bloodshot, confused.

"You know what I'm talking about, Maggie. Our experience. It's a hell of a coincidence that it's all of us, together again. Here."

Och, she went there. Our *experience*. It sounds like something her parents called the kidnapping, as if to make it more woolly, bearable. Something they could refer to without the scary. Except that's not possible. It's all scary. Calling it an *experience* is kind of terrifying in its own way, too. Minimizing. We've had years of hushed tones and euphemisms.

"We're not all here, Steph."

"Yes, Nicholas isn't, obviously." She flutters her hand at me, as if that's not important. Which is fitting, because we've all tried our best to forget Nicholas.

It feels so weird to hear his name spoken out loud. Nicholas McDonal, the boy who moved away after the kidnapping. My parents took me out of school, but Nicholas's folks went one further and moved country. None of us kept in touch, none of us even spoke of him again, until the news came through last year that he'd died by suicide. And even then, we didn't discuss it much. We all felt guilty, no doubt, for not reaching out, but also, I think there was another reason. Nobody wanted to talk about what pushed Nicholas to take his own life, because maybe whatever it was lingered inside all of us too.

"And obviously Cass wasn't there, ten years ago," Steph continues. "But the twins, Ant, you and me and Ben. I didn't sign up for this trip. Ben told me that you and Ant didn't either. Lawrence, I can see choosing it, perhaps, but Sebastian? No way. Don't you think it's deeply weird?"

Deeply. And then again, maybe not at all.

I've thought about it a lot, of course I have. What were the chances that the six of us would be randomly selected, out of a year group of approximately three hundred kids? Statistics isn't my strong point, but I'm going to guess pretty low.

I think it was Dad.

He's a teacher, he would have had access to the system. How hard would it be to fix things? After all, he's the leader of this trip. I think he probably thought he was helping, that he would take us out here to heal us, once and for all. Slay those demons, that's what he said.

I've thought it was him for a while. I've never asked him about it, because everything kicked off after the writing was quite literally on the wall about his affair at school. I didn't say anything to Ben or Ant, because I didn't want them to hate him, even after my mother and I moved out, I hated him with all my heart. And that's the same reason why I say nothing to Steph now.

"Look, I think we should get going, catch up with the others. Ben's lost his pack, and Ant and my dad might be—"

"I mean, what were we all thinking by agreeing to come here, actually? These hills?" Steph's laugh is a high-pitched wobble, and, oh hell, things are sliding into the realm of unhinged again. Don't want to deal. I stare up the rock face, praying to any mountain gods that are listening to send someone down here to relieve me of Stephanie, but none are listening. Steph clearly thinks something's funny, because she's still giggling.

"The cave, *our cave*, is literally a skip and a jump from the other side of this mountain. Your dad knew that, we all knew that. Coming here was asking for trouble. Whatever happens is our fault."

"Och, Steph." I suck air through my teeth, feeling my heart thud in my chest, my cheeks flush hot. "That's not a great thing to say, under any circumstances." I'm shaking, and so help me, I should not engage, but I can't hold back. "None of it was our fault, not today or yesterday, certainly not ten years ago." I dig my nails into my hands to stop the rage that is rising in my chest. "And this is nothing like ten years ago. *He's* not here."

Him. The driver. The one we never, ever mention. And I just did.

Steph starts, looks around her, frightened, as if I might have invoked something, and it freaks the hell out of me, because maybe I have. The original bodach.

What the hell do I know? She might be right. His spirit could be here because he died in these mountains. Do I believe that? Okay, yes, the cave isn't far, as the crow flies, it's not in this valley, but it's closer than I've been in years, on the dark side of Cairn Gealach. And I'm about to say something, really go there with Steph, because she has me rattled, but suddenly she snaps out of it, slaps me on the back, smiles brightly as if the last couple of minutes were a waking dream. Real Steph and Real Maggie are here now, and we're back to awkward, polite half chat.

"Ben will be back down to this ledge in a minute,

wondering why we haven't moved. He's terrified of us talking to one another..." She finally starts up the rocks again, like none of that exchange happened. I give her a few seconds of space, and then a few more. Don't want to catch up.

This section is way steeper. I've got to stay in the moment, on task. It's a gift, because I have to pick the best line up, forget about Steph, concentrate on finding handholds so if my feet slip on the slick rock I won't go tumbling down. I take off my gloves, jamming my fingers into cracks like I'm free soloing El Capitan. Yeah, those dudes have nothing on me, they don't have to work with borrowed hiking boots, a heavy backpack, and an even heavier shit ton of post-traumatic baggage.

I reach to grasp a ledge, squeal like a boy, and recoil as my hand touches something weird. It's springy and rubbery and doesn't feel like anything belonging to the natural world. Pulling myself up, I clap eyes on it from the safety of the ledge. Huh? At first, my brain can't brain. A tangle of beige strings, clumped together. A strange plant, a—? A fungus among us? Nope. I poke it, gingerly. *No way.* I pick up a string and hold it up for the smell test.

Yup. Ramen noodles.

What are they doing here? I scan the ground, and sure enough, there's an orange plastic wrapper, torn in half, fluttering under a bush. Where did this come from? I glance about, and a little shiver of fear runs through me. Someone else has been here, probably in the last twenty-four hours; any longer than that and these noodles would surely have been eaten by a hungry Highland critter. So, who dropped them? Could it be the same person who left the knife outside our hut last night? Or, there's a perfectly innocent hiker nearby, maybe someone who can help us out of here. But how come we haven't seen them, or them us? They would surely realize we need help. Why haven't they made themselves known?

It makes me climb way faster.

And in spite of the adrenaline, my stomach rumbles. A shame the damn noodles weren't in their packaging; we could have used them. I don't think we're desperate enough to eat noodles-gone-wild yet. After a few minutes of hauling ass, I look up to see a large, flat section, a place to rest, stand up, and catch my breath before heading up what is hopefully the final stretch to the shepherd's hut. Can't be far now. I take my pack off, shunt it up the side of the rock like I'm chancing a shot from the center line, and crawl after it. Steph is waiting for me, slugging on a bottle of water, a slightly patronizing look on her face, *I beat ya.*

"I heard voices up ahead. I think we'll catch them if you can go a bit faster."

I grunt as I pull myself onto my feet. She smiles sympathetically and turns around to continue climbing.

"Whoa!" Steph shouts as a shower of little rocks rains down from somewhere up above. "Be careful, we're below you!" She turns to me. "Hey, I was right, the others must be just over that ledge—"

And in that second, I see the rocks come again, this time so much bigger, and I think I shout *watch out*, and I definitely dodge, but maybe I only thought the warning, because Steph doesn't move, she just looks at me like I'm deranged. And there's one huge stone, and it bounces off the rock face, arcs in the air, and I see it hit the back of Stephanie's head—no, I hear it. It's a loud crack, sharp and terrible and sickening. There's a split second of blank surprise before Stephanie's eyes roll back into her head and she falls forward like she's been shot.

I cry out—this time, I know I do. It fills my ears and bounces off the cliff face, echoing around the valley. But for Steph, it's too late.

CHAPTER 12

God. Oh god.

"Steph!"

She's not moving.

I'm pressed into the side of the rock face. _There might be more._ I look up, a smattering of tiny stones fall, and I shrink back.

"Stephanie!"

She is quiet, lying completely still, face down. Her hood has fallen over the back of her head so I can't see where the rock struck her.

Okay, it might be nothing. She might be messing with me. _The sound of the rock, the crack..._ She looks like a toddler who has fallen asleep, or is refusing to move, acting out a silent tantrum.

"Please." My voice is a whimper. "Are you okay?"

Check her, you stupid coward. There are no more rocks! Go to her!

I look up. There might be more.

What's wrong with you? Help her!

"Stephanie!" I shout, loud enough to hear my voice rebound back to me in an echo. "Are you hurt?" She doesn't look hurt, she looks dead. *How do you know what dead looks like? Move! Go to her!* Oh, I remember what dead looks like. A motionless shape on the ground.

"Hey, are you okay down there?" Ben shouts from above. "Steph?" He starts to scramble down to us. "What the hell happened? Did you bash into her again?"

"Of course I didn't!"

"So, what, you pushed her?" He tumbles down the final section and lands next to me on all fours, eyes flashing. "Did she fall?"

"No! There was a rock—rocks came down—no, don't!" I shout as Ben rushes to Steph and skids to a stop on his knees. "The rock hit her head hard, Ben...I don't know if you should move her..."

"Stephanie?" Ben doesn't care what I think. He slowly peels the hood from her head and his whole body recoils when he sees what lies beneath. I look too. Instant hot, bitter bile jumps to my throat. Steph's smooth, black hair is wet through with blood. So much blood that I can't see any wound, only hair soaked with thick, sticky, scarlet blood that is trickling down the side of her face and her neck. "Oh god, Steph." Ben looks around at me wildly. "How do we stop the bleeding?"

"Shit, Stephanie!" Cass appears and runs to Steph. "Her face is in the mud, is she breathing?"

"Should we move her?" I approach cautiously, like it's all my fault.

"She'll suffocate if we don't!" Ben screams back at me, but he does nothing. Typical. He doesn't want responsibility.

"She needs space to breathe!" Cass makes the decision, scraping the mud from around Steph's face, finding some makeshift stone tool and digging frantically. "Support her head, carefully!" Ben snakes fingers around the sides of Steph's head and her neck, it seems so tender a touch.

"Is she breathing?"

"I don't know," Cass says, leaning in low. "Can you feel her pulse?"

"I can't tell." Ben shakes his head. "My hands are numb. I can't feel anything. Stephanie!"

Oh god, this is awful, wake up, please... My gut twists as I stare at that terrible head, the blood pooling, it's running over Ben's hands.

Okay, keep calm, that's actually a good thing. It means her heart is still pumping, doesn't it? I fall on my knees at her side, take her hand. It's cold, but that doesn't mean anything. It's frigid and she's not wearing gloves. I think I can feel blood thudding in my fingertips as I press them along the inside of her wrist, but that could be me, my blood, my heart beating so hard.

"Come on, Steph. Please tell me she's breathing," Ben pleads with Cass, who ignores him, keeps scraping a hole underneath

Steph's face. I shove a hand up Steph's jacket, under her fleece sweater and thermal tee. It feels invasive and I'm shocked at the warmth, but yes, thank god, I can feel the rise and fall of ribs swinging up and out, little, juddering movements. She's alive.

"She's breathing!" It comes out like a silly giggle, and I hate myself. "Her lungs are moving."

"Doing great, Steph. We've got you." Ben leans down to her, then up at me, tears in his eyes. "We need to stop the bleeding."

"Okay, I have bandages." My pack is off to the side, and I jump on it, pulling out clothes and random items frantically, until I find the compact first aid kit I almost didn't bring because I thought it was overdramatic. There are all kinds of zippered sections in the pack. I open everything with fat, useless fingers, before I find one large, padded dressing in a sterile wrapping— which is pointless, because I'm pulling it apart with filthy hands and wondering what bad germs I'm about to be putting into Stephanie's head. "Here, and there's bandage to wrap around." I look at Ben and Cass. "Should I put pressure on?"

"I think so." Cass wipes her hands down her pants. "I'll help."

"How?" Ben says. "You'll push her face into the ground."

"Recovery position." Cass takes a breath. "We need to move her onto her side. There's no reason to think her spine is broken, is there? We should move her in case she pukes or something. Then dress the wound and add pressure to stop the bleeding." Ben and I nod, grateful to be told. "Go gentle though. There might be, like, bits of brain sticking out." She looks at us.

"What? I didn't know how to say it." She starts to sob, rubbing Steph's back. "I'm sorry. You know what I mean."

I nod, because I do, and wish that I didn't.

"Clean the wound first." Ben picks up Steph's drinking bottle and pours some water over her head. Probably not ideal with the backwash and all, but better her own spit than anyone else's. "It's deep." Ben's voice wavers. There's an oval-shaped gash the length of my finger; it looks like a smile with a pair of swollen lips, a mouth leaking blood. I hover with the dressing, feeling more inadequate than ever. "Let me." Ben takes the dressing, and I happily relinquish it. He presses it, firmly but gently, and I unravel a long bandage. Together, the three of us work to wind it around her head. The red bleeds through very quickly, so I find some gauze and we go around with the bandage again. And then Ben kneels there, both hands on the back of Steph's head, his teeth gritted, like he's quite literally pressing life back into her.

"We should keep her warm." With fumbling fingers, I untie the waterproof bag holding Steph's sleeping bag and groundsheet, wiggle her feet in. Cass and I rock 'n' roll her ever so gently to get her covered. We've done everything we can think of to do.

A few minutes pass, or maybe half an hour, I have no clue. My legs have gone numb, we're all kneeling around Steph, Ben with pressure on the wound, Cass holding her hand. I'm lower down. I have my hands on her legs, rubbing them like that will do something. *What the hell do we do?*

Steph doesn't wake up. She doesn't move or make any sound. We check her pulse again and again, her breathing. She's still with us, but we're stuck, not knowing what comes next. The rain stops, wind drops, the mist thickens, swirls around us. God, shouldn't one of us go for help? But where? Who's going to help us, exactly? Maybe it's enough just to be with her.

"I don't think I should press anymore," Ben says finally.

"I bet the bleeding has stopped." Cass steps up with the decision. "I think you've done it."

He nods, takes his hands away, stares at them because they're covered in blood, and wipes them across his chest. On his pale blue, mud-splattered hiking jacket there is now a patchy, dark-red handprint over each booby. We all stare at his front. Ben looks panicked. Cass blurts out a laugh, then sinks, crying quietly.

"What should we do now?" I try to save Ben; he's stuck in time, looking down at his jacket and the blood.

"Caw-caw! Caw-caw!"

Our heads whip up. A call from above, somewhere in the fog. *Dad?* No, it's Lawrence and Sebastian, climbing down to us, noisily, cheerfully. I don't think they realize what is going on until they're practically on top of us.

Seb swears heartily.

"What the actual?"

"She fell?" Lawrence goes into Action Man mode, crouching down beside me. "Any broken bones?"

"A rock hit her." Ben tells him about the head wound, shows

136

him our bandaging efforts, and I can see Lawrence grading us on our lack of skill. "She was with Maggie."

"Ouch, did Maggie go ape on her?" Seb cringes. I take back my earlier thoughts about not wanting him ground to porridge in the landslide.

"Don't." I grind my teeth. "We were just standing here talking, about to climb up, and some rocks fell on us."

"You were arguing." Seb crosses his arms.

"Were you pissy with her, Maggie?" Ben said. "Did you start something?"

"No, of course I didn't start something." I gulp. "What the hell would I be 'pissy' with her about, Ben?"

"Oh, I can guess why," Seb snarks.

"Stop it!" I stagger to my feet. My legs are rubber and my toes are completely asleep, but I have to get some space. I find my pack, rummage in it for god knows what. Anything.

"So where are *your* injuries?" Seb's actually following me.

"What?" I splutter.

Seb blinks at me, mouth in a hard line. "You said rocks fell on *us*. I don't see you with any ouchies from the big, bad wocks."

"Zip it, Seb!" Cass growls at him. "Maggie said there was only one rock. She wouldn't lie."

"Well, no, I didn't. There were plenty." I frown. "I don't know how many, but the one that hit Steph was the biggest."

"Really?" Cass frowns back. "I thought you said only one."

"Does it matter? I wasn't really doing a full rock classification as they rained down on us," I snap at her. "It all happened so fast. I was facing the crags, Steph was looking at me. It hit her and she literally fell where she was standing." I blink at them. "The rocks came from up there, obviously. Let's face it, one of you probably dislodged them when you were climbing."

"Seriously, what?" Ben comes at me.

I hold up a hand. "And if that happened, if one of you kicked rocks down, that's a total accident. But don't go blaming me, because if anything, I am least to blame in all of this."

"And that's what's most important, Ms. Least to Blame." Ben's sarcasm cuts deep, and he turns away from me, in disgust. "You guys reached the hut and it's still standing?" Lawrence nods. "Great, because we need to get Steph there. It'll be dark soon, and we're not spending a night out here."

"How the hell are we going to move her?" Seb looks sulky.

"Muscle," says Lawrence.

"And brains." Ben looks around. "There must be something we can make a stretcher out of. This groundsheet, we can tie it to a couple of branches or planks or whatever."

"Yeah, this place is *so* littered with planks." Seb rolls his eyes. "And I can't see for all the trees and their convenient branches."

Asshole.

"Just look, okay?" Ben shouts at him.

We split up and hunt, only Cass staying by Steph's side. I move sideways, scared to go up or down at first. Prickly gorse bushes is about it, knots of sharp grass, ferns. Nothing vaguely suitable. The idea of successfully constructing anything that is going to help us drag Steph up the crags seems kind of ridiculous. But we have to try.

"Hey! Found something."

Ben's voice, somewhere above and to my right. I climb, tentatively, in that direction. As I pull myself up, I see him standing there with something large, flat, and black in his hand.

"Look familiar to you?" He's waving the thing about. It's rectangular, made of plastic, startlingly out of place—and yeah, it does look weirdly familiar. "Big clue on the other side of that boulder."

I walk around the rock and stop in my tracks. There in the long grass, it looks like someone upended a trash can. Sodden cardboard, food wrappers, smells of spices, coffee—oh, and look at that. Several packets of Super Noodles, mostly intact. And a few feet away, a black plastic box missing a lid.

"The crate...?" I pick up a carton; a dozen eggs, all gloop, except one lucky, smooth, brown specimen, perfect and intact in the middle of all the debris.

"How did this get here?"

Lawrence appears from above, with Seb panting behind him. Ben shakes his head. He doesn't care, he's got bigger concerns, but Lawrence looks incensed.

"Someone must have thrown it from the top!" He looks around at each of us, like there's going to be a big confession.

"I found some noodles, farther down," I blurt, like this is some kind of alibi. "I mean, I didn't realize that they had come from the crate, I couldn't even figure out what they were, at first."

"Did you pick them up?" Lawrence yells at me. "We need food!"

"No, they were disgusting."

"Yeah, and most of this stuff is completely unusable!" He picks up a wet box of crackers that instantly falls to pieces in his hands. He swears, seemingly much more bothered about the crate than an unconscious classmate, but this is his way of showing he's devastated by what's happened to Steph. "Someone sabotaged us!" He storms up to his brother. "If you've done this, I'll throw you off the hill."

"What?" Seb steps backward in exaggerated indignation and nearly does Lawrence's job for him. "You're such a sad sack. Don't be so friggin' dumb. I might hide the crate just to piss you all off—but I didn't—and no way would I throw away our food."

The logic is sound. I believe him, and I can see Lawrence does too, but Lawrence needs someone to get angry with. "Naw, you'd go goblin mode and eat it all yerself, yer greedy bastard!" he screams at his twin.

"We don't have time for this." Ben tosses the lid aside and pushes past Seb. "Most of the space meals are intact. Gather anything edible. We'll carry Steph in her sleeping bag."

I put the egg in my pocket, and we climb down to where Steph and Cass are, in the same exact positions we left them. I load Steph's pack on my front with my own on my back, Cass carries the food, while the boys endure the slow, tortuous nightmare that is hauling Stephanie up and over the crags. Lawrence hauls from the front, Seb mainly gets in the way, and Ben barks instructions and tries not to cry. It takes forever, and throughout, she sleeps.

By the time we reach the hut, we're all in tears, except Lawrence, who never learned how. Tears of desperation, fear, hopelessness—the tears roll, though I scrape them away from my eyes because I don't deserve the relief.

CHAPTER 13

"What are we going to do?"

"Nothing! We can't do anything!"

"If only we had a flare gun, does anyone have a flare gun?"

"Yeah, in my pocket alongside my satellite phone and my helicopter!"

"Seb, you say another word and I'm going to shut you up forever!"

"Like you did with Stephanie?"

I scan the hut wildly for something to throw. Luckily for Seb, I don't find the axe, but rather *The Book of Saints*, which bounces off the side of his forehead with a satisfying thwack.

"Ow, you bitch!" he screams at me. "See? Like we needed any more proof? She's trying to bash me like she frickin' stoned Stephanie! Och!" He stops in his tracks, face frozen, and for a second, I'm genuinely frightened that I might have knocked him out. "*Stoned* Stephanie." He picks up *The Book of Saints*.

"Remember what it says in here? Saint Stephen was *stoned* to death! It's fate! This book is cursed."

"What the actual—?" Ben spits, I scream in frustration, and Lawrence makes to rugby-tackle his twin before someone else does.

"Stop, everyone, just stop!" Cass is small but mighty, her face tear-streaked but firm, her arms outstretched, fingers trembling. "You are upsetting Stephanie."

We all look at Steph. She seems pretty out of it. Completely out of it, actually. But it takes the wind from our sails.

"I don't want to hear any more about stoning. I am lighting a fire." Cass's voice wobbles. "The rest of you, see to Steph, and manage. Your. Shit."

Sometimes it takes an outsider. We heed her words, and she lights the fire, so efficient, focused, plowing everything into this one task.

We do what we can to make Stephanie comfortable, or at least that's what I'm telling myself. I don't think she's aware of anything. It was certainly a blessing on the journey up the crags, Lawrence was not exactly careful. It's lucky for her she's so petite, otherwise it would have been near impossible. I'm sure that if I had been knocked unconscious, I'd still be lying on that rocky outcrop.

The sleeping bag we used to transport her in is trashed, so I give her mine, which feels like the right thing to do. Because of course I feel guilty; generally, if not specifically.

"Thanks." Ben hangs Steph's bag over the rafters. "Hers is soaked through."

"Yeah, I think she peed herself," I whisper to him. "If you can take the lads off somewhere for five minutes, I'll get her cleaned up." He looks shocked. I don't know if he's horrified that Steph has bodily functions, or the fact I'm appointing myself as her nurse. "There's more firewood stacked in the back of the outhouse, go fetch." He gulps and nods, and I reach out and clasp his arm, briefly. "Don't worry."

I have no idea what I even mean by that—because there is every reason to worry—but it does something, and he somehow manages to convince the twins that what they really want to do is venture outside yet again and carry more heavy stuff.

Cass and I peel off Steph's waterproofs and leggings and find dry clothes, her slender legs floppy and surprisingly heavy to handle. The only way to dress her is by rolling her onto her back, so Cass kneels and cradles her head in her lap to protect the wound, while I struggle with a pair of thermals.

"It's okay, Steph, you sleep tight," Cass says, softly. "We'll keep you safe. Leave everything up to us." She looks at me, and whispers confidentially, "You know, she's such a control freak she'll be feeling you dressing her and knowing she could do it all way better herself."

"Yeah." I manage to smile, although this whole thing is making me feel so uncomfortable I want to puke, and Cass is only adding to that feeling.

"Do you think we leave our bodies when we're unconscious?" she asks wistfully, stroking Steph's cheeks with her thumbs. "Do you think she's hovering up there, looking down on us?"

God, I hope not. I look up before I can stop myself, and I can't stop the shudder either.

"Pity she can't float down the valley and get us all help, eh?" Cass chuckles, but she looks desperate, like she's going to break down again.

Urgh, I've been hoping the boys wouldn't come back too soon before I covered Steph up again, and now I'm praying they come in right now because I can't deal with this eerie shit that Cass is throwing out.

"How's that bandage holding up?" I'm all bluster and practicalities.

"Still there." She pulls at it a little. "You did a good job, all things considered."

"Looks grubby, though. Should we change it?"

"No. Might make the bleeding start again."

I nod, the door flies open, and a huge pile of logs with Lawrence's legs enters. Cass and I maneuver Steph onto her side again, in front of the fire, cozy in my sleeping bag. She's breathing. It's shallow, but steady.

Ben sits by Steph and holds her hand. Lawrence and Cass gather pans and noodles and get busy cooking, and Seb collapses on a sleeping platform with a huge moan like it's him who's the victim in all of this.

Outside, the light is fading fast. I didn't think I had any more nerves to jangle, but suddenly, I'm hit with a streak of pure panic. I don't want to be here, I don't want to spend another night in this horrible hut that might landslide down the hill at any time, with Steph's mashed-up head and her judgmental spirit floating in the rafters—and some rando, crate-stealing knife wielder on the loose. It's too, too much. But what's the alternative? There is none.

God, I need to breathe.

This air is thick with smoke and the smell of pee and damn curry powder. Why always the curry powder? I never want to smell that again in my life—and before I know it, I'm putting on my jacket, heavy with wet, clumsily grasping for the door latch and stepping outside again.

I breathe. I pee in the outhouse, walk carefully back, my head on swivel at anything that moves. Devil's Chute has all but gone, and I don't dare get anywhere near the edge that remains. It's raining still. I'm not sure the hut will survive another downpour, and every minute we stay here feels like we're gambling with our lives.

Back inside, food is ready. Ben ladles out noodles and brown water into tin bowls.

"We didn't cook all of the food. We should ration what we have."

"No danger of me wanting seconds. These taste like butt," Seb says, shoveling them down anyway.

"So you know what butt tastes like," Cass states. "Just as well. We run out of food, we might have to go cannibal."

"Truth." He smirks at her. "If Steph doesn't make it, I could fancy a little Chinese."

"You did not just say that." Ben stands up so quickly he sends his bowl flying.

"Calm down, pal." Lawrence grabs his leg and swings around to his brother. "And you, you dick-brain—" He leans over and slaps Seb over the head. "Shut it."

"I'm sorry, I should know better than to set up his stupid jokes." Cass throws a muddy boot at him, but it only makes him cackle all the more.

"How can you be like that when she's lying there like that?" I shake my head. "You don't care about anyone except yourself."

"Ow, your words. I'm so hurt, I need a bandage." Seb rolls on the floor. Lawrence pummels him some more while he groans. "Can you wrap me up too, nurse? So Ben, *seriously*, did you throw the rocks down on your girlfriends? Because don't worry, there isn't a court in this land who'd convict you if you did."

Ben curses at him but sits down, picks up his bowl. He's defeated; we all are. Not by Seb, but by everything. Even Lawrence has stopped now. He collects our bowls and dumps them in the sink with a clatter.

"We need to make a plan," he says. "Obviously, we can't move Stephanie anywhere better than this today. Tomorrow, who knows if the hillside will still be standing. If anyone has an idea, speak now."

"Rig up a proper stretcher, carry Steph over the top," Cass says.

Seb snorts. "You're not suggesting we attempt to lug her up a friggin' mountain?"

We all think about it.

"Should we move her *at all* with a head injury?" I mean, more than we already have. Does it even matter anymore? Truth is, I cannot imagine how long it would take and how difficult it would be to get her over Cairn Gealach. The expedition was going to take us another two days under normal circumstances, and we left normal behind long ago.

"She stays here with you all. I'll swim across the river." Ben strokes Steph's arm. "Hike back to the café, raise the alarm."

"That's ridiculous," I blurt. "It's way too rough, you'll drown."

"Not if I pick the right spot. I'll wear a life jacket."

"You'll sink and perish, my man." Lawrence has torn open a bag of jerky and is helping himself. "It's flood water. Full of debris and mud and gravel. Add fence posts, barbwire, trees, dead sheep. Have you not seen clips of poor losers who've gotten caught in a flash flood? It's like being in a food mixer. Even if they don't drown, they lose their clothes and most of their skin."

"So, we make a raft. There's got to be something we can use around here," Ben says. "We can rip up one of these platforms, or the door—"

"Because the river crossing was so successful last time." Seb gives a double thumbs-up.

"Who knows if we'll even get to the river after that last landslide," Lawrence says. "Cass is right, we'd do better over the mountain. With one change: the girls stay here and look after Steph, and we go fast and hard and don't stop until we're back in civilization."

"Why exactly do *the girls* stay here and look after Steph?" I check Cass for support, but she's staring at the floor.

"Yeah, Benny-boy." Seb giggles. "Don't leave Magnitude alone with Saint Steph, she'll stone her again."

"It was an *accident.*" If there's any rock chucking to be done, I'm going to be aiming them at Sebastian. "We've been through this already, are you dense? It was the rain. The rain caused two landslides that we know of already. The rain could easily set off a rock fall, or at least loosen everything for someone to accidentally kick rocks down on us. Totally stands to reason."

"Does it, tho'?" Seb says. "Thing is, when we were manhandling Miss Thing up the hill, I didn't see any rocks falling, did you? You were below us, did we kick anything down?"

I'm silent, because no, there was nothing. I couldn't even see the place where the rocks might have fallen from, and you can bet I looked.

Seb's living his best life, reducing us all to silence. He smiles.

"So someone threw those rocks down on purpose. And if it wasn't Monster Munch Maggie, where were the rest of you when the rocks fell?"

"Yeah, good point, Sebastian. Where were you?" I point at him. "Because you disappeared for the longest time."

"He was with me," Lawrence says. "Mostly."

"How do any of us know where we were when the rocks fell, if we didn't even realize they were falling?" Cass says reasonably.

"I thought I heard Steph scream." Ben frowns. "I was already on my way down again, to look for you both. Thought you'd been too long."

"No, she didn't scream," I say. "She said 'whoa,' something like that, when the first shower came down. But it wasn't a scream."

"There were two rock falls now?" Seb raises his monobrow.

"I made a noise." I ignore Seb and look at Ben. "Might have been me you heard. I saw the big rock coming at her and I…" *What did I do?* "I think I shouted. To warn her."

"You *think* you did?" Cass says.

"It all happened at the same time." I rub my collarbone. It aches. Maybe something did hit me. "I definitely cried out when she fell." I think I did. Did I? I'm sure I would.

"I know one thing," Ben says. "No rocks came past me." He looks toward Cass. "Did any rocks fall past you? You were farther down."

"No, I just told you. And I was above you, Ben," Cass says. "I thought I heard some yelling. I actually thought it was Lawrence shouting for Seb, and I was confused because I assumed they were ahead of me and the sound was coming from down the hill. By the time I arrived at the ledge, you were already there with Steph and Maggie. So I must have been farther away."

"And you guys dumped your bags at the hut and came back looking for us? And you were together?" I look at Lawrence, because I'm done engaging with Seb. He nods.

"Yeah. Apart from when he took a piss over the edge."

Seb grins. "My humongous water-cannon caused an avalanche, respect due."

Ben's face is thunder. "The only answer is, I must have dislodged the rocks, because I was closest, but honestly, I don't remember doing anything that could have caused that. God, if I've hurt her, I won't forgive myself."

"Unless the bodach was doing a little target practice," Seb says. "I mean, come on, we've all been thinking it, haven't we? Somebody swiped and dumped that crate. Somebody was lurking around last night and dropped a dirty great hunting blade, and reclaimed it this morning." He squints at us. "And don't tell me you all haven't felt like someone was watching us? On the hill? At the river? Steph saw him in the woods and paid the price."

"Don't be pathetic." Lawrence groans. "How could anyone watch us in the mist? And what, you reckon they would stick around when there's a sodding landslide? Who would even bother with a bunch of kids anyway?"

We all think about that one.

Cass stands up. "Did we bolt the door?" She grabs the dilapidated chair. "Lawrence, do me a favor and close that shutter. If anyone needs to pee, go now, and go with someone. And then we lock down tight until dawn, barricade this door, whatever we need to do."

"Wait, really?" My chest hurts at the idea of being locked in here with no easy escape route. "We honestly think someone is trying to do us harm? I mean, my dad's still out there! And Ant!"

"Maybe the bodach already got them," Seb says. "Or, no—the bodach *is* Ant, and it killed your dad, Mags, and now it's coming to get us, one by one." Seb spits.

I tell him where he should go and how he should do it.

Ben squares up to him. "You are this close to me kicking your face in."

"Woo-hoo! Bring it, bro!" Seb laughs. "Pity your ninja sidekick is already down and out. Never mind, you've still got She-Hulk on your side." He grins at me. "Or maybe she isn't."

"Want to find out?" I say.

"Calm down, ladies." Lawrence looks frankly embarrassed at our little display. "We can secure this place and still get the hell out in a hurry if we need to. Even if all of this is just a product of my loser brother's imagination."

"Aw, you hurted my feelings!" Seb pouts.

"So that's the plan, right?" Lawrence says. "Tomorrow morning, we go over the mountain. I don't give a crap who comes and who stays with Stephanie, but if you come, you've gotta be fast." He leaves to close the shutter, we do what we need to do, and within a few minutes we're piling things against the door, getting busy with the barricade.

"This makes me nervous." I kick a wedge of wood under the door. "Whoever stays here tomorrow—what if there's another landslide?"

"Wanna put up a tent? And what if the nutcase is out there with the knife?" Cass says. "We didn't find it with the crate, did we? It means whoever took it still has it."

"They'd better not come near me." Lawrence is fashioning another door wedge out of firewood with his penknife, and he flashes it in the air. "Size isn't everything."

"You better hope," Seb says.

"I meant to say, we shouldn't all go to sleep," Ben says. "We should take turns sitting up with Steph and watch over her, because if she gets worse in the night—"

"Or, if Dad and Ant make it here—"

"Maggie," Seb groans. "Face facts. Daddy dearest and the freak aren't coming. They are either fish food, ten feet under the mud, or halfway to Norway by now. The chances of them knocking on that door tonight are less than me winning the Eurojackpot and giving you losers a single penny."

He beams at us, drops an invisible mic.

There is a deafening thump at the door.

CHAPTER 14

We all jump back so far from the damn door we nearly bring the rear wall down. Ben falls over Steph, Seb rolls and collides with the bookcase, and Cass nearly winds up in the stove. Everyone freezes, eyes glued to the door.

"Don't answer it!" hisses Cass.

"Wasn't gonna." Seb is sprawled under a pile of stuff that has fallen off the shelf.

The door doesn't move. I steady my breathing and strain my ears but there's no sound outside except for the wind.

"Probably something blown against the door," Lawrence whispers, and he really doesn't sound so convinced. "Give it a moment."

"If it was my dad, he'd call out."

"So, who the hell is it?" Cass carefully picks up a pan and holds it up like a weapon.

"Whoever, I'm ready for 'em." Lawrence finds his penknife on the floor and brandishes it.

"What, you going to pick stones out of the killer's hooves?"

"Shut up, Seb!" Ben whispers. He tiptoes toward the door, remembering to collect the small axe on the table. Cass shakes her head no, but he holds his finger up to his lips. "I swear, there's no one there."

"So what's with the axe?" Cass has a point.

"It wasn't a knock." Ben ignores her. "Maybe the hut is shifting on its foundations. It was kind of like a *thunk*."

"Shucks, you really thunk that?" Seb is so annoying.

"Foundations?" I feel prickles up the front of my neck. "Great. This is exactly why I was worried. What if we're all about to slide off the hill?"

"No way, that would be so much louder. We'd feel it under our feet," Cass says. Nerves firing, I have to clench my fists to keep it together as I move toward the door.

"Screw this. It could be rescuers. We need to look outside." I glance at Cass. "I mean, I'll take a pan, obvs." She throws me hers and grabs the chair, which will work really well if it's a circus lion out there.

"Get ready, everyone." Lawrence stands with one hand on the latch, the other grasping the little penknife. "Three, two, one…" He gives the countdown like we're all going to charge, when in reality of course we're all going to shrink back 'n' see.

He opens the door.

Plop.

We all stare at the thing that has fallen in through the door. A backpack.

"Ben, that yours?" Cass squeaks. Ben shakes his head. Not sure how he can tell, because it is absolutely covered in mud. Not splattered or stained. It looks like it has literally been dipped in chocolate pudding. "So whose is it?"

"More to the point, why has someone flung it against our door and left?" Ben says.

"I don't like this…" Cass shakes her head.

"Could it be an animal?" I'm freewheeling, lightheaded. "Maybe a reindeer caught it on its antlers…" I shut myself down before someone else does.

"Think they can make fools of us… Yo!" Lawrence calls as he sidles up to the door, kicks the pack to check it's not going to bite, and leans out of the doorway. "It's way early for Santa to be visiting!" he shouts. "Come out, come out, whoever you are."

No reply but the wind.

"Open it!" Cass says. "Open the pack."

Yeah, nobody's in a hurry to do so.

"They could have food." Seb's not moving. "Or maybe…a bomb."

"That's the dumbest thing you've said all day, and you already set the bar so high, bro." Lawrence bends down, pinches the first of the clips. The strap pings back, making us all jump.

"Maybe we've gotten this all wrong," I say. "Maybe whoever is out there is hurt, confused…or lost like us."

"We're not lost," Ben mutters.

"Okay, stranded, whatever."

"And maybe it's the bodach. Remember him?" Seb trills.

"No." Ben snorts. "Because he's in your imagination."

I'm done. "Last thing I heard, mystical mountain bogeymen don't have backpacks. I'm going out. Where's a headlamp?" Cass hands me one, Lawrence finds another, and Seb kind of dances behind us, making quiet *woooo* ghosty noises as Lawrence and I walk slowly but determinedly outside.

Yikes—it's colder, cold enough to snow, but I don't care about that. I clutch the light in my slightly shaking hand and shine it toward Devil's Chute. Nothing. Across the front of the hut past the window, all clear.

"Here!" Lawrence hisses at me, pointing his light down on the ground. "That look like a print to you?"

"Bigfoot!" Seb whispers.

Not unless the Bigfoot's wearing hiking boots. At least I *think* it's human. But impossible to be sure in this mess of mud.

"Over there!" Lawrence grasps my arm, he's looking toward the outhouse. "Can you see…?"

"It's the ghost light!" Seb squeals, and I gasp and cover up my headlamp. There's a glowing orb; dim, bouncing through the air toward us, a will-o'-the-wisp, a Glenshee faerie, one of the wee folk. The three of us flatten ourselves against the wall of the hut. Ben and Cass peek out and we shush, gesticulating for them to fall back, and *ohmigod*, the orb is still coming.

And it is humming a tune.

Something that sounds so familiar, something that grips me around the neck, presses heavy into my chest so that I feel like

I'm suffocating, and so help me, I cling to Lawrence's arm and make myself as small as I can.

The cave. The humming.

I'm there again. It's dark and terrifying and I can't escape. The humming gets louder, the light gets closer, and I see the outline of a figure. Lawrence's body stiffens for action. Seb whimpers. I want to close my eyes, but I know that won't make me disappear. It didn't ten years ago and it won't now...

"Rooaarrr!" The monster raises its arms menacingly and jumps toward us with a splash of mud. "Hey ma peeps, am I pleased to see you or whaaat?"

Lawrence fumbles with his light and swings it upward, onto a dirt-streaked face that blinks and backs off.

"Don't blind me, dipshit! Like I haven't been through enough already?"

I take a step toward the monster.

"...Ant?"

"Yeah, who'd ya think, Swamp Thing?" Ant cackles at me, their voice even croakier than usual. "Although covered in all of this crap, I guess I could forgive you for making the mistake."

"You're okay!" I rush, throw my arms around Ant's smelly self, and squeeze, hard. "Holy Mother of God, it's amazing to see you!"

"Nope, I'm not her either, but yeah, go ahead and worship me if it makes you feel better." Glorious, human, and very corporeal, Ant pats me on the head. I squeeze some more and they yell at me to stop, but I don't.

Ben and Cass rush for a hug too, Lawrence gives Ant a clap on the back, and even Seb ruffles their hair, which elicits several choice curses.

"What were you playing at?" Ben laughs in relief. "You throwing your pack against the door freaked the hell out of everyone!"

"Not on purpose, I swear!" Ant laughs back. "Truth is, I saw that outhouse and thought all my prayers had finally been answered. I've been holding on so long it was like pushing out a rugby ball."

"Oh god, you're so gross. I love you." I hug them again and whisper, "My dad?"

Ant nods. "I think he's okay."

I feel my heart leap into my throat. "You *think*? He's nearby?"

Ant shakes their head. "Sweets, I need to sit down before I fall down, ya know?" They shudder, and for the first time I notice the grip of their jaw, the water in the corner of their eye. This is all a front. Ant is demolished. I nod, furiously, and they clasp my shoulders. "Don't fret, I'll tell you everything..."

"Come in, get warm," Cass says.

"Absolutin' tootin'—hey, where's Steph?" Ant wobbles toward the door. "Am I hungry. Ate all my supplies already. Mungo said there was a crate of food here. We need to get stuck into that, pronto."

"A lot has happened..." Cass begins, but Ant's already at the steps. They start, turn around to us, and hike a thumb in Steph's direction.

"Er, tell me she's just had a really long day."

Ben shakes his head. Ant frowns, rushes to Steph. We all bundle back inside, lock the door, and give Ant the story. Ant gapes at us, holding Steph's hand, their eyes getting wider and wider. I don't think I've ever seen this kid sit so still so long.

"Very bad scene." Ant whistles when we've told them the worst of it. "No lie, our girl Steph's been out this whole time?"

Ben nods. "Hasn't even moved." He looks as sad as I've seen him, and that's saying something. "She...makes these little harrumphs when she sleeps, sometimes, but not even that."

My heart hurts when he says it, and I'm instantly beating myself up inside, because that's so not the issue here. And the Dad question is killing me. It's all I can do to stop myself shouting, "Dad! Tell me about Dad!" but it feels shitty to shift the focus from Steph.

"So let me get this straight." Ant springs up, goes to the door, like they need movement to process the information ricocheting around their brain. "There's someone out there, for real? Someone who hurt Steph?"

I lift my hands. "We...don't know. Yes, Steph thought she saw someone in the woods, and yes, the crate and the knife have gone missing. But there might be other explanations for that. And the rockfall was an accident."

"You all hope!" Seb brays.

"Well, aye." Ant looks at him. "You an' all, pal. Because if there *is* someone coming for us, you're the slowest in the herd."

"Go jump off a cliff."

"Och, I already did." Ant smiles broadly, and spins around to face me. "Mags, I'm gonna tell you about your dad. I know you're pissing yourself to ask. But lads, I really, really need a refuel, so those leftovers you found from the crate, can I have some?"

"Yes!" I remember the egg in my pocket, and remarkably, it's still intact. That egg must have a superstrength shell after all it's been through. Nevertheless, Cass heats a pan and mercilessly cracks it into some oil she rescued, and the hut fills with one of the best smells in the world. Ant peels off muddy waterproofs, rakes sludge out of their hair with a borrowed comb, and washes up in the sink. When they're done, Ben finds crackers, Lawrence donates some jerky, and Ant perches on the platform beside Steph and enjoys the weirdest meal in the world.

It's all I can do to not ask. Finally, Ant takes a long slug of water from their refilled bottle, and exhales deeply.

"So, *The Tale of the Runaway Dinghy.*" There's a rueful half smile. "Or, another title, *So Sorry, It Was All My Fault.*"

"No." I manage to keep my voice even.

"Don't argue." Ant wags a finger at me. "It was my stupid fault we lost the boat, my fault your dad went in the drink. But the good news is, he pulled himself back in. He'd hurt his leg in the water, but he was totally fine, not bleeding or anything."

"He has a bad knee." I bite my lip.

"Yeah, so I'm giving you all the deets." Ant nods at me, vigorously, and I nod back, mainly because yes, I want it all. The truth feels terrifying, but I have to have it. Ant takes a breath.

"So. There was some crazy log flume action while your dad got his mojo back, but he grabbed the paddle and steered us true. The river got narrower, but uh-oh, it was *so* much rougher—rapids, high cliffs on both sides. Kind of fun and completely petrifying, all in one." Ant's eyes flash. "At one point we got into this whirlpool." They blink at the memory. "We were stuck, it was sucking us down at the front. Thought I was going to be like that guy in *Jaws*, you know? When half the boat sinks and he slides down, and the shark pops up and is like—" Ant opens their mouth wide. "Chomp, chomp, chomp! Come to Mama."

I give Ant a look. "But you made it."

"Yep." They grin. "No idea how, but suddenly something went 'pop' and spat us out. He was paddling like a total machine for the side once we got clear of the cliffs, and he's telling me if anything happens to him, or we get separated, I have to find the shepherd's hut, and that's blowing my mind, because I'm thinking, no way am I letting you go, dude. And then suddenly there was a tree, and he shouts at me to make a grab. I snag a branch and hold on for dear life, but—" Ant looks around at us, the spellbound audience. "The boat keeps on keepin' on, under me, and there's a split-second choice to be made here: branch or boat. And I chose branch."

"You fell in?" Cass asks, and Ant nods.

"That was the worst part. The full-body baptism…" They chuckle, all knuckle-cracking and flexing of limbs, letting those wiggles out. "I mean, I nearly drowned, whatever, but it was also kind of hilarious." Ant looks at me. "Your poor dad, yelling, and me gasping and bobbing downstream. But then I hooked another branch and I did it right this time. Pulled myself to dry land."

"Thank god." Cass shakes her head.

"Oh, He probably had something to do with it because I wouldn't put bets on me making it otherwise." Ant winks at her. "And Mungo, bless 'im, he was paddling for Scotland, but it was useless. He saw me stand up on the bank, and he yeeted my backpack out of the boat on to the rocks! I'm like, what the whut? But then I realized he wanted me to have my stuff whatever happened to him."

"And what did happen to him?" I can barely breathe.

Ant grimaces, looks up at the ceiling. "Maggie, I was cold and wet, shivering so hard I couldn't stand up straight. But the last time I saw him, he was okay, I swear. Paddling, in control."

"You followed him down the riverbank?"

"As far as I could go." Ant bites a knuckle. "But I couldn't catch him, and the sides got too high for him to land. An' I thought, he's told me to find the shepherd's hut, but it feels all kinds of wrong to leave him. So I just stood there. And then the thunderbolts happened, so I crawled under a bush. For the whole night."

"Oh my god, Ant!" Cass says.

"Wore all my clothes and piled everything else on top of me like a hedgehog." Hands come up like paws under Ant's chin. "Survived."

"You weren't scared?" Cass says.

"*Rattled.*" Ant leans forward and stares at her. "But even that gets old after a while. You psych yourself out, you know? There's only so much you can take before the brain...shuts down."

"Like you've got a brain," Seb drones.

"And Dad never came back?"

Ant glances at me, kind of deflates, and slowly shakes their head.

"I waited as long as I could." Ant takes my hands gently. Their fingers are rough and cold, and as they squeeze mine, I feel sick for making Ant feel guilty. Waiting was more than I did. "I absolutely believe he's alive and kicking, Maggie. And I think he must have decided to keep going, send in the troops to get us out of here."

"Yes! That's what we said earlier." Ben puffs out his chest, and my anxiety threatens to bubble into anger. He knows nothing. Dad wouldn't leave Ant alone, not unless there was absolutely no other choice. Maybe if we were all together, he would make the hard choice to leave us, but he wouldn't risk Ant fending for themselves. Something must have gone wrong.

"Tomorrow," I say to Ant. "First thing. You show us how you got here. We follow the river as best we can, and we find Dad. And even if we don't, that's our way out of the mountains and home."

"What about Steph?" Cass says.

"No way am I leaving her." Ben folds his arms.

"And we're not carrying her either," Lawrence says.

"But we've got to try!" I start.

"Whoa." Ant flings up a hand. "Don't waste your energy spitting at each other. The way I came isn't open anymore, why do you think I look like this? The whole of the hillside flippin' fell off, and I was on it when it happened. Only just escaped. There's no going back."

"The landslide?" Lawrence says. "We were on the other side. Must have been some ride." He looks almost envious.

"Never want to do it again." A cloud moves over Ant's face. "I'd been going in circles looking for the hut, I was exhausted but hyper, kept thinking the hills have eyes, the whole bit. Truth is, I gave up. When the earth started to slide, I gave in to it. But I guess it didn't want me. It spat me out."

"How did you find us?" I ask.

"Luck." Ant shrugs. "There was a break in the mist. I saw smoke in the sky, kept heading for it. Then it got dark, and I was screwed until I spotted a life jacket by the woods, and another at the bottom of the hill. Figured it was your clever signposting." They give a thumbs-up. "The only way was to climb, but it took an hour in the mud. Yeah, sheer luck. I only hope I haven't used it all."

I'm wondering if Ant might have used up our luck too.

"You said you felt like the hills have eyes," Cass said. "What exactly did you mean by that?"

Ant drums a beat on their legs, looks embarrassed.

"You know, the bodach thing. You said it happened to you too. You start seeing shadows, feeling like you're being watched. Imagining stuff."

"We didn't imagine the crate smashed on the crags," Seb mutters.

"But you don't seriously think there was someone out there, watching you?" Ben leans toward Ant. "Like, give me a specific example."

"I dunno." Ant stims faster, paddling fingers on their thigh. "Just before it got dark. I saw the smoke coming from your fire, had to walk through the woods—what was left of them—to get to the bottom of the hill." They clasp their hands together tightly to stop the drumming. "That was the time I felt the most scared, out of all of it. Really thought being strung-out tired had chased the fear away, you know? Nuh-uh." Their eyes glow in the half-light as they lean forward. "The fear came back—BAM!—like electricity shot through my veins, man. This feeling of being stalked. Every hair on my body standing on end, I'm fight-or-flighting, firing on all cylinders—and I flew, flew, flew like a bat outta hell with rocket boosters." Ant exhales hard, sits back, and blinks rapidly. "I mean, do we have bears here?"

"Course not," Seb grunts. "Not since the Dark Ages."

"Hmm." Ant shrugs. "People are always talking about rewilding, thought I might have missed some new bear update." They pull a face. "Wasn't trippin' though. There was something on my tail."

"I don't like this," I say. "Too much to be coincidence."

"We need to leave." Lawrence stands up, checks the door again. "And from what Ant says, there's no way out east of here. So it's back to our original plan."

"Which is?" Ant asks.

"Ben, and whoever else wants to, stays here with Steph. The rest of us are going fast, and going north. Tomorrow, we hike out over the top of the mountain."

CHAPTER 15

I sleep heavily, but my dreams fight me, and I wake, sweaty and frantic, pushing away the jacket that was over my head.

Morning?

My heart thumps loudly, resonating off the wooden platform underneath my back. It's okay, I'm not on the ledge. I'm here, in the hut. Sounds of wind and rain, and Seb's snores, slowly pull me back into the real world.

Damn, why am I so cold?

I gave Steph my sleeping bag. As I reach for my jacket again, the shutter over the window rattles in the wind. Is that a crack of something approaching daylight? Please let it be. I *can't* with these dreams anymore.

Twisting around, I see Steph, lying there. She hasn't moved. But she's going to be okay. She's going to be alright, because we're getting out of here and we're going home.

Somewhere in the middle of the room, there's movement.

Lawrence flicks on the hurricane light. He must have had last shift watching Stephanie. We took turns staying awake through the night, for her, and for…other reasons. I went first, propped myself up by the stove and jumped at every creaking of the rafters, every gust of wind, finally handing over to Cass when my eyes could no longer stay open, and burrowing under my coat. Seb declined to be included in the night watch. Nobody pushed it. We all said Ant shouldn't have to take a shift, though they wanted to, and nobody fought that, either.

I wave at Lawrence, and he nods back. He's dressed already—but does he ever undress? Prepped for action, always. He's crouched, rolling up his sleeping bag.

"What time is it?"

"Seven," he says without looking at his watch. "I'm leaving as soon as I'm ready." *Shit.* He will, too. Better get up and get my stuff stowed.

Yes, it was an easy decision to choose climbing Cairn Gealach over staying here with Ben and Stephanie. Though not for the reasons anyone might imagine. Fact of the matter is, I should go because I'll make it. I'm fit and strong. I might be terrible on an inflatable boat, but I have more stamina than any of these kids, even Lawrence. He keeps talking about going fast, but it's not going to help Steph if we kill ourselves. It'll be a marathon, not a sprint.

"Going outside for a few." Lawrence grabs the axe and makes for the door. The unspoken part is: *if I'm not back soon, come looking…*

I organize my crap, and by the time I'm stuffing the last of it into my backpack, Ben and Cass are awake.

"Lawrence says he wants to go as soon as possible. Jesus!" I jump; it's Lawrence himself, outside the window, opening the shutter. The sun's not fully up yet, and rain streaks the glass. For once, I don't care. Can't wait to be away, I'm strung so tight. I pull on my waterproofs as Lawrence comes back in.

"Steph okay?" Ant sits up sleepily, rubbing their eyes.

"Still the same," Ben says. "Did anyone see her move during the night?" Nobody did. Ben gazes down at her and I can almost smell the guilt radiating off him. I feel it too, because I'm abandoning them both, and what's more, I'm happy about it.

"So." Ant springs to their feet. "Who is staying here?"

"I'm going." *Whoa, idiot.* Mustn't sound too keen.

"We've got to take advantage of every minute of daylight." Lawrence has no similar qualms, kicking Seb, who is the only one still asleep. "We'll leave when this slob gets it together." Seb groans dramatically, rolls over, and I can see Lawrence fighting himself not to kick again. I was thinking he might be glad to leave his evil twin behind, but it seems like the decision was never in question.

"I'm definitely coming with you guys," Ant says. "Not that I don't care about Steph, obviously, but you know I'll drive you crazy if I stay cooped up here, matey."

"No bother." Ben's face looks so pale and drawn, way older. "I don't expect anyone to stay unless they want to. That includes you, Cass."

"You're sure?"

I can't read her expression—relief, or regret?—but at least she has the balls to look him in the eye, unlike me. "We'll set you up with plenty of firewood before we leave, and you can have most of our food."

"Er, no. We need calories to get over that mountain," Lawrence says.

Ben holds up a hand. "I have enough. Not hungry anyway."

So we hustle, eating a few soggy crackers as we don water-proofs and stack our packs by the door. Ready. Ben is sitting by Steph, holding her hand. I hover, agonizing. She has my sleeping bag, but hers is still damp with pee and rain, and how the hell can I claim mine back? As I'm dithering, Ben takes off his sweater and chucks it to me.

"Extra layer for you."

"Oh!" It's the one I used to borrow when we were together. Gray marl with fleece lining. I loved how it smelled of him. Sweet torture, now. "I can't. You'll need it. You don't even have the rest of your clothes—"

"No," he says quietly, firmly. "I have a fire." He takes Steph's hand again. "Just hurry. But be safe, yeah?"

I nod, feeling choked.

"Dude, so you know, we're taking the axe," Lawrence says matter of factly. "But you can use this iron bar to beat the guy's brain in, if he comes for you."

Ben nods, grim and brave. Fear grips my heart. This is so screwed up. Ben won't be able to fight all by himself. Tears prick my eyes. I take one last look at Steph and get gone, dragging my backpack outside.

Seb's already there, leaning against the wall, sheltering from the rain. He gives me a snarky look and sighs. *Right back at you, you stupid wanker.* If I needed any more motivation to hike fast, being around him is it.

Cass appears from the direction of the outhouse, red-faced, with an armful of logs. "Not much wood left, but there's a couple of fallen trees up that first stretch." She nods to the mountain trail beyond the outhouse. "Oy, lads," she calls through the doorway. "All hands on deck, and bring the axe. We need to gather more wood for Ben and Steph."

"Och, give it up." Seb throws his head back. "They'll be fine with the logs. Can we just leave already?"

"I'll help." Ben glances back nervously at Steph, but she's not going anywhere. He shuts the door, Lawrence peels his twin off the wall, and we make our way across the mud.

"Hey friends," Ant says breezily. "I'm going to walk around the edge of the landslide. There was a load of branches that fell down, so there might be something burnable I can gather." They skip off toward the slice of hill that is no more.

"Be careful, promise!" I shout after them, and they flash me a cheesy grin. *Oh hell, please don't give us another rescue scenario, Ant.*

"The trees are this way," Cass says, leading us through the entrance to a narrow pass between high rocks. We begin the ascent up a steep, stony trail. It's easier underfoot than the mud, at least. After a couple of minutes, we come to flatter area where the trail splits into three. Cass points up at some dead trees, lying on another plateau above us.

"See, up there? The branches aren't thick. They'll be easy to chop."

"I'll deal," Lawrence says. "We'll get going faster if we split up. The rest of you spread out and find more wood, dry moss, whatever." He jogs toward the trees, brandishing his axe.

"Dry moss? Nothing's dry." I wipe the rain out of my eyes. "Will those trees even burn?"

"Best we can do." Cass starts up the trail on the right. "Ten minutes max, we meet back here, yeah? Only gather dead stuff!" She disappears up the path.

"They're hawthorn trees, they're bad," Ben mutters.

"What?" I stare at him.

He nods, darkly. "You should never bring hawthorn into your home. It's very unlucky."

"Oh, nice catch, Grandma—so would you rather be cold?" I snark, and instantly feel like Queen Bitch, especially considering he gave me his sweater. "Look, let's go get gathering." He lingers, so I continue along the middle trail alone, glancing down at Seb, who has slumped against the rock wall. A flash of irritation runs through me. Seb's going to last half a day at most, he'll slow us down so much. "Coming?"

He shakes his head, barely deigning to look at me.

"Naw. Lawrence will need a hand."

Yeah, right. I'm betting he has no intention to follow his

brother, lazy bastard, but I'm not wasting time. I don't relish going too far on my own, but he and Ben can do their own thing, screw it.

"Okay, fine. Watch out for the bogeyman, tho'."

Because if I shout it, it makes the very notion seem ridiculous, and I am less afraid.

I jog up the trail, finding a few small sticks here and there, but nothing much. There are no trees and very few bushes. Mainly just rocks and the clumps of long grass. Nobody follows me, and after a couple of minutes, my bravado fades. I'm battling waist-high bracken and the trail is obscured. This is useless. The bracken is a mess of brown, broken ferns, tangled tendrils wrapping themselves around my legs as I wade through. I pull at a few fronds. It's wet with rain, but I bet it'll burn when it's dried out, so I gather as much as I can carry and head down the trail again.

God, the smell. *Curry powder!* That's where it's coming from, the bloody bracken! Kind of makes my stomach rumble, though. Breakfast curry, anyone? A day ago, the smell repulsed me, but look at me now. I even chortle to myself. I'll be eating mud pie before this trip is done.

When I get back to the spot where the trail splits, there's no one there waiting for me. Up above, I can see some of the branches have gone from the fallen trees. Lawrence must have taken them down already. No sign of any of the others. So much for us watching each other's backs. I continue along the main trail, and when I pop out of the bottom of the pass, I'm relieved to spot Ben at the outhouse, juggling logs. Beyond him, Cass disappears into the hut. Who knows where the others have got to? Hope Ant hasn't bodysurfed down the hill. I struggle across the mud with my curry-smelling ferns.

"No luck finding anything?" I shout to Ben and he shakes his head, balancing the remaining logs against his chest.

"We'll manage. As long as you guys hurry. It's not like we have to have the fire on constantly." His face is crinkled, I think he's trying not to cry. The burden of staying here with Steph might only just be sinking in, and my heart aches for him.

"I've got enough kindling anyway." I try a goofy smile through the fronds. At the same time, I spot Seb, off in the direction of the crags, the rocky outcrop. What the hell is he doing down there? I look at Ben again. "And as for unlucky hawthorn, I think we're due a whole heap of *good* luck, don't you? Maybe it will reverse the curse?"

Suddenly, a bloodcurdling scream comes from inside the hut.

"Steph?" Ben gasps, dropping the logs.

"Help, someone!"

Oh god, that's Ant. We run inside to see Cass leaning over Stephanie. Ant is frozen to the spot, watching Cass in horror.

"She's not breathing!" Cass feels the side of Steph's neck. "Oh my god, she's cold as ice!"

"Do something!" Ant shouts at nobody in particular. Ben rushes to Steph's side.

"What happened?"

Cass is crying, shaking her head and leaning over Steph.

"Nothing. We just came in and she was like this." She shakes Steph's shoulders. "Wake up!"

"No, you'll hurt her!" Ben grabs Cass's hands, shoving her out of the way. "Stephanie?" He lowers his ear to her face, listening for her breathing, holding her wrist. "She doesn't have a pulse!"

"Chest compressions." Cass links her fingers together, shoves past Ben, puts her hands on Steph's sternum, and pumps hard. "One, two, three, four, five—come on, Steph!" She looks up at us frantically. "How many do I do?"

"Thirty. We did this at school. The paramedics, you remember?" Ant's rooted to the spot, forced calm. "Thirty, and then mouth-to-mouth."

Cass nods and pumps Steph's chest so hard her frail body shakes. Then she pinches Steph's nose gently, leans in to give the kiss of life. *Oh god, she's being too tentative, I can't bear it—*

"Chest again."

"Got it."

"*Ah-ha-ha-ha, stayin' alive, stayin' alive,*" Ant sings, their voice weedy, wobbling. "Come on! *Ah-ha-ha-ha, stayin' alive, stayin' alive!*"

"What the hell?" Ben looks at them, aghast.

"It helps. The emergency doctors tell you to sing that song when you do the compressions," Ant babbles, wiping away snot. "It's the right speed. There's a Taylor one, if that's better? Or 'Baby Shark'?"

"Shut up!"

"Yep. Okay. Okay." Ant nods.

"Come on, come on, Steph!" Cass pumps her chest again, Ant paces in time, and I try my damn hardest to get *baby shark, doo doo doo-doo doo-doo* out of my head.

"Twenty, twenty-one, twenty-two…"

"Oh god, oh god, oh god." Ben grips his head, crouching beside Stephanie's motionless body.

"Come on, Steph, you can do this!" Ant can't stop pacing.

"What's going on?" Lawrence appears at the doorway, Seb behind him. "She's not breathing? Let me—" Lawrence rushes at Cass.

"Back off!" she screams at him, eyes blazing. "Twenty-eight, twenty-nine, thirty. Now the breath."

She does. We wait. Nothing.

Cass wails, restarts the compressions, and we're all just letting this play out. Thirty more. And again. And my nails are cutting into my palms.

In movies, there's always that moment when it's gone on too long, and someone says to stop, to mark the time of death. But nobody does. Cass keeps going, Ant is pacing a trench into the floor, and the rest of us are a stagnant tableau, useless voyeurs, and we're all stuck in this loop. Nobody wants to call it, to make this our new reality, to change Steph's status forever. Everyone is waiting for that last ditch gasp, for Steph's eyes to spring open, her chest to rise again, and for us all to collapse in thankful relief.

But it doesn't happen.

Finally, Lawrence.

"Stop, Cass."

"No." Cass is sobbing, but she's still going, faster and harder than ever.

"She's gone. Stop. Please." I've never heard Lawrence beg before. "It's been too long."

Cass shakes her head. "We have to keep going."

"It's done." Lawrence moves in and physically removes Cass, picking her up round the waist in the same way my dad lifted her out of the river. She screams and kicks, but only for a few seconds before she goes limp in his arms, and they stay there, clutching each other, while she sobs. Ben is staring at Steph, Seb sits down heavily on the floor, Ant is stimming a tattoo on their legs, dancing fingertips.

I can't cry. I'm holding on to everything inside. I grip Steph's cold, cold hand; it's perfectly smooth, the skin waxy, slim fingers graceful in my paw. She's here, but not here. I want to warm this hand, bring it up to my cheek, but it remains cold. We stay like that for as long as it takes Ben to move. Feels like time has stopped.

"We should...we should cover her face."

"Yes." I have no idea why, but it feels right, somehow. Dignified. I carefully place Steph's hand on her stomach, but it slides off, hits the floor, and I feel bad, like I was sloppy.

Soon she'll go all stiff. I chase the intrusive thought from my mind. *And how long before she starts to smell?* I fumble in her pack for her towel. It's small, neatly rolled, with peppermint-green stripes. I hand it to Ben, who unfurls it, and slowly, carefully, places it over her upper half. I think we should move away from her now. But where exactly are we supposed to go?

"How did this happen?" Ben gets to his feet, shaking. "She was okay...when we left the hut."

"Dude," Lawrence starts. "She had a head injury. It was bad—"

"No," Ben says. "She was fine. She was breathing. She was going to live, I know it. Something happened while we were gone. I never should have left her!" He staggers to the sink, dry heaves. I want to go to him, but it's too raw, too scary. After a moment, he takes a breath, composes himself, and a steeliness descends, his face blotchy but expressionless.

"Stephanie is dead," he says, voice eerily calm. "And it's all my fault."

CHAPTER 16

Ben walks slowly out of the hut, shutting the door behind him.

I stare at the space where he was, because anything is preferable to looking at the peppermint-green-striped towel. Even Ant is still. I can hear them breathing heavily, almost to the point of hyperventilating, and I can tell they're trying to control it, and a dozen other impulses, no doubt. And then they crack.

"I'll go see if he's—"

"Leave him!" My voice shocks me. It's guttural, terrifying. Ant tics, a head jerk. *Get a grip, Maggie.* "Sorry. Give him a moment." They nod, wringing their hands, cracking knuckles, trying not to.

"I don't care about you losers. I'm out of here," Seb spits. "If there's a killer on the loose, I'm not waiting around." He glances at his twin—for what? Approval? Dissent? But Lawrence looks away, the muscles in his jaw working. "Well?" Seb gets a little louder. "What's the grand plan? Staying here with a dead body?"

"Shut up!" Cass cries.

"Why? In case I wake her?" he mutters, and we all swear at him. "Be honest. You're worried me shouting will bring the killer back." He shoots a nervous glance at the door. "You're scared? You should be. It's time to *go*."

Cass shakes herself, wipes away tears. "Just be quiet. We need to think what's best." She bites her lip. "Perhaps we should stay here now. Pile everything against the door and wait it out. The weather is better. If Mr. Atkins made it back, there will be rescue people on their way."

"You were all for leaving half an hour ago!" Seb laughs in disbelief.

"Yes." She gets in his face. "But now there's no point, is there? It's too late to save Steph." Her voice cracks. "We might as well make the best of it with a roof over our heads and a locked door, until the rescuers get here."

"They're not coming." Lawrence rubs his face and groans, turning to me. "Maggie, I'm sorry, but if your dad had made it back, they'd be here by now. We'd see a sign. They'd do a fly by. Drones, whatever. Seven kids get stranded in the hills? First light, they're sending in the army."

It's not that I hadn't thought it. I've been trying not to. The weather's cold and wet and horrible, but there's no storm, no reason why the cavalry wouldn't be on their way by now if Dad raised the alarm.

"Daddy's dead too, boo-hoo," Seb snarls. "Mungo got sliced by the bodach."

"Have some respect and shut your trap." Lawrence stabs a finger in his brother's chest, his voice trembling. "If Mungo never made it, we're not expected back until...what the hell day is it now?"

We all pause, because normally it would be Stephanie speaking up with the answer, because Stephanie would know.

"Damn it!" Lawrence mutters, counting on his fingers. "It's Sunday, and we won't be missed 'til late tomorrow. The original plan has us meeting our ride home in the north parking lot, the other side of Cairn Gealach. So we go there, leave now. Basic rule of survival: keep moving." He heads to the door. "Take anything useful from Stephanie's stuff. We're out of here."

It's decided.

———

"Rain's stopped, that's good."

Ben doesn't answer me, but at least he's still walking.

It took an achingly long time to persuade him to leave the hut. Maybe an hour of me nervously watching the door out of the corner of my eye and pretending not to. I don't know what happened to Steph, but I do know I want out of here. Feels like we're provoking the Fates by staying.

I told the others to go ahead, and Ben sat by Steph's body and cried quietly, on and off, and endured me bending his ear with fuzzy crap like: *she'd want you to go* and *it's not your fault this happened*. It's so hard to make the decision to abandon your loved one, but he's done it before. I found Steph's compass and gave it to him, telling him we *needed him* to get us home. That worked.

An hour is an honorable time to hold fast, after all. Once the decision was made, Ben clasped Steph's hand once more, and I left to let him say good-bye alone. It's not that I don't care. It's *because* I care that I can't, won't, process what has happened yet. Right now, I need to focus on getting us caught up with the others, and over that mountain.

After traversing the narrow pass—me, looking up and pushing down the panic, Ben in a daze—we've emerged onto open hillside. Thank god, nowhere for anyone to hide and surprise us here. The slope is wide and featureless, with curved sides disappearing off into oblivion. It's heavy going through the wet peat, but the trail is well marked toward Cairn Gealach. We can do this.

"The mist has cleared. That's a good sign. Once we're over this crest, we might even be able to see the others." Jeez, I'm peppy as hell, filling the silence, scared that if I give him space, Ben might suddenly change his mind, run back to Stephanie. "Even if not, we know the route they're on, so no worries, eh?" The plan is to summit and get as far down the other side as we can before sundown, make for that parking lot.

We walk on in silence, and I rack my brain for something more to say. But maybe it's okay, maybe he's committed. He's overtaken me. That's positive, right? I think he's cried all of his tears, for now. He's probably just numb, needs time to—

"Who was first back to the hut?" Ben stops, and I nearly crash into him.

"What?" My brain scrambles. "You mean when we went out collecting wood?"

He nods, impatient. "Ant, or Cass? Did Seb or Lawrence actually get back before us, and go out again? It's possible."

"Um…"

Ben's forehead tenses, his eyes darting over the bleak landscape. "I didn't find any wood up the pass. I bumped into Cass, and we came down together. Ant was already near the outhouse. Took me less than a minute to pick up the logs. Before that, I didn't see the twins, or you. But that doesn't mean someone couldn't have entered the hut when I was up the pass, or in the outhouse."

"We should hurry to catch the others." I smile weakly. "We can talk about this later."

"I want to talk about it now." Ben glares at me. "Precisely because we're not with the others. We were away gathering wood, what? Twenty minutes, twenty-five? That's more than enough time."

Oh, Jesus. To do what, exactly?

"You don't think that one of us…?"

It sounds preposterous out loud, and as soon as I leave that *dot dot dot* hanging, I feel ridiculous, like Ben is going to turn around and laugh in utter contempt and disbelief, tell me that's not what he means at all, am I stupid? But he doesn't.

"Sebastian's been very quiet." Ben stares into middle

distance, his hazel eyes bloodshot. "And nobody knows where he was when Steph got hit by the rock."

"No, but I don't think—" Got to keep walking. He'll follow if I go, but he reaches out and catches my arm.

"Maybe Seb caused the rockfall." His voice rises. "Not deliberately to hurt anyone. But maybe he was dicking around and it went too far."

It doesn't sound that outrageous. It's the kind of thing Seb might do. But not after the landslide. None of us were in dicking-around mode. We'd dodged death. We were focused on getting to the hut, to safety. At least, most of us were... Lawrence said Seb was with him, but what would it take for Seb to set some rocks falling? A few seconds when Lawrence didn't have eyes on him? Ben sees my hesitation.

"What if Seb knew he had hurt Stephanie—even if he didn't intend to—and he came back to the hut before anyone else, noticed she wasn't breathing, and just...didn't do anything?" He grips my shoulders, his eyes searching mine, face flecked with dirt and streaked by tears. "It would be so much easier for him to do nothing, and we all know Seb takes the easy route. What if he was worried Steph knew it was him who threw the rocks? Way better for him if she never woke up."

"That makes no sense." I break away from his hold. "Steph couldn't have seen who caused the rockfall. She was facing away from the hill. And I can't believe Seb would be that cold."

"Okay, so what is the alternative? Maybe he's right, and there's a bloody bodach that sneaked into the hut while we were out and finished her off!" He's yelling now, spit flying out of his mouth, all that emotion transferring into anger with me, because that's easier, familiar. And I'll be his whipping boy, this once, because I still love him enough to help him bear this unfathomable weight. "I didn't believe her, Maggie! She said she'd seen someone. I told her it was shadows! But what if I was wrong? Ant thought there was someone in the woods. We've all felt it, and I thought it was our imaginations, but what if Steph was right and whoever it is killed her?"

"I don't know." I really don't. My head feels fried. "I think... Steph's injuries were way worse than we hoped, she slipped away, and there's nothing we could have done that would have changed that." I feel a new surge of tears, but push them down. *This is not about me.* "But yes, of course, so much weirdness happening, I'm scared." I take his hand. "Please come. I need us all to stick together."

Just walk, keep walking, gamble that he'll follow. And so I do, and after a few seconds, I hear him let out a yell of frustration. At least it's worked; he's coming after me. Not going to think too much about what he said. It's all understandable—Ben's overloaded with guilt and grief, so he's searching for answers. I don't blame him for running every possibility through his head. In some ways, it's easier if Steph didn't die because we were careless, or clueless. He wants someone to blame, someone not him.

He catches up with me and we ascend silently, in rhythm, eventually reaching the crest of the hill. And then there's another crest, and another, in that totally frustrating way that saps your soul and makes you feel like the mountain is trolling you, but we stamp out our sadness into the hill, physical pain suppressing anguish. As we finally drag ourselves up the last hilltop, we're rewarded with a full view of the task in front of us.

There's a dip below, a small woodland, and behind it, the mountain. Cairn Gealach, immense and proud, takes up most of the skyline; a sleeping giant covered with a muddle of brown and gray stone. I think I can just make out where the trail winds around near the bottom, with vivid bluey-greens of under-growth, and the dotted yellow of gorse bushes. As I trace the way up, I lose track of how we'll scale this beast, past the paler heights of sheer rock faces that lead to a rounded peak, lightly dusted with snow.

"How long will it take us to get up there?"

"A few hours," Ben says. "If the weather holds, we'll be on the other side by nightfall."

If the weather holds. And our luck.

I jump. Figures come into view to the side of the woods. The others, waiting for us, in a field of bracken. So glad to see them, whether they're there because their feet are sore, or they actually care about us. Strength in numbers.

Turns out, it's neither sore soles nor kind souls that are holding them in place. A disagreement is brewing.

"Are we sure there isn't another way around this wood? Argh!" Cass throws her head back in frustration as Ben and I approach.

"Naw!" Lawrence, already forging ahead toward the tree line, shouts back at her. "Sheer drop on the left."

"And on the right?"

He stops, turns around. "It's pointless, you've seen the map. Unless you want to add a whole day's walking."

Ant pulls a face at me, and nods toward Ben. *How is he?* I subtly give them a thumbs-up.

"Ben, thank god you're here." Cass flaps the good map at him. "Look at this. You agree with me, we don't have to go through the trees, do we?"

"Hundred percent we do." I step in to save Ben, because the last thing he needs is to get between Cass and Lawrence. "If we go around, that's another couple of foothills to climb before we even get up the mountain. It's a massive diversion."

"We divert, big deal." She groans in frustration. "So sorry I don't want to go through the frickin' creepy woods after what has happened! Come on! At least on the hill, we're in the open. In there…" She looks around, shudders. "And what about rescuers? They won't see us! It's smarter to play safe."

"Anyone got paper and pen?" Ant asks. "We leave a paper trail. It worked for me with the life jackets."

"Huh?" Cass frowns. "Nobody's going to spot a piece of paper!"

"Yeah, they will, if they're looking. I would have." Ant takes some clear, plastic sandwich bags out of their pack. "I've got these to put them in. We'll just draw arrows, so they know which way we've gone."

"Sounds good." I find *The Book of Saints* in my pack. I shoved it in there before we left the hut, when Ben wasn't looking. Useful to have paper, after all, to start a fire or leave a note. But also, I couldn't ignore the sneaking idea that maybe having all these saints along for the ride could bring us better luck. I tear out a bunch of half-blank pages. "Er, Cass has a pen." Cass raises an eyebrow at me, but gives it to Ant.

"Nifty directions for anyone who's stalking us," Lawrence deadpans.

"Just draw the arrow going that way!" Cass points around the wood. "Because we're diverting!"

Seb groans in exaggerated frustration and looks expectantly at his brother to watch the fireworks; we all do, because Lawrence hates to be challenged. But his face is placid as he slowly reverses through the bracken, holding out a hand to Cass.

"Do you trust me?"

She starts, awkwardly.

"To do what?"

"To have your back. A quick in and out." He smiles at her and waggles the axe. "Me and my little chopper will get ya through, I promise."

"Your little chopper, that's the truth," Seb snorts.

Cass gives a sardonic laugh, blows out her cheeks. "When you put it like that…"

"I guarantee nothing bad will happen to you." He's pulling the full, cheesy sigma face now, and normally Cass would be giving him shite about it, but either she's wrung out, or in his thrall. "Deal?"

"Deal." She takes Lawrence's hand and walks off with him into the woods.

"Oh, the ick." Seb retches. "You sad, sad sacks." He follows them, making an impressive array of regurgitative noises.

"What just happened?" I mutter to Ant, and Ant shakes their head, leaves the note spiked on a bush, as we set off into the wood.

"They've flirted *brazenly* all the way. I cannot process. D'ye think they're in shock?"

"We move quickly!" Lawrence shouts back to us. "In a straight line! In and out!"

We go. Hard enough to move quickly through the woods, although the drive to stay together is strong, and that means matching pace with Lawrence and Cass. As to staying on a straight course, it's impossible—trees, ditches, tangles of briars, all the fun of the fair. Lawrence is following his nose, because Ben has Stephanie's compass, and nobody's taking it away from him. Once, I glance back at Ben and gesture, *Huh?* But he doesn't seem to care. Lawrence is moving so quickly, with Cass by his side, that I can barely keep them in my eyeline. Ant, just ahead of me, has gained ground on them. Maybe Ant's the person to trust in this situation, because somehow, they found their way before. Okay, so I'll risk losing Ben to keep Ant in sight...and after a minute of careering wildly after them, pack jiggling uncomfortably on my back, I wind up with neither in view.

Shit. Where did everyone go?

"Wait!" It's Seb, somewhere in my wake.

I start running again, in the best-guess direction. And thankfully, up ahead, I spot Lawrence and Cass. As I draw closer, Ant emerges from left field and skids to a halt beside them.

"Don't tell me, we're lost."

"No," Lawrence says. "But there's that." He points at a gulley in front of us, thick with thorny brambles, waist-deep. "Better to go around." He slaps his pants. "Okay! Left or right, to keep due north?"

"We need Ben and the compass." I turn and holler. "Ben!"

"Whaaaaaa!"

Our heads whip around at the horrible yell coming from somewhere in the woods behind us. Instantly, my hackles are up. I call out again.

"Ben?"

"Jeeeeeeeesus!"

"That's Seb's voice." Cass pants. "Didn't you guys keep an eye on him?"

"What the hell has he done now?" Lawrence grunts, but he's already ditching his pack and jogging back in the direction of the scream.

"Probably messing with us," Cass starts, but then there's a wail—Seb?—and crashing noises, like an elephant is charging through the undergrowth. Lawrence breaks into a run, and Ant follows. I throw my pack off and make chase too, because sod the twins, but I don't want Ant or Ben getting into any more trouble.

The crashing noise stops. Lawrence screeches to a halt.

"Seb! What you playing at?!"

"Over here!" Ben's voice rings out from somewhere beyond a thicket of brush, followed by a low moan. Lawrence spins, picks up a branch and bashes his way through. Ant and I follow him down a short slope, where Sebastian lies, his arms over his head like he's fending off invisible blows, Ben standing over him.

"What happened?" I look at Ben.

"I just got here too." He seems out of it, disoriented.

"You okay, you waste of space?" Lawrence crouches beside Seb, levering his brother's arms away from his face. "Did you fall?"

"Jumped." He's winded, fighting for breath. "To get away."

"What from?" I wheeze back at him, hands on my aching ribs. "You scared the life out of us."

"Yeah? Good." He sits up, scuttles to his feet, looking around, shaking. "I saw it. I saw the bodach."

Cass arrives. "What the hell?"

"Someone's out there. I saw whatever Steph and the freak saw." Seb snatches the branch from Lawrence's hands, does another three-sixty, like he's expecting something to jump out at any minute.

"Bullshit," Lawrence says, but he reaches into his jacket for the hand axe, and that's it, we're all casting around for weapons in the undergrowth.

"I knew it, I knew it." Cass finds a stick taller than her. I grab a rock. We all back into each other, circling, scanning the surroundings. "What do they look like? Is it a man?"

"Aye." Seb nods, head on a swivel. "Tall, dark—"

"And handsome?" Ant shakes, giggling nervously, leaning back on me so much I'm almost falling over. They've got half a holly bush in their hands, and they waggle it as warding off a flock of pesky sparrows.

"It's not funny, he's out there!" Seb hisses. "Just like Steph said. He's following us."

"Which direction?" Ben asks.

"Don't know. I ran. Could hear him coming after me, so I just booked it, jumped down here."

"Helpful," Lawrence mutters. "Come on, show yourself, you coward!"

"Shut up!" Seb whimpers.

"There's six of us. Whoever he is, he doesn't stand a chance." Lawrence shouts again. "Keep tight in the circle. United we stand."

"Does he have the knife?" Cass whispers. "Because if he does, I'm thinking we won't be standing for very long."

"God, I don't know," Seb says. "I think…he was holding something. But his hands were down by his side. I couldn't see what was in them."

"So how the hell do you know that he was holding anything?" My throat feels dry, blood rushing to my head. "Keep sharp, get ready, everyone."

"You been watching us, screwing with us?" Lawrence yells,

swiping at the air with his dinky axe. "Ya wee feardie-cat, I'll give ya a beatin'! Let's go!"

Oh god oh god oh god. We watch the undergrowth. It's not like we've even got the high ground. If this man's got the hunting knife, and he's as big a psycho as it looks, we stand no bloody chance. I feel Lawrence's shoulders to my left, Ben to my right. We're pressing on each other, facing out, keeping the circle strong. Every leaf that quivers, every bird that startles out of a tree, every raindrop that makes it down below the canopy is giving me a heart attack. We keep revolving, a lazy Susan of over-wound and under-armed teens. I am literally counting the seconds until someone—anyone—flinches and makes a break for it, and that will be Game Over. We'll scatter, and the bogeyman will pick us off one by one, because that's how they do it.

Round, and round, and round...

"Don't think I can do this much longer, folks, just sayin'," Ant sing-songs. "Flight's taking over fight again."

"Stay with me, Ant." My voice is low. "He can't take us all on."

Round, and round, and round...

... and then we stop, stock still. Straining to hear. Tree trunks creak. Far above, wind buffets leaves. And we wait.

"Do you think he's gone?" Cass asks finally.

"If anyone was ever there," Ben mutters.

"I saw him!" Seb turns and grabs Ben by the shoulders. Seb pushes him, hard. Ben staggers backward, rolls over, and glares up at Seb. And that's it, the magic circle is broken. Got to get everyone out of this wood before chaos reigns and we lose each other.

"We're leaving." I haul Ben to his feet. "Which way to the bags?"

Seb laughs. "He's probably waiting there for us."

"Don't be stupid," I snap at him. "Stay calm. We'll get out. If he was going to attack, he would have done it by now." I don't believe a word I'm saying, but I'm shocked at how convincing I sound. "Now, Lawrence, got that axe? Watch our backs. I'll lead with Ben—you have the compass. Let's get the hell out. Keep tight, everyone." To my total shock, they all do what they're told, and we begin to slowly, carefully, fearfully, pick our way out from the ditch and up out over the bank of brambles.

"Wait, where's Steph?" Cass says, then stops, claps a hand over her mouth. "I—I forgot. So stupid." She looks at Ben. "I'm sorry—"

"It's okay." Ben nods at her. "Hopefully she's watching over us."

"Wish she was map reading," Seb mumbles. Lawrence thwacks him on the chest with the blunt end of the axe.

"Stay alert," I hiss.

"We're not out of the woods yet, *lol*." Ant squeezes my arm. "Don't fret, I know the way back to the backpacks." They swallow, smile, all dimples and shakiness, and my heart clenches for them. I nod, and off Ant goes, leading the way. We all follow, with darting eyes, jumping at every shadow. Incredibly, with only a couple of pauses, Ant gets us back to the spot. There's no sign anyone has rifled with our stuff. Hurriedly, we shoulder the packs, Ben points the way, and we are free and clear. I've never felt so relieved to see the end of the trees, and we don't stop running until the mountain makes us.

CHAPTER 17

___

It takes us all day to summit. The first couple of hours we're motoring on nervous adrenaline, breathless and red hot, moving like we've got a fire under us, looking back for our bodach and blocking out thoughts of the friend we left behind, eating up that rocky trail as fast as we can. Fear is a performance-enhancing drug, but Ant was right: eventually the brain taps out. Inevitably, terror melts away and our pace slows. The hike gets steeper and the hard work begins.

And the doubt. Did Seb actually see someone? Could he be making it all up? Or maybe he's lost it; I wouldn't blame him.

The ascent drags, sweaty and difficult, rocks made slippery with drizzle as we snack on the go, not wanting to stop, telling ourselves we're halfway now, we *have* to be, because can't you feel it? The air is sharp and thin, it's so much colder, a slick of ice on the ground, which suddenly turns into a thin layer of snow. And the old enemy, mist, descends, settling heavy on me like a depression, accompanied by the knowledge that we're hidden by it, and any kind of air rescue is definitely not on the cards. But at least the trail is reassuringly constant, with markers pointing us ever upward, encouraging us to dig in, to ignore aching shoulders, heavy legs, and burning lungs. My mind rolls over positive reinforcements on shuffle, like bad memes flashing in my mind's eye, until I feel like I'm losing my grip on reality, with earworms of my own making.

It's darkest before dawn.

Just put one foot after another.

Failure is not an option.

Because time runs on, and what's the alternative? Stopping? Can't. We owe it to Steph to make it. If she were here, she'd be leading the way. Ben knows this, and he's taken charge, driving up the mountain, focused beyond all distraction. All I can do is commit to the next one hundred steps and count them all out loud, painfully, my back crushed under the weight of my pack, my hair blowing in my eyes. I promise myself I'll make it to the next peak. And then the next, and the next. I smash them, kill them off one by one, until it gets done.

"Need to pee," Cass groans from behind me as, bent double, we pause and try to catch our breath. "No cover."

"So?" I pant back at her. "You got plenty of fog."

We've hit a plateau, the first flat section for ages. I can't even see the next ridge because the mist drapes around us like a thick, suffocating curtain. Cass heads off into the fog, instantly disappears. I bend over again, hands on knees, my thermals wet with sweat, some kind of hot, drippy liquid flowing freely out of my nose, and I don't even care.

"Seriously. This is it?" Ben stands a few feet away, twisting around, examining where we've landed.

"This is what?" I'm exhausted, but I can't allow myself to sit, even pop a squat, because I'll never get up again.

Seb comes in last and sprawls on a rock. He's panting and simultaneously eating something, furtively, giving me serious food rationing anxiety. Lawrence is rejigging a broken boot lace, and only Ant seems energized, as quick and alert now as they were in the woods.

Ben strides over to a shape, looming out of the gloom. "Here's the cairn!"

Huh? I follow him, *got to keep moving*, and my foot cries out, but I ignore it. It's been hurting all the way since I decided that we probably weren't being chased; a sharp stabbing pain that has evolved into a dull throb running along my sole and up the back of my calf. I wonder what gangrene feels like. Or tetanus, or lockjaw—that's a thing, isn't it? *Be thankful. If you're walking, you're alive.* The thought is a bolt through the temple, cold as the freezing mist.

Ben turns around, his face relaxing momentarily.

"We're here. We're at the top."

I stare at the shape behind him. The cairn of Cairn Gealach, a marker to show we're at the summit. Sure enough—it's a pile of rocks, quite literally. No sign or fluttering prayer flags, only a cone of gray rocks slotted together, signifying that, *woo-hoo,* we've made it. Rocks. I hate rocks. After this, I never want to see another rock again.

"You sure?" Lawrence calls. "This is the actual summit? How come it doesn't look like it?"

"What were you expecting, a visitor's center and a medal?" Cass reappears.

"Nope, but a view would be nice," I murmur. It's underwhelming and unnerving at the same time, because the mist makes it feel so claustrophobic, and yet one wrong step could mean a fatal fall. *On a good day you can see Ireland!* my Dad had enthused. But right now, I can barely see Cass.

"Take a second to pat yourself on the back, but no more!" she calls out. "We keep going, find the trail down. Hard part might be over!"

"Home straight!" Ant cries too. "Pen, Cass? I'm leaving another note, so they'll know we headed down this way." They scribble an arrow on the page from *The Book of Saints*, wrap the paper in plastic, and leave it sticking out of the cairn. "Let's go!"

The words give me a lift. We made it. And downhill must be easier than up, no? Quicker, too. Maybe we really get all the way to the bottom before dark?

Spoiler: it's not easier. Ben finds the trail and leads the way for as long as Lawrence will let him. The route's not as well marked as the one we came up. This is obviously the road less traveled. As I'm lowering myself onto my butt for the umpteenth time to get down a particularly gnarly section, the rain kicks in. *Argh*, I'm lagging behind. Ben forges ahead again, driven by grief, or maybe by the need to not let it in. Ant, I'd expect to be quick, and Lawrence and Cass seem to be an item now, side by side. I can hear actual laughter and bants as they go. Totally weird, given the circumstances, but I guess it's good to have a distraction. Maybe that's why Seb is speeding along to keep up with them, to kill their vibe. Whatever he's doing, he's left me for dust, and that's shameful.

"This can't be right."

I hear Cass's voice. As I carefully maneuver myself down the latest section of rock, I can just make out the figures a few feet away, by the edge of a path. Slithering onto my backside, I hit the ground, my fall broken by a carpet of springy heather. My pack falls off.

"The trail marker points down there," Ben says, as I drag my pack and walk toward them. "But the path's gone, it's nothing but loose stones, sheer scree. We'd kill ourselves."

"Another landslide?" Cass leans over to look.

"Might only be the first part." Lawrence shrugs. "We could slide down and find the rest of the trail intact."

"Yeah." Ben's face hardens. "Do you want to go ahead and let us all know?"

"I will!" Ant grins.

"Whatever it is, no you won't." Urgh, this damn pack is caught on the tangles of heather. I tug and fight, it finally releases, and the recoil makes me stagger to the edge.

"Ha, ha!" Ant catches me before I slide off down the scree. "What, you want to go first?"

"Definitely not." I cling to them, teetering, calves on fire, until Ant pulls me back from the brink. "Thanks, mate. I owe ya."

"So, if we're not going that way," Cass says, "what's the alternative?"

Ben sighs, studies his map again. I look around, not that there's much to see, but because I've just remembered what the alternative is. Dad told me all about this part of the mountain, even showed me a YouTube video. I remember, because it was so damn cool and totally off limits. He said there was no way that any sane head teacher was going to sign off on *that* risk assessment paperwork.

"The alternative route"—I clear my throat—"is traversing an arête."

"An a-what?" Seb sighs.

"Thought you'd studied the map, Sebastian?" I mutter. "An arête. You know those clips you see of adrenaline junkie dudes with cameras on their heads, walking along a spine with a sheer drop on either side? That spine is called an arête. Like a dragon's back."

"Sounds trippy." Ant is practically jumping for joy.

"Last trip you'd ever take." I wonder if I should physically restrain them. "You have to crawl like a baby if you don't want to fall. And there's no way we should be attempting it in mist and rain."

"Hey, it might be easier if we can't see the drop," Cass says.

"Let's test that theory out." Lawrence grabs the map. "Which way?"

"No!" My voice sounds scratchy and weak.

Ben points numbly. His eye sockets are dark and his hair plastered to his face. I think he's nearly done. And I don't have it in me to argue with Lawrence. We trudge after him down an easy section. As we descend, the mist thins, but the rain gets worse, turning to stinging hail. Little white balls of ice batter my hood, pinging off the ground in a way that makes me wobble. I almost keep pace with Lawrence this time, not wanting to lose him, and when he stops a few feet away from me, I know he's found the start of the arête, because he begins to chuckle.

"Jesus. Are you kidding me?"

The dragon's back. An arc of mountain, the beginning just visible. The trail is all of two feet wide at most, but it's not really a trail, more a jumble of mismatched rocks, topped with a light sprinkle of snow, that only a goat would be happy walking over. On either side, the mountain drops away steeply into the sea of mist below.

"How high?" Cass breathes.

"High enough," I answer.

"Not too high to try," Lawrence sing-songs.

"Bro, *you* are high if you think I'm going to try." Seb looks the happiest he's been all afternoon at this clapback.

"It takes, like, five or six hours to cross." Something like that. I can't remember exactly. Whose counting at this point? "That's in good conditions, which we don't have."

"Six hours?" Cass sinks onto her knees. "Big nope."

"Aw, spoilsports!" Ant leaps lightly onto the first section, arms out. "See? Easy!" They turn to face us, smiling brightly. Above, the sky cracks with a loud roll of thunder. "Shit!" Ant jumps out of their skin, a rock shifts, their foot shoots out, and they land on all fours. "Oof!"

"Ant, for god's sake!" I scream at them and fling out an arm, my own feet very firmly planted on safer ground.

"Cheers, sweets." Ant's smile turns rueful, and I haul them in quickly as the thunder rolls again, followed by a shattering of sheet lightning directly overhead.

"Debt paid," I breathe, and Ant nods, hugs me. The touch feels good.

"Guys, over here!" Ben calls from somewhere back into the mist. "There's shelter!"

We stumble-run away from the arête, following Ben's voice to a flat section of rock with a massive overhang, a chonky chunk of granite forming a roof overhead, and plenty of room to shelter underneath. We drop bags on relatively dry ground and stand there, backs against the wall, jaws dropping as the sky is lit up by flashes, the mist giving it a weird pink hue.

"Makes sense to stay the night," Lawrence says. "We can pitch our tents under here. Start early tomorrow."

"What happened to stay moving to survive?" Seb moans at him.

"You want to crawl along that ridge in the dark, be my guest." Lawrence shrugs. "Try pulling the big hero move. I'd love to see it. And the next time I'll be seeing you is in hell."

Seb looks furious, but there's no argument. Everyone already knows he won't dare to go solo.

Another whole night of delay, another night that Dad has to survive out there, on his own. My chest aches with the thought, but we're too exhausted to do anything else. A knot of disappointment and defeat curdles in my gut, but the storm is back, and it feels all the closer and more dangerous now that we're up here in the clouds. For now, we're pinned.

We put up the tents, which is always a joy, especially when you're cold, wet, and aching to collapse. There are only two remaining, which will be a squeeze, but I'm happy to have roomies. My tent houses me, Ant, and Cass; Lawrence, Seb, and Ben are in the other. Despite the fact there's ample room under the overhang, we set them up side by side, as close as possible.

"We can build a fire over there." Cass points to the end of the overhang. "Boil water for space meals. It'll do us good to have something hot inside us." I can tell Seb is finished by the lack of the obvious jokes.

"What do we use for fuel? We're above the tree line," Ben says.

I cast my eyes around. There's a surprising amount of dry crap under the overhang, dead ferns and the like, but it's not going to take much time to burn through it.

"The heather. The ground before the arête had loads of the stuff. I kept tripping over it. It's got these really dense, woody stems."

"Won't burn, it's too wet," Ben says.

"Wanna bet?" Lawrence holds up a small, yellow canister.

"You have *lighter fluid*?" Cass gawps. "Score. You kept that quiet earlier."

"Last resort." Lawrence shrugs. "And credit where credit's due. It was his idea." He nods a head toward Sebastian. "He's only just finding out I snuck it out of his bag, the wannabe arsonist."

"Better an arsonist than an arse," Seb mutters. "See. I told you it would come in useful."

"Och aye, you were talking like we were going to have barbecue up here," Lawrence snorts. "How did that turn out for ya?"

Seb's face is pure hate, petulant like a toddler's. Lawrence laughs, we all laugh. It's mean, it's petty, but we need it.

Lawrence risks himself in the lightning to gather enough heather to douse in fluid and set alight with a whoosh. In no time, Cass has rigged up a pot of something squeezed out of silver pouches, bubbling away over the fire at the far end of the overhang.

"I might not even need these now." Cass holds up two logs and I stare at her in disbelief.

"Don't tell me you carried them from the hut?"

"Yup." She nods proudly. "Five of 'em, in my pack. Figured they might be more important than deodorant and a change of clothes."

"Ew, glad we're not tent buddies." Seb wrinkles his nose.

"Oh, me too." Cass smiles sweetly. "This is veggie chili, you gonna be hotboxin' tonight, and no mistake."

We drag rocks around the fire to sit on, and practically melt our jackets, we get so close. There's not much chili to go around, but it's something, a shared meal.

"Lightning's stopped," Cass says. "And the mist looks like it's clearing again. Do you think there's any chance they'll see our smoke?" She scrapes the last of the food out of her tin cup. "Or, you know, if there's a drone or a helicopter looking for us, they could be picking up heat signals."

Lawrence looks at his watch. "Too late, it'll be dark in a few."

"What about satellites?" Ant says. "Point the spy cameras this way!" They jump up and duck out of the overhang, waving at the sky, twerking. "Yo! Come an' geddit!"

"Yeah, I don't think they will have involved NASA for a bunch of missing Scottish teenagers," mutters Ben.

"Or even an English one." Cass raises an eyebrow.

"Whatever, I'm glad we lit the fire," I say, taking a sip from my bottle. "Keeps away the wild animals." *And the evil spirits.*

"Any wild animals come near me, they'll end up in the pot." Lawrence snorts.

"Do you think we're safe here?" Cass says. "Not from animals, but…"

"From the dude my brother thought he saw in the woods?" Lawrence stretches out his legs and flexes his arms. "If the bodach makes it all the way up the mountain, fair play to him, he can have me."

"It wasn't a bodach…" Sebastian says, unusually quietly, gripping his cup. "I know I said that, but I didn't want to tell you the truth."

"Big surprise." Lawrence grunts.

"What are you talking about?" Cass frowns at Seb.

"I saw...Nicholas." Seb looks up at us. He has our attention. It's like we all stop breathing for a moment. Even Ant stands still.

"Nicholas."

It's not a question. I say it before I can help myself, my mind racing, because I already know full well who he means and I really don't want to.

Seb's face is expressionless, lit up by the glow of the fire.

"I wasn't going to say, but since you're doubting me, you get to deal with it too." He crosses his arms over his chest, as if preempting the attack. "It was Nicholas McDonal standing there, staring at me with dead eyes. I swear on my life."

CHAPTER 18

———

"Uh-oh," Ant breathes.

"What the hell, Sebastian?" Lawrence's face is contorted with pure disdain. "Don't shit us like that—"

"I'm not shitting you—"

"Just shut up!" Ben yells at Seb. "Why can't you ever give it a rest?"

"You're disgusting, Sebastian McTavish." I shake my head.

"Hold on, who the hell is *Nicholas McDonal*?" Cass asks. When we don't answer, she stares at us until her brow twitches upward and her mouth drops open...and she gets it. "You mean the other kid on the bus? Back when you all were little and... you know?"

"Yes, the other kid," Lawrence growls. "Who now solely exists in my brother's imagination."

Cass frowns. "But...isn't Nicholas McDonal dead?"

"Exactly."

Seb's shaking. His eyes are actually filling with tears. "It was Nicholas in those woods. Unmistakable."

"Sebby baby, you're sleep-deprived!" Ant blurts out a laugh. "How would you even know what Nicholas looks like when we haven't seen him for years. He left school—what, the same time as you did, Mags? Right after what happened."

"Yeah, and he moved to Italy or Spain, somewhere like that." I hug myself. "And now *he's dead*, Sebastian, you utter wanker."

"Believe me, or don't." Seb's eyes are wet, but his mouth is set in a line. "I know what Nicholas McDonal looked like because I saw a photo when he killed himself last year, *obviously*. And I'd recognize him anywhere. You don't go through what we went through and not recognize each other. Even if we looked completely different, there's an *energy*."

"An energy!" Lawrence snorts.

"I'm telling you." He shakes his head and shudders, but his voice is calm, and that's the most unnerving thing, because it's the part that makes me want to believe him. "Nicholas's energy. He was tall, skinny—"

"Slenderman." Lawrence laughs.

Seb ignores him. "He had long, straggly black hair and he wasn't wearing hiking clothes, not even a jacket. He had on black jeans, black sweater."

"Well, you can't be right about that. No one would survive long out here with no outer layer." Ben pouts at the idea.

"Beside the point, Nicholas frickin' killed himself!" I groan.

"So, you're saying it's Nicholas's *ghost*?" Ant's eyes shine wide with relish. They jump up and down on the spot, fingers a-tap-pin'. "Seeking vengeance, and returned to the earthly realm to clobber us!"

"Whoa. Wait. What?" Cass holds out her hands. "So this Nicholas died by suicide, for real? Why'd he do it?"

"Why do you think?" Sebastian's voice rises for the first time. "Because a man abducted us when we were kids, kept us in a cave, and tried to kill us when the moon was full. Kind of sets you off on the wrong foot in life." He signs a cross on himself, wipes away a tear. "Nicholas never got over it."

"How would you know, ya idiot?" Lawrence sneers. "We hadn't heard from him in years!"

"But now you reckon he's *here*?" Cass glares at Sebastian, who shivers. "Tell me straight, guys. Is it at all possible he's still alive? And why would he be out to get us?"

"Yeah, exactly, thank you." I feel the pressure in my chest. "*We* didn't do anything to Nicholas! For sure, he died. Tragic, but that wasn't on us. And no, ghosts are not bloody real. Even if they were, I happen to think humans are the ones to be afraid of, and most of you sitting around here should know that!" I can't help my voice rising, *got to get a grip.*

"This is all stupid." Lawrence throws his head back. "Don't listen to a word this fool says, Cass. That poor bastard's dead, and my brother is losing his tiny little mind."

Cass nods, turns, and screams in my ear. My body lurches, and I see her staring at something behind me. I twist around.

"What?!"

Ant's dark, finger-length hair is standing up from their scalp. It's a frizzy mess even at the best of times, but this is something else. It moves, ever so slightly, dancing, alive, as Ant blinks at us, a bemused look on their face.

"Lookin' at me?"

"You're fecking possessed, I knew it!" Seb screams, leaping to his feet, moving as far away from Ant as he can, and it sets off a chain reaction, we're all backing off.

"What is it?" Ant says, and their hands move up to their head, like they can suddenly feel what we can see. "Ooh, hello, Medusa. Bet it looks awesome."

"It looks...unreal." I take a step toward them. "Good and bad." I reach out a hand, touch—

"Argh!" I gasp, as the jolt shoots up my arm. "Electric shock!"

"Your hair too!"

"Huh?" I put my hands up, can feel the crackle of my curls twisting into the air. "What's going on?"

"Static electricity," Ben says. His hair is determinedly flat, and Seb hasn't really got any, but both Lawrence and Cass have rogue strands reaching to the heavens.

"Holy hell, the friggin' fire is singing now!" Sebastian shrieks.

"What are you blethering about?" Lawrence is trying to flatten his do.

"No, listen, he's right." I stick my hands out, bending low. "God, it's the cups! The metal cups are humming!"

"No, no, no, this isn't good," Ben says. "It's static electricity. It's interacting, charging everything that will conduct it.

It means it's highly likely there'll be a lightning strike, right here."

"Well, aye!" Lawrence says, throwing his hands up. "We've had all that already. But it's not even thundering now."

"No, this is different," Ben says. "Even more dangerous. It comes out of nowhere. Builds up, invisible. It doesn't even have to be stormy, it can be bright sunshine sometimes—then bang! You're zapped."

"But we're alright as long as we're under this rock, yeah?" Seb is whimpering now.

"Not entirely," Ben says. "Lightning can penetrate rock, actually."

"Can it, *actually*?" Lawrence snarks. "So what the effin' hell are we doing under here?"

"Oh jeez, oh jeez, oh jeez..." Seb's spiraling, quite literally, spinning in an ever-diminishing circle, hands to his face.

"Peeps, I really think we should keep moving," Ant says, jogging in place. "Cut 'n' run. We can make it down the mountain."

"In the dark over the dragon's back?" Seb screams at them. "When did it get so dark? This is all too weird!"

"Chill, please, everyone needs to calm down," I start.

"This is just...science—we're a little unglued because of the electricity," Ben says. "It does this. The static makes people act wild. Like, drunk, irrational, confused." He grabs Ant. "You're not going anywhere, please. We need you here. It's only the electricity hyping you up, it'll pass."

"Okay, okay." Ant backs into the wall and slides down it, beating a rhythm on the ground with their hands, head whipping from side to side. "The static is making me erratic! The static is making me erratic!" They giggle dementedly, like a creepy circus clown. Out of the corner of my eye, I see Lawrence grab something from Cass and shake up his water bottle, and a few seconds later he beckons to Seb.

"Here, have a drink. It'll be okay."

"No!" Seb backs away. "You put something in that!"

"Like what?" Lawrence laughs. "Believe me, if I had anything worth spiking your drink with, I'd have gulped it down myself by now!"

Seb nods, takes the bottle, even lets Lawrence put his arm around him as he chugs the water down, his eyes still wide but his breathing steadying. After a minute, he lets Lawrence lead him back to their tent, and they disappear inside.

"My hair's dropping." Ant looks sad and glad at the same time.

"Yeah, the metal has stopped humming. That's reassuring," Ben says.

"Okay." Ant exhales. "Not just me. It's the sparky air doing its thing."

"I need this shitty day over." Cass kicks the tin cookware so that it is outside the overhang. "There. The rain'll do the dishes and if the lightning wants to strike something, win-win."

We don headlamps and tentatively line our water bottles up too, to catch the rain, and get ready for bed. It must be all of five o'clock in the afternoon, but the moon is hiding behind black clouds, and it's dark as midnight.

"Hey." Ben takes the iron bar out of his bag and hands it to me. "You take this, keep it by you."

"You believe that Nicholas crap?"

"I have no idea what I believe. All I know is, if anything comes into your tent that shouldn't, whack it and ask questions later."

That is, if I don't electrocute myself on the damn thing.

The tent is dry at least, I think, as I roll out mats and pick the spot in the middle for warmth, because poor Steph still has my sleeping bag. I suppress a shudder when I think of her there at the hut, alone, cold as stone. It makes me feel deeply sad, but also so grateful we're not still there. I don't know if I could have done that, slept in a place with a dead body. *Steph is a dead body.* Still can't believe it.

Ant crashes first, easily, all tuckered out. I'm endlessly grateful that we got Ant back. This could have been so much worse. Got to think of the positives. I put the iron bar between mine and Ant's sleeping mats. Tomorrow we'll be off the mountain. And Dad? Can't go there now.

I fetch my toothbrush from my pack, lined up with the others against the wall of the overhang. Does it really matter if I don't brush my teeth? Of course not. But maybe it's the little things that keep you going, the well-worn routines. I suck in the cold air, and as I retrieve my water bottle, Cass and Ben are at their backpacks, headlamps strafing. By the end of the overhang,

Lawrence is chucking one of Cass's logs on the fire and sitting back down on his rock. I squeeze toothpaste and walk over as I brush.

"How's Seb doing?"

"Knocked out." His face is tired, grimy, but somehow still beautiful, made amber by the fire.

"Hmm." Supposed to brush for two minutes, but that's not going to happen. I rinse and spit. "You put something in his water, didn't you?"

"Seemed like a good way to go." Lawrence shrugs. "Only a handful of Cass's magic pills to calm him down. He'll thank me tomorrow. Always did get cranky if he didn't have his naps." He chuckles half-heartedly, stretching out in front of the flames. "I'll keep watch, can't sleep anyway. Ben, you can take next shift."

"And wake me up when it's my turn, too." *And please keep that fire burning,* I almost say.

"Yeah, I reckon you'd knock anyone's lights out, Maggie." Lawrence doesn't look at me. I don't know if I should be pleased or insulted.

I walk past Cass, back to the tent. Ben gives me a look and I mouth, "Good luck." He gives me the briefest nod as he heads off to the boys' tent.

And so to bed, fully clothed. Trying left side and right, never getting comfortable. Cass doesn't come in. Maybe she's taking next watch. I hear the low murmur of voices by the fire. Silly me, she must be with Lawrence. God, those two are getting cozy. It must be nice to have someone right now. And then the wind picks up a little, the rain gets heavier, and I sink into the darkness.

———

Next thing I know, I can hear the zipper on the tent flap.

Cass.

How long have I been asleep? Eyes are glued shut. I'm lying on my side, willing myself to slip back under again before I wake up properly, chasing sweet oblivion. But then, as Cass lies down behind me, I'm suddenly, violently wide awake.

Because I know with absolute certainty that it's not Cass.

Too tall.

Too male.

Wrong…energy.

A streak of fear cuts through my core, heart lurches upward. *Don't scream.* Can't breathe, *must keep still, keep breathing, slow and deep*, faking I'm asleep.

What is he doing?

Impossible to be sure, but he is definitely lying down, close enough to snuggle. I feel the heat of him. *Don't puke.* Is that breath on my neck? What next? I wait for the pounce, the stab, the pillow in my face. *Or something way worse?*

Slowly, so carefully, I stretch out my fingers in the dark, feeling for the iron bar I stuck between the two sleeping mats, but Ant has shifted and the mat has moved; the bar is stuck under them. I can't reach for it without giving myself away.

Stupid, stupid, stupid.

I should have made sure I had that bar in my hand, but I was so undone, so wrecked. All the more reason. *Think!* I rack my brain as cold sweat trickles down my back. The body behind me shifts slightly. I am going to vomit, every cell in my body is vibrating. *Toothbrush!* It's in my jacket pocket. If I grip it firmly enough, if I exert enough force, can I stick him in the neck, and get out of here? What about Ant? No way of waking them without him knowing. I move my hand, ever so, ever so slowly, easing it into my pocket until I can feel the bristles, damp and slippery beneath my fingers.

He's to my right. I'm right-handed. That's not good. If I turn over, I'll need to stab with my left.

This is why you practice, my dad says. *You practice with your weak hand, because sometimes your only option is to take that shot.*

I silently pass the brush into my left hand. Fingers are numb and tingly, been lying on them, but they're waking up quickly. I listen for breathing, but it's all rain and wind. *Shite.* The boys might not hear me yell. I'm going to have to do enough damage to buy time to get Ant out of here without any help from the other tent.

My god, what if he got to the boys already? Who was keeping watch? Did he get Cass?

Don't think about it.

If he knows where we're sleeping—and he probably does, because he will have been watching—he'll know it's Ant and me in here. Would he presume we're easier to pick off first? *He better think again.* My left arm is crying from numbness, but I've had much worse. When I move, I'll have to be so quick. Use the momentum of the turn to hammer the brush home. Shall I aim for neck? Or face, or belly? God, let's just hope I hit something. And follow it up with an iron bar.

Here goes.

I lean in on my right hand, ever so slightly, and push off with as much force I can, springing around one-eighty degrees and bringing my left hand and the brush down, harder than I've ever dunked before.

And I'm blocked.

"Ach!"

An arm, flung across mine.

"Jesus, Maggie!"

I drop the brush.

"Ben?" I rasp, scrabbling in a pocket, flicking my headlamp on. "Oh hell, oh hell, oh hell!"

He's lying there, grasping his forearm, face screwed up in pain.

"I think you've broken my arm, you maniac."

"Maniac?" I hiss at him. "You're the one sneaking into my tent, what the frick did you expect?" I rub my arm where it hit his, like it hurts too, but I have no idea if it does, I'm so overdosed on adrenaline and some kind of hot rage I can't fully explain.

"I'm sorry, I guess I did tell you to hit first and ask questions later." He's prone, looking up at me. He actually looks scared. I still have the high ground, literally if not metaphorically. I back off, and he sits up, blinking in the light of my headlamp. "Had to sleep somewhere, didn't I?"

"What's wrong with your tent?"

"Cass and Lawrence."

"What?"

He grips the top of his nose. "I know. It was terrible. I was fast asleep. Next thing, there's some unholy orgy going on."

Yep, definitely going to puke my guts up.

"Don't tell me Seb too."

"God, no!" Ben shudders. "He was out cold, asleep, but there's him on one side, me the other, and the filling to this gross sandwich is a fumbling mass of...*urgh*. And the sound effects." He rubs his face. "How can they, even? After everything. After Steph."

Yeah, I hardly think they will have been thinking about her. At least, I really hope they weren't.

"Maybe it's life-affirming, or something? Tragedy throws people together."

Ben actually chuckles at this. "Steph'd be majorly pissed off to think they're having a grief-shag on her account, I can tell you that." The soft laughter turns to tears and shuddering, and before I can think better of it, I'm holding him, and he's crying harder and laughing too, and telling me I'm hurting his arm and that I'm a bloody liability, and we stay like that for so long, too long, until I reach over and flick my headlamp off and I hear Ben's breathing settle and become regular.

I should have known it was him, lying beside me. I didn't

recognize his energy. And that makes me sad. Finally, I allow the stinging tears to overtake me. But I'll hold him in my arms for now, and we'll try not to think about what's right and wrong.

I listen to the gusts, every now and then wondering if I can hear noises of mad love from the next tent, and really hoping that the bulging of the tent walls and the keening noises are only the wind. It's nearer to Ant's side, thankfully, and Ant sleeps on. They never woke up when I attacked Ben either. *Weird*, I think, as I drift off to sleep.

CHAPTER 19

I wake up with a jolt, sweat running off me. The tent sides are flapping in the wind. The noise must have woken me.

Is it morning? There's a haze of light outside the tent. I sit up, search for my headlamp, and switch it on. The wind is buffeting the sides, and there's that flapping noise. I shine my light toward the sound. It looks like one side of the tent has come away slightly from the pole at the top corner. I knew we'd done a half-assed job setting up. No wonder I'm so cold.

God, I'm hungry, too. I think that was the last of the proper food last night; we'll be down to trail mix dust now. When I get home, I'm going to demand a huge breakfast, whatever time of day or night it is. Bacon, eggs, fried bread. Finished off with a donut. Jeez, I can almost smell the bacon! My stomach feels like it's turning in on itself.

At least you're still alive! Steph won't be demanding anything from anyone.

I jump as Ben snorts and rolls over. Might as well get up. I'm never getting back to sleep.

Wait.

I look at the flap of tent again, reach out a hand to touch it. That hasn't come away from the pole. The material is torn. Floor to ceiling. Diagonal. Something about it…doesn't seem right. I lean closer, feel along the edge of the fabric. There's no fraying, the tear is completely clean, straight…not like a tear at all. This is a cut.

I spring back from it like it's going to bite me. Someone slashed our tent. With a blade. Maybe a big hunting knife.

It's happening again.

Terror compresses my chest. I feel a rush of adrenaline so strong it threatens to make me pass out on the spot. *Not now, Maggie.* Whoever did this could have done a lot more. Why didn't they? Were they disturbed? Maybe they just want to scare us? Well, it's certainly working—

What's that?

There's a light, flickering, somewhere outside. He's there!

I shrink back, my hands clutching at my neck. The light's not moving. It's only the fire, maybe the embers flared up, it's the glow of flames I can see.

Okay. I grapple for the iron rod. Need to wake everyone up, but I need to do it silently. Lawrence first. If I can just creep into the other tent…he has the muscle.

I crawl forward to the zipper on the tent door, slowly, oh-so-slowly easing it along, around and up, pausing to listen, but all

I can hear is the wind and the crackle of the fire. As the tent flap gapes open, I stay absolutely still, making myself as small as possible, and take in the view of the overlook and beyond. The breaking dawn could work against me. Can I crawl out and into the other tent unnoticed? I look toward the fire, and in the glow, I can see a large, dark lump of something partially obscuring the flames.

What the hell is that?

My nose is hit with a sweet 'n' salty, meaty smell, hit so hard my stomach curdles. It's not all in my head after all.

And it's not bacon.

Before I can question the wisdom of it, I stand on shaky legs and stumble toward the six rocks and the orange glow. There's a lot of smoke, the flames are dancing. They're burning bright because there's something large fueling the fire. That's what I can smell. And I know exactly who it is.

Because this is happening by the book.

"Lawrence!"

Lawrence is lying face down across the fire.

Is this a prank? Please let this be a prank. Do something!

"Somebody, help me!" I yell, throwing caution to the wind, as the iron bar drops from my hands. I move as fast as I've ever moved, and before I can blink, I'm hauling Lawrence off the fire. But the fire comes with us. His jacket is in flames, melting, sticking to him, and I'm beating the flames down with my bare hands, screaming.

Roll him.

That's it, roll him, extinguish the flames—but he's unwieldy, so dense and heavy as hell and it's not doing any damn good. The flames find an escape, licking around his body for oxygen, for life.

"Please, somebody help!" I cry, tearing off my own jacket, thudding it down onto Lawrence's chest, his head, his stomach, desperately trying to suffocate the flames. I cannot bring myself to look directly at his face...

"What are you doing?"

It's Cass's voice. I don't look. I must kill the flames...

"Stop it, Maggie!"

She's screaming and grabbing me and then she gets a hit of the smell or maybe a look at Lawrence's face, and she backs off, retching.

"Jesus Christ!"

"Maggie, what—?"

Ben and Ant are there, in the mix. Someone pulls at me. I fall over backward. I can hear shrieking and the thud of boots stamping out embers, and for a second, there on the cold, hard ground, I wish I could faint, check out, let someone else handle this. But I'm sickeningly conscious.

"Look at his face!" Ant is on the ground beside me, holding me. Ben has extinguished the last of the flames, backing away from Lawrence, who is lying on his side a few feet away, facing the deadened fire. Cass is crouched by the backpacks, crying. I make myself look at Lawrence this time, really look. Get it over with.

Lawrence's face is cooked on one side. Chargrilled. One eye is swollen shut, his face a mass of bloodied blisters. I gag so hard it jolts my entire body, but I can't tear my eyes away from poor Lawrence. All of his hair is gone, apart from the flop of blond right on top; that one section miraculously escaped, the rest has singed away, his eyebrows too. And worst of all is his mouth, warped into a snarl, those perfect teeth shockingly white against blackened lips.

"Lawrence! Lawrence, mate!" Ben sounds like he's begging, trying to make himself get closer to the smoldering body, and failing. "You're okay, you're going to be fine, we've got you."

"It was Maggie!" Cass wails from the other side of the fire. "I came out of the tent and she was hitting him. She wouldn't stop!"

What? Cass's eyes lock on to mine, and the intensity scares me. "No, I was putting the flames out. He was on fire. I was hitting the flames with my jacket!" I scrabble to my feet, holding out my smoky jacket and at the same time kind of clinging to Ant and them to me, and it's just as well, because I'm not sure I can feel my legs.

"She did this to him!" Cass is crying, doubled over, looking up at Ben with big, wet eyes. "I saw her, she was setting him on fire and hitting him!"

"Have you lost all grip on reality?" I yell back. At least, I try to yell, but it comes out like a wheeze and a cough. "It wasn't me!"

"Of course it wasn't." Ben straightens up. As fast as my relief at him believing me settles, my world starts to spin. God, I think I'm going to pass out. "We need to help him." Ben sets his jaw, takes a breath, steeling himself to deal with Lawrence. I will myself not to faint. Ben's words sound distant, like they're being carried to me on the wind. "I'm getting a sleeping mat. Cass, please, help me move Lawrence away from the fire, back against the wall." Cass shakes her head, crawls even farther away, and it's like it's all happening in slow motion. Ben fetches the mat, slaps his own face with his hands, as if pumping himself up for a fight, and moves in to pull Lawrence himself, twisting his face away so he doesn't have to look, gritting his teeth. I know he's trying not to puke, not to breathe in the smell.

"Why did you do that to him, Maggie?" Cass cries.

"No. Stop. Not me." I can hardly find breath to speak. Oh, I'm sinking. I might get my wish and check out of here, but I really don't want to anymore. Got to warn the others. "Listen to me. There's someone here. Our tent was slashed."

"What?" Ben stares at me, and somehow, I manage to move, staggering toward the tent, pointing.

"Here, look, a clean cut. Whoever did this must have attacked Lawrence, pushed him in the fire." The others just stare at me, gawping. I hunt around in the dirt to retrieve the iron bar.

Cass's voice is a whisper. "The man from the woods? Or... Nicholas? He's here?"

"Someone is." I put my half-melted jacket back on. "Get weapons. Now."

They must comply, because I slide down to the ground by

Lawrence, gripping the iron bar, and the world stops spinning, and the next thing I know they're all crouched next to me, firing out whispered questions.

"Did you actually see someone?"

"They pushed Lawrence in the fire?"

"Where did they go?"

"What should we do?"

I shake my head. I don't know anything for sure except that I'm slipping. I press my back into the wall to try and shake the feeling like I'm going to fall off this mountain into a bottomless void.

"I didn't see anyone. Woke up and saw the slash, and then…" Oh, this is going to sound so twisted. I lower my voice so Lawrence can't hear. "I could smell him burning."

"Shut up!" Cass slaps her hand over her mouth.

"I came out of the tent, and he was face down in the fire. Didn't you hear me call for help?" I bury my own face in Ant's filthy jacket, breathing in, the smell of the soil momentarily blocking out the burning. I wish I could hide in it forever, but I force myself to come up for air.

"I heard you." Ben has moved. He's found the medical kit in my pack, and he's fumbling to unzip it. "We need to fix Lawrence up, fast. Keep alert, keep eyes open."

Ant nods, standing up too, swinging the axe. "If the prick is out there, I'll see him."

Cass is fiddling with Lawrence's penknife, and I am never letting go of that iron bar again. We take a couple of uneasy paces forward, holding the line. If anyone is coming from the one-eighty degrees in front of us, we'll be ready. But there are other places to lurk, we all know it. Around the end of the overhang, or on top of it. Someone could be crouched directly above us on this rock roof, and we'd never know it. I shudder, grip my bar because that hurts, and pain is good. Wounded animals are more dangerous.

"I need a hand here," Ben says.

"Wait until the coast is clear!" I hiss at him.

"Mate, I don't think Lawrence can wait."

Cass swallows, shakes her head.

"I'm sorry, I can't—"

"Make it quick." I move to Ben. "What do we—?"

"Not even sure." He rifles through the med bag, various white-packaged items with words on them that I can't read, the letters dancing in front of my eyes.

"He's breathing." Ant looks back at us, and I feel a punch of love for them. How they can tell he's breathing, I don't know, because Lawrence's chest is a mess of black and red melted stuff. "Bloody hell! What about Seb! He's still asleep. Shouldn't we get him?"

"No frickin' way. Not yet." Ben rips open a sachet. "Anti-burn gel, Medica-Soothe. That sounds right, doesn't it?" He looks at me. "On his face?" I nod, because what do I know? "And there are wipes…? Should I put on gloves?" His face convulses. "Oh god, I'm sorry, it's just so—"

"Here." Ant skids over to us, grabs the gel. "I don't mind." They squeeze the gel on Lawrence's face, the whole lot. Ben hands them a wipe and they dab the goo all over. It's kind of fascinating in a terrible way.

"Gah!"

Lawrence roars, jerking upright and stumbling onto his feet, good eye blinking, his jaw moving up and down like he's forgotten how it works.

We scream. Probably not the best move. He stares at us with the one eye, wide and frightened, looks down at his chest.

"Whaa—?"

"Lawrence, it's okay. You should sit down, relax!" Ant, soothing, casual—how do they do it? "You had an accident, but we're going to make you better and—"

"Aargh!" He puts his hands up to his face, feeling, and shrieking. When he pulls his hands away, half of his face-skin comes away too.

"Oh, gonna be sick!" Cass runs off to the wall.

"Lawrence, you need to sit down," Ben shouts. "You'll be just fine."

Lawrence doesn't look just fine. He looks terrifying. Frankenstein's Monster bad. And the worst of it is, the full realization is dawning on him.

"Wha...ma face...?"

"Please, mate." I get as close as I dare. "I know you don't take orders, but imagine I'm my dad and do what you're told, yeah?" I try to chuckle, make it light, putting my burned hands on his burned arms. Ant's there too, and together we gently guide him back onto the sleeping mat.

He looks at me. "Wha—"

"Ssh!" I smile, tight-lipped. "We're going to make you feel better, but you've got to stay still or we don't stand a chance, you understand?" He doesn't nod—I'm not sure that he should—but there's no fight. "Painkillers, Cass." She's bent over by the wall, wiping her mouth. "Where are they? He's going to need them."

She nods, staggers off to her bag.

"We think someone pushed you into the fire, Lawrence," I say, trying to focus on the good eye and ignore the rest, but even that one is shot with blood and soot, and swollen, no eyelashes. "Do you remember?" He just stares at me, as if I'm speaking a foreign language. "Did you see anyone?"

"I…" His good eye darts to where Cass has appeared by my side, then it rolls back in his head with a grunt. She rattles the bottle of pills at me.

"Crush 'em up, put 'em in water, like with Seb." I turn to Ant, lower my voice. "Think we should try a bandage on his face. Can you handle it?"

Together we stick a white rectangle of gauze over the bad half of Lawrence's face. If that doesn't sound easy, it's not. Cass returns and hands me a water bottle.

"I'm sorry I said what I did." She blinks at me. "I panicked. So dumb. I realize you were trying to help him."

"That's okay."

We're too late with the drugs. Lawrence has slipped into unconsciousness again, and thank god for that. We try to cover his raw, burned chest in gauze, but nothing will stick.

"We should move him into the tent, keep him warm," Ben says.

"Yeah, but tell Seb first." Ant pulls a face.

"Tell me what?"

Seb is standing there on bare feet, swaying, sleeping bag wrapped around his shoulders. He leans over and peers at his twin. It must be the most screwed up thing to see the mirror of your own face toasted and bandaged that way, but his expression doesn't change.

"Is he dead?"

"God, no!" I get up, go to touch his arm, and he flinches. "He fell in the fire. At least…" I look to the others, wondering how far to go, but no one steps in to stop me. "We think someone jumped him."

"What?"

"Someone slashed our tent," Ben says. "And we found Lawrence, er, face down in the fire. We haven't seen anyone, but these things didn't just happen by themselves." Ben's being oh-so-reasonable, like we're trying to work out who ate the last of the jerky. Seb swears, mightily, rubbing at his eyes with fists, like that will wipe away this nightmare.

"You out there!" He swipes the axe out of Ant's hands and stomps to the outskirts of the overhang. "You wanna come and face me, you coward!" He beats his chest. "Where is the bastard? Dead or alive, I'll take him down!" He's puffed up and wobbling like he's drunk, pacing the length of the rocks, stumbling over the bracken, a silhouette of a deranged ogre, taunting the rising sun. "That really you, Nicholas? Show yourself! I'll smash yer bones with ma axe! Come at me, bro!" We all hold our breath as Seb paces, roaring clouds of smoke into the cold air.

"Get ready," Ben says through gritted teeth.

"Good. Flush 'em out." I'd rather fight than live in the agony of anticipation a moment longer. I grip the iron bar with both hands, my shredded palms burning, and wait for the attack.

But no one comes.

"Chickenshit! I'm done being scared of you!" Seb turns, walks back to us, and sinks to the ground by his brother, deflated.

"Whoever it was, they've gone," Cass says, with more volume and confidence than I would have guessed she'd be able to muster. "They knew what was coming. You chased them off, Seb."

He nods slowly, eyes on his twin.

"Is this like Stephanie? Do we have to wait for Law to die before we can go home?"

Behind him, Cass silently bites her fist, tears in her eyes, as Seb rocks gently back and forth. Jeez, those pills got him good. Or maybe something that was already very thin snapped.

"Don't be soft." Ben walks up and punches him lightly on the shoulder. "Lawrence is too damn stubborn to die."

"Aye, you're not wrong about that." Sebastian chuckles softly. "If he wasn't, do you think I'd not have finished him before now?" He stares at his twin, and his laugh turns bitter. "You all don't get it, tho'. You all think you're so clever, but you're ignorant. How can you not see what's right before your eyes? Denial. Safer that way, is it? Not now. It's just as well you have me to connect the dots."

"Don't be daft," Cass says. "Come back into the tent, we'll take care of it all. You rest up for a while."

"You know what I'm talking about." He points at me. "In the hut, I saw you reading that book. I bet you brought it with you too. You understand, don't you, Maggie?"

No, don't make me say it out loud. I feel my throat constrict like I'm going to cry, and I know I can't feign ignorance.

"What is he talking about?" Ben stares at me.

Seb's mouth contorts into a smile. "Ant got lost. Stephanie was stoned, I told you that already. And Saint Lawrence? Check *The Book of Saints.* I'll tell you what it says. It says he was *grilled.* Burned, like a piece of meat. Now tell me that's not exactly what has happened to my brother."

"That is...ridiculous." Ben's face twists in disgust.

"He's telling the truth," I mutter. They all stare at me in shock, even Sebastian's eyebrows are raised. "On my life, it hurts me to agree with him, but you can't deny that this is all going down according to our saints."

"You honestly believe that?" Ben looks in pain, shakes his head.

"Give me another explanation why we're being hurt, one by one! Think about it!" I turn to Ant. "This is about what happened to us ten years ago. The cave. The driver, he was...ill, he wanted us sacrificed to God, didn't he? And it was because we all have the names of saints."

Ben, Cass, and Ant are staring at me like I've lost it.

"Sweets," Ant says. "We've dealt with so much. I get why you see a connection. But this is *out there*."

"*The Book of Saints* was left for us to find, I'm sure of it." I make for my pack. "The driver never fulfilled his destiny, did he? We never met our fate. Now someone is finishing what he started."

"You're exhausted, you're strung out, you're not thinking straight—" Ben stutters.

"You really think it's Nicholas, Maggie?" Ant's voice sounds so sad, I look up from my pack. I want to cry.

"No," I croak. "I've no idea who's doing this, but what I do know is in here." My hands close around *The Book of Saints* and I hold it up for them. "We can see what's coming to us. Someone is trying to kill us the same way as our namesakes."

Cass snatches the book from my hand, runs to the end of the overhang and throws it into the air, high and long, tumbling out of sight. "That's what I think of your book!" She screeches at me. "I'm not part of this, and I refuse to be! Seb's in pieces, and you're only encouraging him!" She goes up to Sebastian. "You need to rest. I'll take care of these losers." She puts her arm around him, and amazingly, he lets her lead him back to the tent and help him in.

"I swear it's not just coincidence! Lost, stoned, and grilled!"

Ant and Ben are silent. Ben won't look me in the eye, and Ant is drawing a circle in the dirt with their boot. Oh god, I know how I sound, but I need them on board. Haven't got time for them to decide whether I'm losing my mind or not.

A second later, Cass emerges and beckons us to the edge of the overhang, talking under her breath.

"Awk-ward! Sorry for the performance."

Ant stares at her. "Huh?"

"I had to get that book out of here. He's *obsessed*. Was muttering about it in the tent last night in his sleep." She exhales. "Maggie, you might be on to something, for all I know, but don't trigger him. If Seb explodes, we don't know what the consequences will be. And we need to focus if we're all going to make it out of here alive, right?"

"Um, okay. Yes, of course." I'm not sure my brain is moving fast enough for this.

"Great." She pats me on the shoulder. "Do your thing and plan a route out." She looks at each of us. "And if you see anything sus—anything!—scream and I'll come running." She grimaces at Lawrence. "Let's get him inside too. I'll watch them both."

We drag Lawrence back to the tent on the sleeping mat, and once we've got him inside, Cass fixes us with a stare. "Don't dawdle. Patrol and plan. I've got a horrible feeling we don't have long left." She zips the tent closed.

"What was that?" Ant whispers, as we walk away. "You really believe it though, don't you, Mags? The saints thing."

"I do." I turn and look at Ben. "I know it sounds messed up, but you see the truth, don't you?"

"The truth? Doesn't matter." Ben shakes his head. "But you and Cass are both right about one thing. We need to get off this mountain before our time runs out."

CHAPTER 20

Patrol and plan. A quick sweep, and hunt for the trail out of here. Sounds organized, sensible, like we're calm and in control.

I feel anything but.

The truth is out there. I said my piece. Cass deflected Sebastian. I have no idea if the others think I'm insane, but they're choosing not to engage any further for now. And I can't process what it all means either. At least I'm not entirely alone in my madness, if that's what this is.

As I step out from underneath the overhang, the palms of my hands throbbing with burns, sickeningly sticky and feeling like they're glued to the iron rod, I'm anointed by the finest of Scottish drizzle. I blink away the gentle wet.

While we were in our world of trouble, the sun has risen, casting a beautiful peachy glow over the mountains, like we're living in a different story entirely. It's utterly beautiful. The grand curve of the arête takes my breath away, sweeping around to the left of us, before it swings, dramatically, right and connects us to the hill north of here. And hidden behind the bottom of that hill is our destination, the parking lot. I wish we could fly, because it feels like it wouldn't take more than a few minutes to reach safety, salvation. Surely, now that the worst of the storm has passed, there will be others heading out here?

I scan the hills for movement, friend or foe, but there's nothing. The landscape is eerily still, hardly a breeze; no sheep bundling clumsily down a hillside, no crow soaring above us. Anxiety tightens a band across my gut. We need to move, now. Could the arête be our way out? But damn, it's long, and high, and treacherous. How are we going to get Lawrence across?

I do a cursory sweep of the trail back toward Cairn Gealach, not wanting to stray too long, keeping out in the open, before heading back quickly to the overhang. As I approach, Ant jumps down from above.

They smile ruefully. "So, there's no one up there. Can see for miles around. Whoever was here has gone to ground."

"And no sight of anyone coming to help us?"

"Oh, silly me." Ant pouts. "Forgot to mention. There's a helicopter hovering over Cairn Gealach and a squad of Mountain Rescue coming up the trail."

I push their shoulder.

"And a Saint Bernard." Ant pants at me, tongue out. "With a bottle of rum around his neck."

Saint Bernard. What did he die of, I wonder?

Ant's being overly normal with me, cheery even, and I grin back. Fake it 'til you make it.

"Where are the binoculars?" Ben's face appears around the side of the overhang, his face flushed puce, his eyes shining like they haven't for days. "Found something."

We shoot each other a look and run, Ant naturally overtaking me, Lawrence's binoculars bouncing on their chest. We reach the end of the crag, but Ben's already disappeared, his voice coming from somewhere behind the corner of rock.

"Get over here!"

We follow, edging around the overhang on a narrow ledge, until we're almost directly behind the spot on the other side of the crag from where the tents are. Ben stands a few feet away looking west, chest heaving, his arm out, fingers stretched and pointing across the valley. Below us is a short drop, leading to a sweeping downward slope and an opposing rise up to the dark, jagged peak opposite. This would be a relatively easy hike for someone wanting to surprise us up here. But that's not what Ben is so excited about.

"Look! It's a bloody building!" Ben jabs at the air with his finger toward the opposite peak and seizes the binoculars from Ant, almost strangling them in the process. "On my life, please let this be what I think it is."

"A building?" Ant says. "Another shepherd's hut?"

Ben shakes his head. "Way better than that."

"So, what?" I squint in the direction Ben's looking. "You're looking at that dark, flat rectangle, at the top, on the left? It's just a rock."

"No, it isn't." He stands there, binoculars clamped to his eyes, elbows on his chest. "It's man made and ugly as hell. I can see the end of a wall, a roof. And see that skinny, pointy thing coming out of the top?"

"It's all in shadow, how can you even?" I screw up my face. "A tree?"

He lowers the binoculars, looks at me. "It's only a frickin' antenna. That building over there is a weather station."

Ant stares at him. "What, with, like, scientists and food and phones?"

"Wouldn't that be sweet!" He barks out a half laugh, excitement barely contained, moving down the ledge until he can go no more, and taking another look. "No, most of these weather stations are unmanned. They're literally one room, a concrete box. But hello, *antenna*! That could mean a radio, some way to communicate, send a distress signal!"

"Oh my god." I swallow. "We could radio for help?"

This might be it. This might be where it ends.

And a concrete box. It's safe inside a concrete box.

"We really could do that? Talk to someone, send a message?" Ant looks like they're going to make a run for it already.

"Got to try!" Ben's flat out chortling now. "We have to get over there! This is our best chance."

I'm sold. "Get our stuff, get the others." I start moving back around the side of the crag. "Cross fingers that Lawrence is conscious!"

Turns out, Lawrence has juice and then some. When we

return, Cass is practically sitting on top of him to stop him leaving the tent. We explain the plan, pack up in record time, and boy, is he down to move. He's not making any sense, but his legs still work. It's his hour of power, after all. We need to get him to the weather station before he crashes and burns—oh god, bad choice of words.

It's Seb who's the problem. He's so strung out, paralyzed by the situation, Lawrence's face, his own pills, and muddled brain. But once Ben mentions that there might be food, something shifts and he's on his feet and heading toward the ledge before the rest of us.

"I've got a good feeling about this," Cass says. "Things can only get better."

I'm trying to keep excitement down. There are no guarantees of anything. But as we descend into the dip, Ben and Ant on either side of a scarily determined Lawrence, there's a bounce in my step. We're covering ground faster than I'd dared to dream, although once again, the weather is turning. For the first time, it is snowing. Fine flakes floating down like ash. The wind drops, and the snow falls. It feels like relief, the relief I won't allow myself to feel yet, no matter how hopeful Cass is, how compliant Seb is being, or how Ben is walking with his head held high for the first time. Ant keeps turning around and giving me a cheery thumbs-up, and against all expectations, Frankenstein's Lawrence is powering through, leading the charge. Me? I feel in stasis; the world around me, buffering. But maybe, just maybe, this is the new beginning, the reset.

Ben and Ant are up ahead with Lawrence, Seb is stumbling after, and Cass and I are bringing up the rear. I think she wants to hang, to make up for whatever happened earlier. I don't bear any grudge. Stress, trauma, or as Ant puts it, "the sparky air," is to blame.

"This is wild. It's so pretty!" Cass wipes snow from her face. It's red like she's been punched, but her eyes glow. "Christmassy!" She leans toward me, like she's telling some big secret. "I hated Christmas when I was a little kid. My grandparents did all the religious stuff, but no gifts, no decorations, no fun."

"What, no presents?" I'm on automatic, lengthening my stride. Don't want to let the others get there first and give me spoilers, I want to discover the good or the bad right there with them. "Brutal. And no tree, either? That's my favorite part." Yeah, although come to think of it, the smell of pine forest might hit different now. I walk faster.

She sniffs. "Kids don't get to decide for themselves, do they? When we make it out of here, I'm going to choose all fun, all the time. Steph has shown me, life's too short."

Urgh, tacky. Too soon. I keep going, looking ahead. Lawrence has reached the top. It's actually terrifying how well he's doing. I pray to all the mountain goddesses that Ben is right about this place.

As we scramble up the final section, the snow peters out, and I see the building properly for the first time. A concrete box, yes, with one door and a long, narrow, rectangular window. On one side, a huge water barrel. On the flat roof, there are—I don't know, weather instruments? A metal cylinder, a little paddle, spinning in the breeze, two sets of solar panels. But we're all looking at what I'd first thought was a lonesome tree. A tower fixed to the roof, maybe ten feet high, with a large antenna sticking out of the top and two smaller ones halfway up. My heart flips.

"Three aerials." Ben exhales.

"That's good?" Ant says.

"Guess we'll find out."

Nailed to the edge of the roof, there's an official-looking sign. I reach up and clean the snow off it with my sleeve. Red lettering. There's a rope attached to the sign, with a fist-sized rock dangling below. The sign reads:

HIGHLAND WEATHER FORECASTING STONE

Stone is wet	Raining
Stone is dry	Not raining
Stone casts a shadow	Sunny
Can't see stone	Foggy
White on stone	Snowing
Stone jumping up and down	Earthquake
Stone gone	Tornado

Silly. But it chokes me up, because it reminds me of dad jokes and normalcy. This sign is evidence that there are nice, boring, safe people out there, the ones who wrote this sign, the ones who carefully tied this rock and chuckled to themselves as they did. There is a world beyond our current terrors, of routine, and numb comfort, and wholesome silliness, and I want to be back in that world, with those people, my whole being aches for it. I clear my throat, hold back the sob.

"Told you, Scotland does have earthquakes."

"Ad-ock!" Lawrence croaks, from beside the door. "Ach! Ach!"

Door's padlocked. He wants the axe, which Ant has been clutching this whole time. They move in and swing the axe down once, twice, and the magical third time, and the padlock gives up. Lawrence busts through the door and stumbles inside, and we rush in after him.

A single room, narrow. Light coming in from the window. On the right, a long, wooden desk with a single chair. Incongruously, to our left, a huge, beaten-up, tan leather recliner, into which Lawrence immediately sinks, his race run.

"Are those the radios?" Ant points at two black metal boxes on the desk. They're shoebox-sized, encased in thick, gray, insulated padding and bracketed to the table. The box nearest to us has a single button and a little red light, the other houses a small LCD screen with numbers on.

"Let's see." Ben leans over, examining them, feeling around the back. "Hmm, they probably collect and transmit the information from the measuring instruments on the roof, but it's all internal."

"There's nothing we can use to speak to someone? Send a signal?" Cass's voice wobbles.

Ben rubs his face with both hands and crumples forward onto the tabletop. "Don't think so."

Sebastian swears, backs up against a wall, and slides down it like a broken egg.

"I'll get into the back of them. There might be something…" Ben finds Lawrence's penknife and fiddles with the casing of the first box, while Cass collapses on the floor. Ant ducks under the desk, looking for something—anything—that might help us, but there's very little here. On the other end of the table I unzip a first aid kit, find a pack of silver heat blankets, two grubby mugs, and a tub containing half a packet of oat cookies and some sachets of hot chocolate. But I can't even get excited about sugar. *Please, won't fate give us a break?*

But it is not to be. Ben dismantles both boxes, stares, swears, sighs, rebuilds them, and switches everything on again, like the conscientious geek that he is. Eventually, throwing the penknife back on the desk, he storms out of the building, slamming the door so hard the air pressure hurts my ears.

I sit on the desk, exhausted, feeling hope drain out of me like blood from my veins. Not sure what I was expecting—maybe a microphone, some dials that would make white noise while we turned them, ever so carefully, to the sweet spot, until we heard the voice of a friendly-sounding Mountain Rescue person? Or a Morse code machine, that we could tap up and down, *dot-dot-dot, dash-dash-dash, dot-dot-dot,* SOS, Save Our Souls. Save Our Skins, more like.

"Can I eat one of these?" Ant says, holding up a cookie. "There's enough for one each."

"Gimme." Seb holds out a hand. "How do they make hot chocolate here if there's no kettle? Stupid bloody weather station."

"Yeah, because that's what's disappointing." Ben appears in the doorway, his face red and blotchy. "I'm sorry. There might be a way to make something here send a signal, but it's beyond me."

"Okay, okay." Cass dabs away tears with the heels of her hands and wipes them down her legs. "On the bright side, those cookies weren't stale. Which means people come up here regularly. We could secure this place. If the desk gets pushed against the door, no one's getting in. There's the water barrel outside, and we have purification tablets. Seb, we should leave you here, safe with Lawrence, while the rest of us carry on. Like now. Where's the map?" She rifles in Ben's pack and finds it. "Okay, we're way off the original trail anyway, so we go in the most direct route out of the mountains. There's a ravine immediately to the left of us, more mountain to the right. So I guess we literally go around the building and continue over the hillside, pretty much in a straight line until...here!" She taps the map. "There's another way, northwest. We can reach the car park eventually, see?" She traces it with her finger. "And it's downhill most of the way. Easy compared to what we've already done."

Ben has the binoculars. He lets out a deep sigh. "Okay, let

me walk over the crest of this hill and recce the route, see what it looks like. Check these guys have what they need, then we'll go."

"Be careful. That ravine looks pretty bad." I hand him the axe. It's battered and blunted after its run-in with the padlock, but it's still the best we have. "And we don't know who's out there. Be quick."

"I will. See to your hands, yeah?" he says. "They'll get infected if you don't."

I nod, and he leaves. We put the wooden chair against the door and Sebastian parks himself on it.

So hard to pick up and go again. But that's what it takes.

Lawrence is passed out on the recliner. God, his face is a mess. And there's still that burned smell, although maybe it's my hands I'm smelling. The top layer of skin has completely come off my right palm and fingers, my left is almost as bad. Maybe I'll have no fingerprints after this. I hope I can still play ball. I mean, if I live long enough.

I squeeze antiseptic gel onto each palm, which sends electric pain up the underside of my arms, and—*Jeez!*—a flurry of curses flying from my lips, while everyone watches, because they're too done in to do otherwise. At least Ant helps me bandage my palms.

"I should have known. You want to abandon me here," Seb says, leaning sideways on the wooden chair, which creaks and threatens to break under him. "And I have no choice in this."

"It's for the best. Suck it up," I say. No fuse, no filter. Can't deal with his crap while every nerve in my upper body is screaming. The pain has kicked in so strong. Heaven knows what Lawrence will feel like when he next wakes up.

"Calm down, hen," Seb grunts. "I'll stay. He is my brother. Anyways, this way, the killer gets you, not me."

"You think that Nicholas's ghost is doing this? Or what? The ghost of the driver, come to finish the job?" Ant paces, ready to be out of this prison. "Too bad for you, ghosts can walk through walls."

"Freak, you're phenomenally stupid." He shakes his head. "Didn't any of you bother to read *The Book of Saints*, after what was said?"

"You saw me throw that rubbish away." Cass gives him a look.

"Maggie gets me." He winks at me. I scowl back. "So let me tell the rest of you guys. Nicholas was *murdered*. It only looked like suicide. Saint *Nicholas Owen*. He was tortured to death, but his torturers lied and said he'd done himself in, because they didn't want to admit to killing him. Look. It. Up."

"The book is gone!" Cass groans.

"Nope." Seb smiles. "Mags picked it up again. When she thought no one was looking."

I roll my eyes. Damn. At the base of the overhang, while everyone was helping Lawrence down, I'd seen the book, lying in the heather. Swiped it up before anyone could spot me—or so I thought. I rise, dig the book out of my pack. The pages are stuck together with wet. I peel them back with clumsy, painful hands, until I find the right one.

"Well…?"

I put a hand up, skim-read it, all the while wondering why I'm doing something that Seb has told me to do.

"It's true." I drop the book on the desk, cross my arms. "So if Nicholas is really dead, who did you see in the woods?"

"Aye, my mind was playing tricks on me." Seb taps his temple. "Here's the thing, tho'. Nicholas was a vision. A whopping, big clue. A clue to search *within*."

We all look at each other.

"Eh?" Ant snorts.

"Laugh all you want. You're the ones who are going down." Seb nods, sage and serious. "By hallucinating Nicholas, my mind was telling me to look within the group."

"What, *us*?"

Seb's mouth curls into a sly smile. "Bingo. I'm talking about the *us* back then. The us in the cave. And what I'm saying is, one of us is the killer."

CHAPTER 21

"Oh, this is too much." Cass buries her head in her hands.

"It's ridiculous!" Ant laughs.

"Why, freak?" Seb snarls at them. "We're all screwed up, aren't we? After what happened to us? And here on this friggin' mountain—ten years later, almost to the damn day—one of us has completely cracked!"

"Who, then?" Cass hisses at him.

Seb rolls his eyes. "Isn't it obvious? It's *Ben*. He's stepped over the edge. Whacked his girl and tried to kill my brother."

"Are you joking?" My throat feels tight. "That's the stupidest thing you have ever said. Ben couldn't kill a bloody rabbit! I know there's no way on this earth he'd hurt Lawrence! And *Stephanie*?"

"You don't know shite." Seb's so calm, it's chilling. "Steph cheated on Ben. With Lawrence. Motive, right there. You didn't know that, did you?"

"What? That's bull," I spit back at him.

"Really?" A lazy eyebrow raises. "What do you think, Cass? Because Steph confided *everything* in you, didn't she? Do I lie?"

"Through your teeth." I look at Cass. "Tell him."

Cass shifts her feet, eyes downcast, and my heart stops beating. "He's... Actually, it did happen. Steph and Lawrence did get together."

"What?" I stare at her. "When?"

She shrugs. "I dunno. A few weeks ago."

"Like, a one-off? Or more than that?"

"More. And, this is so awkward..." Cass exhales, looks toward the unconscious Lawrence, and lowers her voice. "He actually told me that he wasn't into it. He said he'd made a massive mistake. He finished it as quickly as he could. God, I'm being so disloyal to Steph, talking like this—"

"Ha!" Seb blurts. "Not that Stephanie knew anything about loyalty!"

I shake my head. Can't believe that Steph would do that. Or can I? *She always took whatever she wanted.* I'm horrible, how can I think like this?

"And Ben knew?"

"Not immediately." Cass's eyes dart around the room. "But yeah, I think she told him. They had a massive argument a couple of weeks ago. She wouldn't give me any details, but not gonna lie, I reckon that's what it was about."

I sit on the desk, stunned, my heart breaking for Ben, anger punching a hole in my stomach, anger at Steph, and guilt for the anger, because she's *dead*. And Lawrence! How could he? I mean, not that he and Ben were friends, but isn't there a code? Between us all? Didn't we make a bond? Why did he have to do him dirty like that? *Just like Ben and Steph betrayed me…* I feel my head spin, need to walk it off, gulp fresh air.

"This is all dumb-de-dumb-dumb," Ant says, reading me, rubbing my back. "Ben would be upset, angry—but not enough to kill anyone."

"He was talking to Lawrence, last night," Cass mutters. "Outside the tent, when we'd all gone to bed. I was drifting off to sleep and their voices got louder, like, high pitched— laughing, I thought—but could they have been arguing?"

"But Ben came to sleep in our tent," I say. "In the middle of the night."

"He did?" Ant gives me a look.

"Yeah. But only because Cass and Lawrence were apparently…you know."

"Urgh!" Seb says. "With me right there, asleep?"

"No! How sick do you think I am?" Cass's mouth falls open. "I sat by the fire with Lawrence for a while. Ben came out too, and then I went to check on Seb. I laid down in their tent because I was tired. Must have fallen asleep."

"Oh, you laid down," Ant intones. "You were lying in wait for some Lawrence lovin', weren't you?"

"I'm gonna lose ma lunch," Seb groans.

"Okay, sure. Guilty." Cass looks sheepish. "So what? But

actually, I fell asleep. Before Lawrence came back. Or maybe he never did."

Ben said they were hot 'n' heavy. But was he lying? Giving himself a reason to come into my tent, knowing how it would throw me, how I'd never suspect him of doing anything to anyone because he was too busy cuddling up with me?

Don't be so stupid.

Ben wouldn't hurt Lawrence, even if he was cut up about Steph cheating, and god knows, he'd never lay a hand on her. But what if Seb's partly right? Because he's right about one thing, *we are all messed up.* Could Steph's death have triggered something in Ben?

"Ben was creeping around after me in the woods. He was first to find me when I called out, after all," Seb says. "He's never liked me, and my guess is, I'm next on his list. But now he's going off with you guys, and leaving me here, so good luck. Why don't you look it up in the book? See how you're going to die?"

"Wait, what about me?" Ant says. "If this saints theory of yours is correct, how the hell could Ben make sure that I got lost? He couldn't have known that I'd jump back on the boat."

Seb shrugs. "He knows you well, freak. He put your backpack in the compartment at the back of the boat, didn't he? He knew you'd forget it, knew you'd do something reckless like jump back in and jerk the boat free. And he probably had a whole bunch of other ideas lined up to lose you if that didn't play out."

"This is your imagination gone wild," Cass says. "What about Maggie's dad?"

"Meh, he doesn't come into this," Seb says. "He's not one of us. Just like you, you lucky bint."

"Oh, screw you—"

"Ssh!" Ant jumps. "What's that?"

"What's what?" Seb clutches the chair.

"Shit, there's someone on the roof." Cass gulps, standing up and grabbing her stick. We all look up and hear the *plod, plod, plod* from one side of the roof to the other.

And then the smashing starts. Whoever is up there is kicking the shite out of something.

"God, are they trying to break in?" Cass cowers against the wall. "Barricade the door!"

Maybe I hear a grunt, maybe I recognize the *energy*, but I know full well who it is on the roof. Before I can think better of it, I grab my iron rod and run outside.

Ben is a blur of motion, raging on top of the roof with the axe, bashing the weather instruments, stomping on them, scattering them to the ground. His face warped with vitriol, spit flying out of his open mouth, roaring like he's possessed. Through everything, I've never seen him violent like this, and the shock is so overwhelming, a laugh bubbles up from deep within, out of control.

"What are you doing?" I back away. "Why would you...?"

He doesn't answer, doesn't stop, doesn't even slow down.

"Seb's right." Cass gasps. "It was Ben, he's the killer." She screams as he rips a solar panel off the roof and tosses it down on the ground, just missing her, and as she dodges and knocks into me, something switches in my head.

Ben's not Ben; it's the only explanation. Stephanie broke his heart, and so he broke her. He knocked Lawrence out and dragged him on to the fire. He's destroying the signal because doesn't want us to be rescued. He wants us to all die up here, one by one, killing us by the book. And then he can make up any story he likes, and we won't be here to tell anyone any different. Sharp tears spring to my eyes, I feel my knees buckle, and I damn myself for being so weak. *Stop him, Maggie. Scream for help. Run away. Save yourself.*

But I can't. I'm stuck, like I was stuck in the cave, pinned between rocks, unable to escape. I sink into the mulchy ground, feeling all the breath leave my body. If it's Ben who is doing this, maybe I don't want to live.

There's screaming, yelling—Ant—Cass—Seb—all watching him, and like me, they're useless; retreating, in disbelief and fear.

But not Ant. At least, not for long.

"Stop, Ben! No!"

Ant clambers up to the roof with a warrior cry. Ben's climbing onto the transmitter tower now, but it doesn't take Ant long to be on him, reaching for his ankles and clinging fast, their legs dangling. Ant's body weight isn't enough to pull him down, but he can't shake them off either and Ant hangs on, so strong, so agile, finding footholds again, never giving up, tugging like a puppy with a chew toy. Eventually, it's too much for Ben, and he falls. It's not far, but he lands on Ant and the two of them thud onto the roof, in a tangle of all the debris of the smashed instruments. As Ant rolls away, clutching their head, I wake from my stupor, pulling myself up there between them, throwing myself onto Ben.

"…get off me, what are you doing?"

"What are *you* doing?" I straddle him and clasp his wrists, force them down either side of his head. He's stronger than me—that I know—but not in this moment; he doesn't have my white-hot hurt, my desperation. He's weak underneath me, too weak…

"Stop! Just stop, please!" He's limp, motionless in defeat. "I'm not fighting you!" He says, his voice shaking with emotion. "I promise, I'm doing this for the best!"

"How can that be?" I hear my voice rasp, like I'm outside my body, watching from above. "You're destroying the signal!"

"Exactly." He inhales, like this is the last chance before he goes under, the last breath that will ever enter his body. "Because if there's no signal, they'll come."

I stop. Stare into his sad eyes. The red haze clears from mine.

The signal stops, people will come here to fix the equipment. And they'll find us.

"Why should I believe you?" I cry. "Why should I trust you when—"

"When I've let you down before," he says, barely loud enough for me to hear. It's a statement, not a question, and somehow, that's enough.

I let go, roll off him. Lie on the roof, on my back, sucking frigid air in, staring at the sky. The tiniest flakes of snow are falling again, or not even falling, floating, dancing in the air, defying gravity. Makes me feel like I'm going to plunge through them, fall up into the air, so high I'll feel the lack of oxygen clutch my throat and rip my lungs, before I'm frozen solid and tossed out to space.

"You could have just switched the button off on the stupid box inside."

"This felt better."

I shut my eyes and lie there, and there's the clatter of debris as I hear him move away, jump down off the roof. I can't hold the whole picture in my head, it feels full of wool, or mist—yes, this mist that has been there at every turn, it has seeped into my brain, infected it, this miasma of damp, diseased air. I'm so hungry and tired. It's dulling my faculties, making the simplest decision impossible, turning any kind of logical thinking into the biggest mountain to climb.

The wind is picking up again, the tower rattles above, and when I open my eyes again, Ant is leaning over me.

"It's not Ben," I croak. It's not. Of course it's not.

"I know." Ant looks as wrung out as I've ever seen them, feral, wild-eyed, dangerous, and I think I'm seeing myself reflected back at me. I pull Ant in close, a hug, and breathe into their ear.

"Don't tell him what Seb and Cass said. Any of it."

They nod, once, and immediately wince with pain and hold their head. More battle scars. I sit up, untangling myself from a coil of rope that has fallen from the tower. Below, Sebastian and Cass are scuttling back into the weather station, and I know they know it too. Whatever nightmare we just dreamt up was only that. Fake news. Visions from tormented souls. Ours.

———

"We need to bear farther west." Cass stops, scratches her head and squints at the map. "Otherwise, there's some kind of drop in our way."

It's the first time anyone has said anything since we left the weather station and set out on our new route home. Shame sits heavy as rock on my shoulders. I can't believe we let Seb talk us into doubting Ben. Another one to put down to the sparky air. I know Ant and Cass feel it too as we endure twenty minutes of silent trudging, because there's too much that accidentally might be said, and there's a long way to go before we can safely say it. As for Ben, he's disappeared into thought, into himself, hanging back.

"Yet another slope, so what?" Ant leans over Cass's arm to stare at the map. "We can handle it."

"I don't know." Cass frowns. "I think those markings mean it's very steep."

Should have guessed. There's no marked trail here, but the going has been suspiciously easy so far. We've followed drove roads, wee lines etched into the grass made by centuries of sheep traversing the hillside. Haven't spied any sheep, though. If I saw one, I think I'd hug it. And then eat it.

"How much longer will a diversion add?" Ant's impatient. Too long, is the answer. There's every reason to want to pick the fastest route.

We left Lawrence, worryingly awake and writhing in his recliner, and Sebastian, subdued and avoiding any kind of interaction with Ben, but clearly cogent enough to create a barricade behind us. We heard him moving things against the door. We left them a bottle of Cass's wonder pills and promised to hurry.

"Which way is west, anyway?" The map's markings blur in front of me; tired eyes, exhausted brain, can't make sense of the tangled lines.

"We cannot go west." Ben catches up. "The cave."

That stops us. Or, at least, most of us.

"But—" Cass starts.

"It's okay!" I take off my pack. "There's a perfect solution, but I left it behind. Keep walking straight on to the cliff, take my stuff, I'll catch up with you." I turn and run back along the sheep track. God, it feels great to have that pack off me.

"Hey, come back!" Cass calls. "We should stick together!"

Yeah, probably, but I need the space, need to get this done, feel like I'm useful again. I'm headed back to the weather station, back to collect something that will get us down the cliff and means we don't have to pass any closer to *that place*.

I make it back in half the time, and at first glance, the weather station is quiet. Maybe Seb managed to get those drugs into his brother? Hope so. I'll be quiet too, and quick, don't want to interact, disturb, or freak them out that I'm the killer creeping around out here. I pull myself up onto the roof, crawl as lightly as I can to the piles of debris, and find what I'm looking for. Rope. I got it all twisted around my legs when I was fighting

Ben, and it's just what we want now. Climbing rope, two lengths of it, the good stuff. And what's more, there's a harness. They must use it for doing maintenance on the tower. Yeah, they're gonna need more than that to fix the place up now. I coil one of the lengths of rope up like Dad taught me, tuck the harness under my arm, and hopscotch back through the debris. There's a door slam from below, my head turns.

Seb walks out, looks around. Instinctively, I duck down, but he's already seen me.

"Jesus!" He claps a hand to his chest. "What are you doing up there? I thought you'd gone!"

"Needed rope." I hold it up. "There's a cliff ahead. Lawrence okay? What you doing out here, anyway?"

"Water barrel fill up, before it gets dark." He frowns at me. "So, go! Don't want to be holed up with him any longer than I have to."

I jump down off the roof.

"Going. Where's your water bottle?"

He looks down at his empty hands. "Silly ol' me. Forgot it."

Something about the way he says it, slowly, deliberating, as if he's daring me to challenge him, curious if I will. Inside, Lawrence groans.

"We both have jobs to do, better do 'em." He turns, closes the door behind him.

I run back over the hillside as fast as I can.

———

I nearly run over the cliff, it comes at me so suddenly. And it takes a moment to spot the others, they're sitting on the ground down to the left of where I've arrived. As I race over there, Ant shouts.

"At last! Was coming after you, slowpoke. You got what you went for?"

"Yup. We have a kit now." I hold up the rope and harness.

"What's that?" Cass's face blanches, and I unclip the harness and step into it, tightening the buckles.

"Hmm. It's on the X-X-L side, so fingers crossed I don't fall out." Cass's mouth drops open in horror.

"No, no, no! You're not suggesting we climb down?"

"Why, what do you think she went to fetch, an escalator?" Ant snorts.

"But we'll kill ourselves!"

I peer over the side. Well, break a few bones, maybe. The drop looks about the height of maybe two basketball hoops stacked on top of each other. However, this time, I will not be beaten by a pathetic cliff.

"Easy-peasy."

"Totally. And this is the lowest point." Ben steps up. "There's even a rock over there for you to secure the rope." He blinks at me. "Figured you'd gone back for it. I should have thought of it myself."

Yeah, I'll forgive you. You had other things on your mind.

I grab a carabiner off my backpack, clip it on the harness, and lash the rope around the back of the rock.

"For real? You're going to climb down?" Cass says.

"Better than that. I'm going to rappel."

"How, exactly?" Ben says. "Where's your belay device?"

"Dad taught us the old-school ways, remember when?" I unravel the rope. "We just need the right knot."

"I'm down!" Ant jumps up.

"Of course you are. But that's a big nope from me," Cass says. "We can find another route."

"Where?" I shake my head. "We don't have much time before it gets dark." *And I am not going any closer to the cave…*

"Hey, Mags, your hands must be killing you. Let me do the test run." Ben walks up, holds the carabiner clipped to my harness, and fixes me with eyes that may never let me in again. He lowers his voice. "Then we send Cass—you can push her off and I'll catch her, you with me?" He winks, and I feel a twist in my stomach, because he's trying so hard, and it's a glimpse of my old friend.

"Sure." I drop the harness, step out.

"You'll do what now?" Cass says.

He steps in, fastening the harness as tight as it will go, but its previous owner must have been a Highland giant, because it's still loose. I hope to hell I can remember the right way to hitch the rope around the carabiner so that Ben can belay down the rock face. But my worries are for nothing. Dad must have done a great job with me, because muscle memory kicks in, and my cold fingers loop the hitch without thinking. All done, Ben gives me a smile, stands with his back to the edge.

"Here goes."

The rope takes the strain, we hold our breath as he leans further, the rope feeding through my hitch perfectly, and he walks down the cliff, slowly, looking like he's done it all his life. In less than sixty seconds, he's standing on the ground below, beaming a smile up at us as he removes the harness. "Yay! Okay, you're next, Cass. Go on, pull it up."

"Looks like it would pinch." She gestures between her legs. "Doesn't it hurt?"

"Not as much as jumping." Ant grins.

She grimaces. "Fine, I'll do it."

The harness is retrieved, and while Cass steps in and I attempt to adjust the buckles to her smaller frame, Ant lowers Ben and Cass's packs down the cliff. And then the rope is pulled up again and it's her turn. As she backs up to the edge, she groans.

"This feels so wrong!"

"The more you lean, the easier it is," I say. "Don't worry, trust the rope's got you."

She's shaking as she begins the lean. It's so hard to trust. With rappelling, it won't work unless you give up control. You tilt backward, and it feels too far, but you've got to go further, so you bite down on your instincts, and just when you think you're doomed, there's a moment where you get the right angle, you find you can move your feet, begin the descent.

But some people can't give in to it.

I stand in front of Cass, she leans a bit, clutching the rope.

"Further! Straighten your legs." I nod encouragingly. She nods, tries, but I can see the fear on her face.

"No!" One hand shoots out, she grips me, tightly, looks up in horror, and I almost go, I almost topple off, over her, headfirst. In that split second, she looks up at me, and I see the panic in her eyes, it's like I'm locked in her gaze, and this is it, I'm going to fall, I'm going over, and then strong, wiry arms link around my waist. Ant is there, anchoring me on solid ground, and Cass swings away, takes first steps down and shouts out a relieved laugh, and she's safe while I land backward on top of my savior.

"Okay up there?" Ben shouts.

"Yeah! Thanks, dude," I gasp at Ant, who nods from underneath me.

"You owe me one more now."

"Who's counting?" I go to scrabble to my feet—I can hear Ben shouting reassuring directions to Cass—but Ant puts a hand on my arm.

"Hey, while it's just us, super quick..." they say, finger to lips in a hush, reaching out for their backpack. "Need you to see what I found." They pull the pack over and open the front section, and we both crouch there. "Does this look familiar?"

I stop myself screeching just in time, hands over mouth.

It's the knife. The orange, bobbled handle, the long, curved blade. If I was in any doubt, it still has my blood on it.

"Same one?" Ant whispers. I nod.

"Where was it?"

"Seb's pack."

"That motherf—"

"Listen." Ant grabs my arm. "We only have seconds. I've been thinking about it all the way here. Seb put the blame on Ben, but it's Seb who's been doing this."

"No, let's not go there again—" I shake my head. "The sparky air, our heads aren't working right, remember?"

"Maggie, I know I bashed my head but I'm clearer than I've ever been." Ant's eyes bore holes into mine. "There's so much anger inside Seb, especially against his brother. And look at the evidence. Who had opportunity? On the boat, Seb was the one handing off the backpacks. This was planned. He left mine on there on purpose!" Ant's eyes flash. "And you said he disappeared before the rock fall, and he was back near the hut when we went for wood before anyone else! He's the one that's been feeding us wild ideas about the bodach, Nicholas, all the saint stuff!"

Judging from Ben's shouts below, Cass is almost at the bottom. Ant's hand grips tighter on my arm.

"He told us himself—*look within*. There's no mystery man stalking us, Mags. There would be some sign, tracks on the ground. So Steph and I got spooked by shadows? Not surprising, it's frickin' terrifying up here. And Seb played on that, told us he'd seen someone too. But we haven't heard or seen anyone, have we? And who the hell would be after us, anyway? This is *personal*. Seb literally burned his own face. He's always been jealous of his brother!"

Below, Ben cheers, Cass has done it. Ant edges closer.

"Seb's always given me shit. But you know me well enough to know I wouldn't speak against him out of hate." Ant's grip tightens. "The thing that got me thinking in the first place was this: when Lawrence got burned, Ben told Seb not to worry, said that Lawrence was tough, he was too stubborn to die, yeah?" I nod. "And Seb replied, if it was that easy to kill Lawrence, he would have done it before now. *Before* now. Don't you think that's a weird choice of word? Not *by* now, but *before* now! Slip of the tongue. He was admitting he pushed his brother onto the fire! And let's face it..." Ants shakes their head. "Sebastian is the most obvious suspect. By a frickin' country mile."

Fear pulses through me. Can't fault the logic. And Seb was leaving the weather station when I was on the roof. Where was he really going? Not to fill his water bottle; of that, I'm sure.

Ant stares at me. "If you've ever trusted me, Mags, for the love of donuts, trust me now." It hits like a punch to the stomach.

"I do." I say slowly. "And it's Occam's razor."

"Is that what you call this knife?" Ant wiggles it, pulls a face. "Kidding. I know what it is. The most obvious solution is the right one, yeah? But that's why you get it, Mags. You've always been the brains, hen." They look across at the cliff edge. "Here's how it goes. We get Ben back up pronto, and run back to the weather station before Seb kills his brother."

"Yo, where'd you go?" Ben's calling from below.

"Were you not watching me, after all of that? I cooked!" It's Cass.

Ant whispers, *"Just Ben.* Us three. Cass isn't part of this, and we can't waste time persuading her." Ant goes to the edge and calls down. "Ben, Maggie's hands are bleeding really badly. We need to get them patched before she can climb. Bring your first aid kit up!"

"What? I'll throw it!"

"I need help, please!" Ant begs. "Hurry, it's really bad."

"Seriously?" He groans and complains, but after a few seconds we can hear him climbing.

"What do we say?" I look at Ant. "And what do we tell Cass?"

Ant pulls a *dunno* face as Ben arrives at the top. He sees me there, very obviously not bleeding to death, and Ant and I both hush him, beckoning him toward us.

"It's Seb," I whisper, when he's close. "We'll tell you on the way, but we have to get back to the weather station, now!"

CHAPTER 22

———

"Guys? What the hell? Don't leave me down here!"

I feel bad for Cass, I really do. It goes against everything in me to leave someone behind. But Ant's right. There's no time. Besides, Cass was never part of this, we can't drag her into danger. She'll be way safer down there than if she comes with us to tackle Sebastian.

We shouted down a lame excuse about Ant and Ben needing to speed back to the weather station to get more first aid supplies. And in this deception, I'm lying half conscious at the top, with Quick Onset Hand Hemorrhage, or whatever it's supposed to be.

"So pull me back up! I'll look after Maggie!"

But we deserted her, sprinting, fast and free without the burden of our packs. We're doing her a favor. And after all, we left Lawrence behind, and he's the one who needs us now.

"…makes sense." Ben is running the fastest, and I don't catch every word. "…gonna kill him."

Assume he's talking about what he's going to do to Sebastian, and having witnessed him in action on the roof, I believe it. As we get closer, I can just see the top of the tower poking up beyond the crest of the hill. Almost there. I speed up and grab Ben's jacket, making him slow down, and turn to Ant, finger to lips, signaling stealth mode.

"Seb was outside when I was here. Gave me some crap about filling up his water bottle, but he didn't have it with him."

Ant nods. "Can we go around, flank him?"

"Not to the right, unless you want to end up in the ravine." I squint at the other side. "Maybe—"

"No time!" Ben has tunnel vision. He pulls away.

"Okay! But at least hunker down, eyes open." I point to the crest of the hill. "We get up here, we're exposed. If he's outside, he'll see us straightaway."

Ben doesn't argue, but he turns and keeps going. Damn. I shoot a look at Ant, and we follow. Got to keep up. Maybe it won't matter if we don't get the jump on Seb. There's three of us, one of him, and Ant is gripping that knife like our lives depend on it. Seb doesn't stand a chance.

And as we reach the top of the hill, we see he's going to be no threat at all.

In silhouette against the dying light, Sebastian has his back to us, his head down, arms up above him.

He is hanging from the tower.

I slam on the brakes, all air leaving my body like I've been hit by a truck. Beside me, Ben skids to a stop. Ant gasps and slides to their knees.

"Jesus…" Ant's voice is so quiet, I don't hear what they say next.

The figure is slumped, swaying slightly in the breeze, and immediately, I know with no doubt that Sebastian is dead. It's as it was in the artwork, the painting in *The Book of Saints* that Steph said was famous… Saint Sebastian was hung from a tree, and…

I walk, legs shaking, toward the weather station. There's something sticking through his jacket, out of his abdomen and chest.

Arrows.

"It can't be." I stagger down the hill to the building, not wanting to get near, but needing to be sure. "I only saw him half an hour ago." Seb's face is in shadow. He's suspended from the mast, hanging from the piece of rope I left behind, which is looped and knotted around his groin, stomach and chest. The weather forecasting rock swings gently from his neck. The world spins and I stick my hand out to steady myself on something that isn't there.

"Oh god, Seb! I'm so sorry." Ant wails. "How, how? I was sure it was him!"

"Who can have done this?" Ben crouches, looks around suddenly. "Someone friggin' *shot* him with arrows! Come here, both of you—whoever it is can't have gone far." He skitters down to me, as I feel panic seizing up my chest.

"Where's Lawrence, tho'?"

"No way. Lawrence would not do this to his brother." Ant

scuttles toward us. We stick together like glue, just like in the woods, checking every angle.

"Maybe he did, because there's no one else here, is there?" Ben scans desperately. "God, I don't know which is worse."

"I won't believe it. Lawrence couldn't—" I break away, make a dash toward the weather station doorway, not knowing if I'm going to find Lawrence's bloody body, or him hiding behind the door with a crossbow.

"Don't go in there!" Ben cries, but it's too late, I have to see.

The room is empty. The desk has been moved, a barricade, for safety—but it clearly didn't do its job. Or was Seb caught outside? I smell something sharp, sour—pee? The recliner is on its side. Seb's pack is still there, undisturbed, but there's a spilled water bottle on the floor. Was there a struggle? Did Lawrence put up a fight? Or did Lawrence kill his brother? No, I won't accept that. Besides, he's too burned, too messed up, he wouldn't have the strength, and where would he get the damn arrows from?

"Maggie."

I jump as Ben appears behind me.

"We need to get out of here. Whoever did this is close by." He reaches for my arm, tries to pull me out of the door, but I stand firm.

"What about Lawrence? We don't know where he is!"

"I know he's not passed out on that chair." Ben's face is grim. "Look, we don't know what's happened here, but we have to go! Do you want to die too?" He gets in front of me this time, tries pushing. But he should know better. I am the wrecking ball, after all.

"I can't just leave Lawrence!"

"Too late." Ant appears at the doorway, face crumpled, tears streaking their dirty face. "I found him." They point over past the water barrel, beyond the end of the wall where the ground drops away steeply into the ravine.

I run to the edge, nearly over it, falling onto my backside and saving myself just in time. At first, I see nothing unusual, folds of hill, a deep tear in the mountain, with scrubby bushes and a tiny stream running over rocks far below—but then I spot it. Can I trust my eyes? *I know what dead looks like. A motionless shape on the ground.* There's a body way down there, face down, an arm flung up, one leg bent awkwardly at the wrong angle.

"That's him?" Ben clutches at his chest for the binoculars, but they must be in someone's pack, back with Cass at the cliff.

"Lawrence!" I scream. "Oh god! Lawrence!"

Ben claps a hand over my mouth, and I push him off angrily, but I know why he's doing it. There's no doubt now. Someone else did this. And they're still here. Whoever it was is strong enough to overpower the McTavish twins, shoot Sebastian and haul him up the tower, tie him there, and toss Lawrence down into the ravine like a bag of trash. And it took them a matter of minutes.

"Got to run, Maggie." Ben's voice is urgent, in my ear.

"I can't," I say. "We have to try and get down there. He could still be alive."

"He's not, you know it. And even if we could reach him, how the hell would we ever get him back up?" He pulls my arm. "We run!"

"The rope!" I shake him off. "We go back and get it, that way—"

"Not happening. The killer is here, Maggie. We're going. Ant!" he hisses. "Gimme that knife!"

"Not happening either." Ant is pacing, watching our six. "I'm keeping it, *because I'm going to gut whoever did this!*" they scream into the ether. Fear threatens to paralyze me, stick me here to this edge, forever frozen in time.

"Shit, what about Cass?" Ant stops in place. "We left her alone."

Somehow, we run again. Away from Lawrence's poor, broken body. Past the wreck of what was Sebastian, swinging gently, side to side. I can't look at him, none of us can. We take on the hillside behind the weather station again and pour every last ounce of energy and will getting back to the cliff as fast as we can.

And when we're yards out, we shout, scream for her, because *he* might be there, he might be doing something to her right now, he's had all the time in the world while we've been discovering his handiwork.

"Cass! Watch out!"

"We're coming, Cass!"

"We're almost there!"

And then we are there, and she's not.

Below us, only the pack Ben was carrying remains.

"What the hell...?" Ben pants, hands on his head. "Cassia! Where are you? Dammit!"

"She's hiding. She took her stuff," Ant says. "It's good, it's clever. Lying low until we came back."

"Did she see him coming? Cass!" I shout out. "We're here, it's safe! We've got the knife!" *God, I feel so bad, we left her, we abandoned her...* I'm already stepping into the harness, numb hands gripping the rope and yeeting myself off the edge, feet only just finding rock, bouncing down so fast my injured foot cries out when I hit the ground. But there's no time for that. "Where are you, Cass?" I run out onto the flat grass, a clearing, surrounded by hawthorn trees, scrub, and evergreen bushes. Sparse cover, but she'll be here, she will have found a den, a bolt-hole. And it's a good one, because I can't see her.

"Mags, the harness!" Ben shouts from above. I go back, secure it so he can pull it up, and he and Ant tussle over who goes next.

"Jesus, I've just realized, he's probably still up there!" I call to them. "If we couldn't climb without gear, neither could he! Throw the packs, get down here quick!"

The packs thump on the ground, and Ben practically pushes Ant off the cliff first, pulling that harness back up and racing down himself.

"We leaving the rope?" Ant wheezes. "Makes it easy for him!"

"Take the harness off." Ben unclips it. "Nothing much we

can do about the rope, but the bastard's going to get a hell of a friction burn if he tries sliding down."

"Hope he friggin' flays himself raw," I growl. If the killer's gotten this far and has managed to string Seb up, and throw Lawrence down, he's packing way more gear and muscle than we have.

"Cass would make for the car park." Ant picks up the pack Ben's been carrying and thrusts it at him.

I hope so. We spend mere seconds looking for her, staring at the ground trying to track her trail, like we're experts suddenly, mountain people. I think I can see flattened grass leading the way down the hill, but it might have been me when I was looking for her before. She's not here, anyway. Or if she is, she's not capable of letting us know that. I shiver.

"We carry on too, we're not far, we'll catch her. Which way?"

Ben points, we're heading downhill, a trail of sorts, tumbled stones and scrub, maybe a dried-out stream. One foot in front of another, as fast as we can.

"*Straight on 'til morning,*" Ben says, striding out with the axe in his hand.

"It'll take us that long?" Ant says. "It's not even dark yet."

"It's a quote from—"

"I know, *Peter Pan,*" says Ant. "Only my bloody role model, *you addle-headed simpleton*! And if I'm him, that makes you two my Lost Boys."

"Yeah, we're not getting lost," I breeze, going as fast as I dare.

"And if Captain Hook is around the corner, I'll frickin' punch him," Ben sing-songs. We're babbling nonsense, but sometimes that's what gets you through. "Whatever. Let's get the hell out of Neverland."

We descend, fast, risking ankles, and the air changes; it's teasingly warmer, and I feel that terrible hope begin to seep through, in spite of me doing my best not to acknowledge it. We're leaving the wilds behind, we're almost to safety. And although every sinew in my being has been stretched to its limit and my knees are crying out with the gradient, the trail gets easier.

"Getting so close now, I know it!" Ben's leading, Ant not far behind, and they're hyper-focused, gaze down. But my head keeps swiveling. I'm checking the hill, because this is the scariest part, the part where you think you've done it, you're sliding into home, you might begin to relax. That's when they strike.

"Around the hill to the right, at the bottom. We should have eyes on the car park any second now!" Ben's speeding up. I want to tell him to slow, be careful, because wouldn't this be the sweetest time for the killer, to catch us when we see the light at the end of the tunnel? So I hurl myself down there, almost falling, the momentum making me crash into Ant, and the two of us barging into Ben as he stops, suddenly, at a twist in the trail.

Cass is sitting on a large rock, pack off, rubbing her ankle.

"Oh my goodness!" She looks up at us and her face crinkles with relief, tears streaming down her face. "I thought you were all dead!"

We rush to her, hug her, as she batters us with shouts and with sobs, her body shuddering, as she tells us how she panicked and fell, running away, and hurt her ankle. And all the time, I'm keeping one eye on that trail, the path down the hill, the way he'll be coming if he's following us. Because I'm so, so sure he is. He wants this finished.

"Did you all go back to the weather station?" Cass wails. "Why?"

We look at each other. No choice. We have to tell her. Tell her how we suspected Sebastian, but we were so very wrong. How we found him hanging, the arrows, by the book. And how we saw Lawrence, crumpled, far below. And so we do. Quickly, rip off the Band-Aid. Cass's face stretches in shock, horror, and fear. The tears flow again, and she buries her head in her hands and falls to the ground in a ball.

"It's too much..."

"I know...but Cass, we need to keep going. We're so, so close!" Ben picks up her bag. "Can you walk on your ankle?"

"It feels broken." She winces, her eyes screwed tight. "I can't..."

I squat beside her. "Sod this, Cassia. We're not going to let him win. He got the others, he's not getting us." I grip her arms. "You saved me on the riverbank. Right now, this is me paying you back. I'm going to frickin' firefighter-carry you out of here if it comes to it. Now, get your arse in gear!"

Cass looks at me with wide eyes, presses her lips together and nods, but as soon as she tries to stand up, her ankle gives way.

"No biggie. And hup!" Ant takes her under one arm, me the other, and we lopsidedly lift her, take an arm and a leg each, and stagger down the trail, Ben following, dragging bags.

"I thought I wasn't going to make it." Cass sniffs. "I ran and ran, and I fell. Kept thinking whoever got you was going to catch me."

"Yeah, he still might." I twist around, but all I can see is Ben puffing, hefting packs behind us.

The light is fading; the full moon rising. We're almost out of time, we won't last another night here, we'll never see the sun again. But it can't be much farther, and at least when night falls, our ride home is due. We just have to survive a little while longer, and we're home and dry.

"See anything yet?" Ben grunts from behind.

"More of the same." I stumble as Cass sinks to her knees. "Get up! Don't let it beat you!"

I feel the anger well up inside, fists in my stomach, pushing out. Damn to hell whoever has done this and damn this mountain. Damn being cold and wet and laden with dirt. Damn being hungry and terrified, and strung-out exhausted. Damn the sores on my armpits where the pack straps have rubbed me raw, damn my frozen fingers and burned palms, my lacerated foot, my sore collarbone, my aching back, and my dead legs. I am done with this. So done. I will not let it get the better of me. I've beaten these mountains before, and I will again, and screw anyone or anything who thinks they can take me.

Just as I'm running out of things to curse, we come around

the curve of the hill, and below us, it's there. The parking lot. Down this last stretch, a skip and a jump across a small stream, a mere stroll by a clump of small trees, there's a gravel rectangle framed by a smattering of gorse bushes. Thank you, mountain goddesses. There is even a green, portable toilet, and a single-track road leading away. We've done it. We've reached our final destination.

Ant whoops for joy, Ben overtakes and throws the packs down the slope, one by one, and runs after them, delirious. I'm so tempted to do the same with Cass, but I catch Ant's eye, we grip her tight, and take off after Ben, all three of us clamped together in our strange three-headed-monster way, lolloping down that hill as fast as we can without killing ourselves.

"We're here! We made it!" Ant abandons their side of Cass and runs into the middle of the empty space, arms above their head, running laps of the lot. I scoop Cass up in both arms, waddle a few steps farther and dump her onto a nearby boulder.

How good is it to have gravel underfoot? Not natural, mountain gravel, but this horrible bright-gray stuff that the local council bought and recklessly trucked up to the hills to spread, a blot on the landscape. God, how I love it. I kneel painfully on it, bend to kiss it, and then I throw my head back, and laugh, the sound is so deranged it scares me for a second, but I do it anyway.

"Guys! Come here!" Ben calls from the far end of the lot.

"What now?" Ant yells and runs after.

"Don't leave me!" Cass panics, and like the hero I am, I go

and piggyback her to the corner of the lot where Ben and Ant are gawping at something out of view.

And when I get there, I almost drop Cass in shock.

Behind a dense, high gorse bush, there's a car.

CHAPTER 23

We stare at the car, hardly daring to breathe. If we move, it might disappear, like a mirage.

"You can break into that, Ben?" Ant whispers.

"I can."

"Hot-wire it? Drive us home?"

"Just watch me."

I send up a silent prayer of thanks for all those lost days Ben spent in his dad's garage. I would moan at him, tell him he was boring for not wanting to hang out with me, and then bitch about the grease in his fingernails, and gripe that he smelled of oil and machismo. But now he is going to get us home.

He walks toward the car, as if in a trance.

It's an ancient-looking, army-green, four-wheel drive, with a huge grille at the front. And it looks to be in a similar state to us: beaten up, mud-encrusted, and tough as nuts.

"Will it go?" Cass hops after him.

"These things never die." Ben runs his hand over the bonnet lovingly.

"Need something to pry the door?" I start toward the backpacks. "Where did you put the knife, Ant? Or shall we just break the window?" I find my iron bar.

"Whoa!" Ben holds up a hand. He lifts a finger at me. *Wait.* And he tries the door.

It opens.

"No frickin' way!" Ant dances on the spot. "Bloody get in there and get hot-wiring, Benny! I'll get the packs."

"Oh my sweet angel, Ben, I could marry you." Cass opens the back, slowly and delicately climbs in, collapsing on the ripped, filthy seats. "Aaaah! You have got to do this, Maggie; it is amazing!"

So help me, I do. I forget Ant, who is nobly dragging our stuff, and ease myself onto a seat. *Och,* I cannot describe how wonderful it feels as my muscles relax, my aching bones sink into the leather, and my eyeballs roll back in my head. After endless rocks and damp ground and hardness, to sit on something even marginally upholstered is truly an experience out of this world. Ant throws the packs in the back and joins us. In spite of the fear and bitter grief of the past few hours, or perhaps because of it, we lose control luxuriating in those comfortable seats. We giggle and jostle each other for more room, stretching ourselves out as much as we can, with exaggerated groans of ecstasy.

"What's taking so long up front, Ben?" Ant cries. "How come

we're not home already? Actually, can we do a drive-thru on the way? Thick shakes and fries, my treat!"

"That might not be on the menu just yet," Ben mutters, opening the dash, flipping sun visors.

"What's wrong?" The spell has been broken. I lean over. He points to the steering wheel. A black and yellow horizontal bar is clamped through the center of it.

"Wheel lock." Ben sucks in air through his teeth. "Why bother locking your car when you've immobilized it with a steel bar? Makes sense now."

"No way!" Ant's face falls. "So what? We can start the car, but can't turn the wheel? So, we'll just drive in a straight line! It's better than nothing!"

"Yeah, right." Cass huffs. "Want to add 'car crash' to the list of shit we've survived? I don't think so."

I lean closer to Ben.

"You can remove it?"

The muscles in his jaw tense. "If I had the right tools. I've seen Dad jimmy one off before, but I'm not a friggin' car thief. I'll need something to pick it with, maybe—"

"This could help?" Ant holds up Lawrence's penknife. "Much guilt." They look sheepish. "Took it when he was unconscious. Now I feel like all kinds of responsible for what happened to him."

"Don't be stupid." I squeeze their arm. "Whoever did that wouldn't have been stopped by a penknife."

"Speaking of which…" Ben takes the knife, eases out the skinniest blade. "Can one of you keep eyes on the hill, please?

The idea someone's sneaking up does nothing for my lockpicking skills."

"On it!" I open the door, push Ant out. "Hey, take the binoculars and scan the road, yeah? I'll watch the hillside."

"Righto." Ant lifts a hand to their temple, and sits down again, with a jolt. "Urgh. Feeling woozy."

"You banged your head when you were on the roof with Ben," I recall. "Want me to take a look?"

"Naw, I'm just spinning with hunger." They grin at me, but their face is pale under the dirt.

"I've got you, dude." Cass twists around and leans over the back seat, rummaging around amongst the bags. "Picked up some of those hot chocolate packets at the weather station. Can't make it hot, but we've got enough water to have wonderful *chocolat froid*!"

"What she say?" Ant groans.

"She's going to make us a lovely milkshake with backwash water and age-old cocoa powder." I glance up at the hill. "Actually, that sounds totally wonderful right now."

It is. Cass shakes up a bottle of chocolate water, takes a sip, and hands it around. The sugar hits my tongue, tasting sweeter than anything I've ever had before, instant rush. Ben takes a glug but keeps working on the lock.

"Finish it. I'll watch the hill," I say to Ant. "You burn off more energy than the rest of us put together, anyway, you need the calories." They nod, take a couple of hearty swigs from the bottle, and lay their head back on the rest.

"Mags, give me a hand, yeah?" Cass opens the door and awkwardly hops around to the back. "Need to get into my pack properly and pay a visit to the thunderbox." She nods to the portable toilet. "Period's started. Like I needed anything else." She smiles ruefully.

"Oh god, you poor thing." I drag her pack out of the back of the car, she opens it up and finds a small cosmetics pouch inside, and slowly, we hobble to the toilet together.

"Won't be long. Watch my back, will you?"

As she shuts the door, I scan the hill. So far, so good. The light is fading fast, and the moon has already risen over the mountains, full and pale pink. Means snow. Doesn't feel cold enough now we're off the mountain, but you never can tell.

"Hey, I'll see if I can find anything you can use as a walking stick!" I shout to Cass.

I walk past the gorse bushes, squinting at the ground. Hopefully, she won't need a stick, because hopefully, we'll be out of here when Ben beats the wheel lock. I have faith in him. We'll head anywhere people are, hit up the first friendly house we see, and call the police from there. Oh god, please let Dad have made it back. Surely he did? My heart clenches. Don't want to think about him up the mountain. The killer is out there. *Hurry up, Cass, hurry up, Ben.* I glance at the hillside again. Twilight, and that strange rusty glow of winter coming in, I shiver. *Don't be complacent; get back to the car, lock yourselves in, weapons in hand.*

"You done, Cass? Wow." I bend to the ground. "I've just

found you the perfect walking stick, this looks like Gandalf's staff!" I pick the stick up, it's long and sturdy, with a rounded crook on top. "Couldn't be more perfect!"

"Brilliant." Cass appears, smiling. "I'll take it for a spin." She tucks it under her armpit, hops, scrapes the stick back into position, hops again...and makes it all the way back to the car, with me following, casting nervous glances around as I go.

"Getting anywhere?"

I slide into the passenger seat beside Ben and lock the door. The yellow plastic of the wheel lock is off, revealing the steel part inside.

"Progress." He grunts. "Get me a headlamp, yeah? Getting dark in here."

"Sure." I hurry around to the back door, pull my pack out, and toss the headlamp to Ben via Cass. Okay, lock in and sit tight now. Cass can't move far. Ant is still in the same position, splayed on the seat, head back, not moving. Are they actually snoring? Like a hyperactive toddler, when they check out, they check out.

I go to shut the back door, but Cass's pack is still on the ground from earlier. Reaching down to pick it up, I knock it sideways, and something falls out.

The little black cosmetic purse Cass took to the toilet, her period stuff.

I bend to retrieve it. *Huh?* It's heavy. Too heavy. When my fingers clasp around what is inside, I know. Instantly. A wave of cold sweat sweeps over me, and crouching low on the ground,

I unzip the purse with trembling hands and swear under my breath.

A phone.

What the hell?

The screen lights up, I hurriedly shield the light with my hand and force my eyes to focus. A powered up, working phone! And what's more, a little icon shows signal.

Jesus Christ. My mind goes into meltdown. *What? How? Why has Cass got this? And didn't tell us?!*

Okay—she must have forgotten to hand it in to Dad at the café. No, don't be so stupid. *She would have said if she had a phone.* Like, a million times, *of course she would!* When the boat escaped, when we were at the shepherd's hut, when Steph got hurt! It's not like she suddenly discovered it buried at the bottom of her bag, *and if she did, why would she not tell us?!* She had a phone all along, and she never said a word.

She just took it in the porta-toilet with her. *What was she really doing there, making a call?* Okay, this might be nothing, there might be some wild but totally feasible explanation. But why is every cell in my body telling me different? Cass is in the back seat now, next to a passed-out Ant, while Ben works on the lock. My feet feel as if they're nailed to the spot. Should I shout out to Ben and Ant? What will happen if I do? *Just use the phone! Get help!*

"Going to pee!" I call out brightly, as if anyone cared, and I stride off, with the phone clamped under my arm, praying Cass isn't watching me, praying she won't suddenly be suspicious. *God oh god oh god.* What the hell is going on here?

I shut the toilet door, lock it, lean on it, head spinning. Keep calm. Keep focused.

Make the call.

I fumble with the phone, almost dropping it in the toilet bowl, cursing at myself. *Keep it together, Maggie, breathe, get this done.*

The phone's unlocked. Either it always is, or it hasn't auto-locked yet because Cass only just used it. Who was she contacting? *Never mind, act first, ask later.* Call the frickin' police!

I dial 999. Emergency services. Send all of them now, Scotland's finest, and the army, navy, and air force too.

I clap the phone to my ear, wait to hear the ring. Nothing. *Come on!* I look at the screen—

Dialing...

To my ear again—

—*beep beep beep*—

No! Call dropped. Try again, quick!

Call dropped.

I look at the signal icon at the top; damn it, there's only one bar. Dad told me that emergency calls piggyback off any available network, but out here, nothing's guaranteed. *Keep trying.* One bar is one bar.

Dialing...

Call dropped. *Shite, hurry!*

I dial my mother's number, in case by some twist of fate, that will work better.

—*beep beep beep*—

Call dropped.

"Come on!" I shake the phone in frustration, to wake it up. *Och, Jesus,* my head feels full of fog, can't breathe in this airless box, please let this work.

Okay, text! Doesn't take as much signal for a text to send. Quickly, write it, send it, get it done!

"Maggie?"

I jump. Someone's shouting for me, from the car... Cass? *Type, woman!*

Open text messages, new message, remember Mum's number. *Quicker to send a voice note? Yep—*

"Mum, help me," I whisper. "*We're in serious danger, I'm at the north car park—*"

There's a door slam. Cass? She can't walk fast. Ben? I should bust outta here, run to him. There's three of us, and only one of Cass. We can hold her off while we message for help. She's got a broken ankle, it's not like she can run after us. *But who has she been calling?*

I press to send the voice note, doesn't send. *Just text already!*

No! The bar has disappeared. I hold the phone high, stare at it, climb on top of the toilet lid, willing that little bar to come back, but it doesn't.

I can run. I'll run back up the hill if it means I catch a signal—

Scrape. Scrape. Scrape.

I hold my breath. It's Cass and her stick.

"Maa-gee. Whatcha doing in there?"

Scrape. Scrape. Scrape.

I type frantically. Mum help me danger... north car park mountains urgent please killer hurry no joke call police Dad missing

Scrape. Scrape. Scrape.

"Maggie? You hiding from us?"

Only from you. I press send and damn, a little ! appears, it hasn't sent, press send again... a little ! again, bloody crappy mountain, make this work you shitty phone—

"Only, I need you," Cass pleads. "To help me."

Scrape. Scrape. Scrape... Oh god, she's almost right outside the friggin' door.

"Because there's something wrong with Ben."

My blood runs cold. Cass's voice is low, concerned.

"He's passed out, I think." She sniffs. "He really needs your help."

Oh, you bitch, what have you done?

"And Ant's fast asleep," Cass says, and my stomach twists. "I've tried, but I just can't wake her."

Them—I clap my hand over my mouth to stop myself saying it, the other hand thumbing, continue pressing *send send send send* until I think I've broken the phone. Maybe it's my fault, anyway, it's stuck in a loop, like we were stuck in a loop when we were trying to revive Steph, like my whole life is stuck in a loop, because I'm back in the mountains, *oh god don't make a sound, they might go away.*

I never thought it was Cass. She was the odd one out, all this time. Funny, when we found her on the trail just now, it was odd, her face—she was sitting, rubbing her ankle, and when she saw us, she was…relieved. There was no flash of fear, of shock or surprise. She should have been frightened, just for a millisecond when we appeared, before she realized it was us. But she wasn't. Like she wasn't scared the killer was after her. And like she knew we'd be coming…

"Hey, Maggie!" Cass's voice sounds like she's moved farther away, but I didn't hear the stick. "I think I see…lights! Yes! Could be rescuers, might be a car! Going to look!"

Scrape, scrape, scrape…moving faster, the sound going away…

What now? My body's tingling. Do I go? Don't know which way to jump. *Send send send*…nothing.

Silence.

She's gone?

I put my ear against the door. Where was the knife? Ant had it last. Or did Ben use it on the wheel lock? He had the penknife too. If so, Cass might have both knives now. *Oh god, please don't let her have hurt my friends.*

Or maybe I'm imagining this, maybe my brain is misfiring with exhaustion, maybe something else is going on here and Cass is perfectly innocent, maybe she really has seen lights?

No. Don't trust her. I need to act. I'm on my own, it's up to me. Phone's useless like this. I need to go. *Run fast, run like you've never run before, Maggie. Head up that hill again, get high enough to call for help, this one last sprint, you can do it, you're the Wrecking Ball, nothing will stand in your way…*

I'm perfectly still, ear on the door. No wind, no white noise of rain. And no Cass. But I'm not stupid. I turn the lock very, very slowly, ease the door open and peer through the crack and let my eyes adjust to the half-light. I can't see the car from here. There's no sign of Cass. And no lights. Okay, I can see well enough under moonlight to book it up that trail again. I need to go, and go now.

I open the door a wee bit wider. *Get ready to fly, Maggie. If you ever needed to be fast, it's now.*

I leap from the door, gripping the phone, feet skidding in the gravel, huge gasp of air, bent forward, arms bent and ready to pump, muscles contracting, teeth bared—

From behind, a crack.

World goes dark.

I fall.

CHAPTER 24

I'm in the cave.

And I'm at peace. This is home, after all. The place where I belong. Yes, it's dusty, damp, and smelly, but at least I can call it mine. I've returned, but I never really left, did I? Because I'm special. We're all special, the saints. Not everyone has this bond, but we do; the saints all share it, and it's so strong, it's lasted ten years, and will be with us for the rest of our lives. Although…those lives are ending here, tonight.

The bloodred moon shone when he took me out onto the ledge, and it is shining again; it makes me so happy, fulfilled. A loop through time, a loop completed. The joining of the ends, like a circle, like a bloodred moon.

Oh Lord I want to be in that number
Oh when the saints go marching in

Lying here, on this pure, cold stone, I can feel my blood pumping, life flaming through my veins. Just one more push! You can finish this! Pins and needles pierce my skin, but that's okay, it means I'm waking, my body coming back to me. Soon I'll unstick these eyelids, rub the crust away; I'll be able to see the truth, in all of its glory, and it will be beautiful. So, wake up.

Wake up…

"Wake up."

A voice. I open my eyes. It's dark, but there's a light somewhere, flickering, and I'm hit with a smell: musky, strong, and familiar. The air is so heavy with dust and damp, I feel it with each breath, suffocating me, the panic rising in my chest. Shadows dance on the ceiling, as I will myself to move…and a face looms into view, too close to mine, breath warm on my skin.

"Hi, Maggie."

The voice is warm and soft. Encouraging. I shift a little, turn my head, trying to see the face that the voice belongs to. But I can't. Like in a dream; the more you focus, the worse the distortion gets.

Ow.

Head is throbbing so hard I can hear it. Not sure where I end and everything else begins. And memories rush back, suddenly. The porta-potty, the cracking noise, the blackness. Something…got me.

Oh god, the phone.

My hands are empty. I flex fingers, try to move wrists apart.

Can't. Plastic bracelets, cutting into the skin, too tight. *He had to put them on because I was naughty.* Fear, sharp and violently sudden, slices through me, my heart banging, breath shallow.

"Wake up! I can't do this without you."

I look into the brown eyes, inches away from my own. Wide, staring pupils. I know those eyes. And that energy.

The driver?

"You've been out way longer than I wanted. Must have whacked you a lil' bit too hard! Sorry about that. I had to be sure."

The blurred face moves away slightly; a hand comes up and tucks a strand of black hair behind an ear.

"But hey, thanks for the walking stick. Did the job great. I was all for using the iron bar, before; you would've been a goner. Can't have you dying on me, Saint Margaret. Not yet."

The picture clears. Cass.

"What...?" My throat feels blocked, choked, can't get the words out, my brain exploding with pressure. She did this to me? Hands tied in front, I try to roll over on my side, push up on one sore elbow, feel something pressing me down—a weight— but there's nothing, it's only me, I can't...

"Whoa there!" Cass laughs. "You might want to give it a second."

My ankles are tied too. I can make out rough, curved stone walls, an archway or alcove of some kind, and a cluster of candles with fitful flames, jittering in the breeze. Cass's backpack, leaning against a rock.

Wait, *breeze. There's a way out somewhere.*

The fog lifts. I'm really here. I'm in the cave, lying curled up on the same floor I'd laid on when I was six years old and wished myself dead. The cave was blocked off after what happened, how the hell has she done this?

"Why am I here?" I gasp, trying to get up, sit at least, must make myself bigger… Cass leans back on her heels, watching me, an amused smile playing on her lips. "What have you…?"

"I did what needed to be done, Maggie." Her voice is low, dead serious now. "All according to the book. Thanks for finding it in the hut. I guessed it might be you who would. The trigger."

"What?" I gasp. "You mean you killed Steph? How could you? She was your friend!" The words come in a jumble, and I throw them out while I can, my brain threatening to check out of the game and leave me blubbering on the floor. "Lawrence and Sebastian, too? But I don't understand why, how, could you do that…?"

"Oh yeah, you got lots of questions, for sure." Cass sighs heavily, the sound echoing off the walls. "I get it. You want a full and rounded explanation, blah, blah. But I'm not sure you can take the truth, Maggie. You always hide away from it, eh? Sucks for you." She waggles a finger. "Because He sees everything. Ultimately, you have to face up to your actions. You can't hide from Him."

"Who? The driver?" I croak.

"No, silly!" Cass leans in, pushes me playfully, and I rock

back, my head thudding onto the dank ground again, sending waves of pain down my body. "Your Father."

"Dad?" Panic, and hope, pure, agonizing hope; it gives me energy, sears through every atom of my being, and I twist around to look behind me. "Is he here?"

"Nope, wrong again!" The laughter peals out. "Not your stupid ol' dad. Our Father, God." Cass shoots out a hand, grabs my collar and pulls me in so close, I can see the dirt embedded in the corners of her eyes, around the creases of her mouth and forehead. "He was promised souls of the saints' namesakes, wasn't he? And he never received them, not a single one, and that was *your* fault, Maggie. You denied God." She blinks at me, brows knitted together in a frown. *Has she lost her mind? Have I? Is any of this real?* "You know, it fuddles my head to imagine; you deprived the Almighty Creator of sacred souls! How does that even feel, Maggie?"

"Cass." I try to reach out to her with my bound hands, and she throws me off, but this time I save myself from falling on my head, abs crunching as I roll sideways and push myself up again onto my knees. "Please! I don't know what's happened here, to you, but where's Ben? Where's Ant? What have you done with them?"

"What should have been done years ago, Maggie." Cass looks at me sternly. "Ant is sleeping like a baby. Well," she giggles. "A dead baby."

I lurch toward her, but she dodges, chuckling.

"Oh, mate, I'm sure Ant appreciates you caring, but her

number was up from the start. I knew she had to be taken out quickly, she's sharp and she's quick." Cass eyes me. "Unlike some people."

A sob curls in my throat, but I keep it down.

"It's they, not she, and you know it!" I growl. *Can't think of Ant dead, I can't and I won't.*

"No, it's not, Maggie." Cass rolls her eyes. "What God ordained, so shall it be. It is not up to us to question His Will. It is a sickness!" Cass prods her temple. "Anyhoo. It doesn't matter now. Do you remember what it says in *The Book of Saints*, how Ant dies? Not gonna lie, it was a bonus getting her lost like that." She walks over to her pack and pulls out *The Book of Saints*. "Essential reading! We'll need it later. Yeah, I'm glad Ant came back, because *duh*, Saint Anthony didn't die by getting lost. He died from ingesting ergot." Cass studies the book, circles around me, kicking at the dust. "Says in here that ergot's a fungus, in case you're interested, grows on wheat 'n' grass. You eat enough of it, makes you really, really sick." She shrugs. "But whose got time for that? Not me. Shame, because you get these really wild hallucinations—can you imagine Ant tripping?" She giggles. "That would be golden! But sadly, not feasible. So I cheated a little. Popped some cheeky pills in the chocolate drink. Enough to fell a horse. Meh, it's still poison, it counts." She chucks the book on the floor.

"No!" I feel the hot streaks of wet tears down my face, can't stop. "Please...it can't be real, Cass. I think...we're in a bad dream. But we can end it. Your phone. Let's call someone."

"Oh, this is *real*, alright." Her face contorts in anger. "I have felt every kind of pain, don't think it hasn't been hard! Some deaths are a blessed duty, but sacrificing Steph hurt me. Those tears were genuine." She sniffs. "I put a pillow over her face in the night, felt her slip away. She didn't even fight it."

"Jesus, Cass—" I wail.

"Don't take His Name in vain!" She points a finger at me. "It was peaceful for Stephanie, but torture for me. And nobody even bloody noticed in the morning, not 'til we came back from collecting wood!" She shakes her head, aghast. "Couldn't believe how careless, how self-involved you all were. Took *Ant*, of all people, to actually clock Steph had been killed! But"—her mouth sets in a firm line—"I knew then, if I could do Steph, I could do anyone. And so I did."

"You pushed Lawrence onto the fire? How?" I cry. "Did you drug him, too? Or knock him out?"

"Lawrence," Cass exhales. "Well, I was fond of Lawrence. At least, I was fond of what he could do to me." She winks cheesily. "But guys like him are a dime a dozen. Ha! In his case, that's true, because, you know, Sebastian! And let me tell you, those boys are more alike than anyone would ever guess, when they get down and dirty!" She opens her mouth in mock delight, claps her hands, and gives me a saucy grin. "Too much? How d'ya like me now, Maggie?"

The cave is tilting, walls closing in on me. I drop backward onto my butt again, no strength to do more. She's delusional. She couldn't have done what she says. How would she have the strength to haul Seb up the tower? It doesn't make sense. She's standing there, grinning at me, and I try to make out something of the person I know to be Cass, and I can't.

"I think...you've lost your mind."

"No, I lost my *father*." She glares at me. Those eyes. I saw something in them when she rappelled down the cliff. That look of genuine fear, it sparked a memory I wasn't ready to recognize. But I know it now. They were *his* eyes, the driver's. I remember how he looked at me, when I bit his hand and pushed with all my might and he stepped out into nothing.

"You father was...the driver?"

Even in this dim light, I see the color flush into Cass's cheeks. The corners of her mouth turn down, and her hands tighten into fists.

"Maximilian Del Vento was his name! You little shits all know that, but you only ever call him "the driver"! Like that was his only identity!" she spits. "He was a holy man, a servant doing the Lord's bidding, and he was my dad! You killed him, Maggie! You denied God, and you denied *me*." She pulls the hunting knife out of her jacket and grips it, knuckles turning white. "I wish with all my soul that I could kill you now! I never even met my own father, he left before I was even born, but there was still time for us to make that right. Before you took that chance away from me. But you didn't think of that, did you? Of who else you were hurting by killing him?"

"I was six and he wanted me dead." I meet her stare. "He

was going to jump off the ledge with me in his arms!" I stagger to my feet and take a shuddering step toward her. "I was an innocent kid!"

"Back the hell down, Wrecking Ball!" The knife flashes in the candlelight. "You got the better of my father, but you won't beat me. I'll gut you like a fish if you come any closer!"

"What about *my* dad?" I shout. "Where is he?"

She shrugs, barks out a laugh. "I dunno! I'm not interested in his soul. I doubt he even has one, after what he did to your family. Yeah, whatever, I'll admit I slipped him a couple pills in his tea before we set out, put a couple more in his water bottle, but he must have walked them off, because he was still the same obnoxious prick as ever when he floated down the river! That plan worked out, at least." She flings her hands up in the air and screams girlishly. "Oh no, what a dummy! I've dropped the boat's tether! And he figured he'd better swim after it!" She blinks at me. "I really wasn't expecting it to be that simple. Sometimes, God shows us the way."

I turn from her, sickened, and look around—*must do something, hide, escape!* Where? *The archway.* I try to shuffle one foot in front of the other, but my ankles are tied too tight.

"Er, God's not going to show *you* the way, Mags," Cass says. "Not the way out, if that's what you're looking for." She walks toward me, biting her lip in excitement. "I told you, I've got plans, and you're kinda key."

"How did you do it? Get me up here? I see your ankle's all healed. Did God help you with that? Did all of His angels lift Seb up the tower? Throw Lawrence down into the ravine?"

She grins, raises a bent arm, and shows off a bicep.

"Bullshit," I sputter. "You were with us when the twins were killed!" I turn away, shuffle again toward the archway, it's so pathetic, horribly funny, and Cass doubles over with laughter at the sight of me. I'm all but hog-tied, alone, no one to help me. *Unless...* "Where is he? You never said... Where's Ben?"

"Ah-ha! Wondered when you'd actually remember about your true love." She chuckles at me indulgently. "Patience, sweetheart. He'll be here soon."

My heart drops through the floor. What the hell does she mean? Ben is part of this? I won't believe it. But everyone else is dead, and she must have someone helping her. My guts cramp. I'm going to throw up. I sink down to my knees, because if I don't go willingly, I'll fall, and I put my ravaged wrists against the cold ground, head down, blood rushing, thudding in my ears...

"Ben's always late, isn't he, Mags? Boys, eh?"

I squint up at her and she makes a face.

"Steph bitched about it all. The. Friggin'. Time. Smart move, on Ben's part, tho', the lateness. Kept her keen. I think she was *astounded* he had a life beyond her. *So* Steph. Kind of out of character for him, you might imagine, but people can switch, even the ones you think you know—like that!" She clicks her fingers and laughs at the dorkiness of it.

There's a noise from the archway—a shuffling sound. We both turn to look, and Cass chuckles softly.

"Yeah, with Ben you can never be sure what you're going to get."

CHAPTER 25

———

As I kneel on the dirty floor, a figure comes into view, leaning on the wall in the shadows, panting with exertion.

"Finally decided to join us?" Cass says. "What took you so long?"

The figure steps into the light and stretches up tall, one hand on the small of his back, face racked with pain.

"Oh, I dunno. I guess you could say I got a bit hung up."

Sebastian winks at me.

"Hello there, Mega Mags."

"You!" Can't trust my voice. "But I don't—"

"*Understand*!" Cass whines. "Seb, Maggie here is having a really hard time getting up to speed. I thought we were giving them a fighting chance at sussing us out! I mean, you are eternally unconvincing, Sebastian, and I did my very best bad acting. "Boo-hoo! Poor old Steph, oh, I'm afraid of the killer! Ow-ee, I hurt my ankle!" She sticks her tongue out at me, but I'm barely looking at her, because I can't keep my eyes off Seb.

"I saw you at the weather station, you were…dead."

"Yeah." He smacks his lips. "Wasn't it delicious?"

"How did you…?" I gasp. "You were hanging."

"Yeah, you took the harness I was going to use, you dumb bitch!" He glares at me, before snorting with laughter. "Had to wrap the rope around myself a dozen times, it was sooo uncomfortable, and it left a bruise."

"Oh, I am so very sorry to hear that!" I spit at him.

"You were sorry when you thought I was dead." He turns to Cass in mock amazement. "Can you believe it? Mags, Ben, and the freak were totally *sad* about me. I was touched!" He gawps. "I almost climbed down! I never knew you loved me like that!"

"I don't," I snarl. "We were only coming back to the weather station because we were onto you!" I try to get up and move, but my legs buckle. Seb snorts with laughter, and Cass slaps a hand to her face.

"Ooh, the shuffling is *super* cringe. Please don't anymore, girl."

"Ant knew, Seb!" I glare at him. "It was Ant who worked it out, and we ran back there to take you down!"

"But you *didn't* take me down!" Seb crows, and then his face freezes. "Hold up. They didn't take me down. They're all like, 'Oh, save poor *Lawrence*. Let's get a rope, let's jump in the ravine and haul him up to see if he's still alive,' but no bugger checked on me!" He screams. "I could have been okay! If you'd bothered to read the book properly, you'd know Saint Seb didn't die from his wounds! You totally could have saved me, and it didn't even occur to you to try!"

"Guilty," I spit. "Why? Because Lawrence is worth twenty of you. Lawrence has friends, he always comes first. Wow, it must kill you to compare yourself to him every damn day. Did you drag him onto the fire because you couldn't stand to see his pretty face? Or"—I swing around to Cass—"the two of you together? Because we all know that this loser wouldn't have the strength on his own!"

"Och, babe." Seb clicks his tongue at me. "That speech is supposed to get me riled, or something?" He leans in close, grabs his groin. "Truth is, it hits me in the sweet spot!" He reaches out, I knock his hands away with a yell, but he still cops a feel as I fall to the floor, lobster-kicking him hard as I can in the shins. He squeals, his ankles taken out, and crashes beside me.

"Okay, *yawn*. Stop now, you two," Cass drones. "Time's a-ticking. We're on a schedule if we're going to set this happy little scene to frame your murder-suicide, Mags." She smiles at me. "'Cos that's where all this is heading, in case you didn't get the big, fat clues." She pokes me in the stomach. "Maggie couldn't live with being such a fugly bitch. She went on a killing spree, then she jumped off the ledge to offer her soul to the Lord. Praise Him!" She sighs at Seb, still on the floor, holding his shins. "Right, where's Ben? Like now, Sebastian!"

He nods to the archway, and Cass groans, walks through into the darkness, and after a few seconds, lets out a shout.

"What the hell, Seb? What did you do to him? Help me!"

Oh god, no. Let Ben be okay.

Seb gets up, shoots me a dirty look and I'm sure considers a kick, but thinks better of it as Cass screams for him again. She has a hold on him. How did they get to this? I thought she despised him. He disappears down the tunnel, and I look around, desperately. *What can I do? A weapon? Think!*

In my dreams, the cave was different every time. In reality, it's smaller, the roof way lower than I remember. Did the driver really keep us all in this one area? There's another way out, I know it, to the ledge. Which way? Got to hurry, they'll be back soon.

The candles flicker. *The breeze!*

I shut my eyes, turn slowly until I think I can feel it on my face, and look in that direction. Another wall. *But looks can be deceiving.* I caterpillar forward, worm and squirm across the floor, elbows raw, knees scraping, but the breeze is getting stronger, and as I get closer, I can see the posts that have been driven into the rock, and the wood that has been nailed there.

There were selfies, afterward. Kids came up here, stupid teens, camping out in our cave, snapping pics of the place that the driver fell from. So the National Parks boarded everything up.

With numb fingertips, I pull at the wooden boards. The first couple are nailed tight, but the third one I grasp comes away easily and falls to the floor with a clatter. *Oh god, the beautiful outside, the frigid air, the smell of coming snow—*

"Hey!"

Cass stomps up behind me.

"Not yet, hon." She crouches down beside me, strokes my hair. "You're quite correct, that's the way you're going out. But not before you've seen your sweetie, eh?"

I push her, slam her thighs with my tied hands, and she falls back onto her butt, slamming into the wooden boards, and another comes loose.

"Hey!" Her face twists, and I jump to my feet, bend to pick up the board with my tied hands, draw it back behind my shoulder like a bat and prepare to swing, hard—

"Drop it!"

Sebastian is standing across the other side of the cave. At first, I can't make sense of what he's holding—the light is dim, and my brain fried—but then I realize.

"Drop the plank and back off, Magnitude."

A crossbow is aimed at my chest.

"I'm a total amateur with this." Seb grins at me. "It keeps going off when I don't mean it. Ben knows all about that, don't ya?" He steps aside. Ben, lying on a sleeping mat.

"Oh god!" I drop the board, bunny-hop over to him, and Seb falls over laughing. But I don't care, all my attention is on Ben. His eyes are closed, skin pale and clammy, and his chest rises and falls way too rapidly. And I gasp as I see them: an arrow sticking out of his shoulder, another at the top of his thigh. "You shot him? You bastard!"

"Yeah, and those bolts are not the joke shop ones like I had!" Seb's holding his ribs, laughing. "Fooled you suckers, ha!"

"He's bleeding!" I swear at Seb, raise myself up, and face him. "So what now, you're going to shoot me too?" I smack my own chest. "Come on then!"

"Seb, I told you, no more bow!" Cass is on her feet and in Seb's face.

"It was a bolt out of the blue! Geddit?" Seb grins at her. "What, no thanks for saving you from being bashed in the head by She-Hulk?" He pouts. "Anyway. It was totally Ben's fault I shot him. He was too damn suspicious. You got him hot-wiring our wheels and then you ran out on me. What was I supposed to do?"

"You brought me up here in that car?" I cough, looking at Cass.

"Course she did," Seb says. "What was the alternative, carry you?" He blows a raspberry. "It was all in the plan. We left the car there to come up here—together!" He glares at her. "And she was supposed to kill Benny-boy first. But he was running circles looking for his annoying ex, and so it was left to me to pick up the pieces! As usual. But it was kind of worth it. Dude, you should have seen Ben's face when he saw me!"

"I got him out of the car just fine, it was your job to talk him into coming up here, like I messaged you!" shouts Cass. "Not to bloody shoot him!"

"I was aiming for his nob, so actually, he was lucky." Seb pulls a face. "What does the book say? Saint Ben died by sticks being pushed into his fleshy parts? That's as near as damn it."

"Sloppy." Cass tuts, strides over, and snatches the crossbow away from him. "But I guess we're improv-ing this one. Any torture available." She plucks a candle from the cluster at the wall and holds it over Ben, dripping hot wax on his face.

"Stop it!"

She sighs at me. "Don't like the kinky stuff? You're right. I should wait for divine inspiration." She holds the crossbow in one hand, lifts the candle with the other, closes her eyes, and tilts her face skyward, breathing in, deeply.

"Or we could kick the crap out of him. That works." Seb grins.

"To be fair, it does." Cass snaps out of her reverie, tosses the candle aside, and crouches beside me. "Because in our little scene here, Ben is the one who caused you to flip, Maggie. Ben left you, so you don't play by the rules. You mess him up the worst of them all. Maybe like a montage of your best bits? A couple arrows, a light stoning, a little fire play? "Magna Maggie! This time it's personal!" She springs up and kicks him in the head, and I scream.

"No! Leave him alone!" I lean over Ben protectively. "Just tell me one thing: in this lame-ass plan of yours, when do I get to kill you two?"

"Oh, you don't. We're traumatized, but TLDR, we make it." Cass nods sympathetically. "Obviously, for this to work, Sebastian does have to be shot, but I'll make it superficial."

"Yeah, with the joke shop arrows!" Seb cries.

"No, I do have to actually shoot you for real, or at least, 'Maggie' does." Cass air-quotes my name. "Fingerprints, after all. No one's going to believe you if you're entirely unharmed, but I don't have to finish you off."

"You finished me off the other night, alright." Seb licks his lips.

Cass looks at me, makes a distasteful face. "I'm sorry you had to hear that." She shakes her head at him. "Unacceptable, Sebastian." And then she shoots him. In the neck.

At first, I think it's a joke. Seb's eyes bulge and he staggers backward making funny, strangled noises, blood spurting out of his neck in an arc—too perfect, it looks faked, they must have rigged something—

"And one in the abs, yeah, I remember the pic." Cass calmly fires another bolt into his stomach and Seb grunts, doubles over, falls to the ground on his side. His legs bicycle, frantically, in a useless getaway, and he's rotating on his shoulder like he's pulling a twisted break move, or maybe he's a wind-up toy, desperately spinning and leaking dark liquid onto the dusty floor, until there's no more power, and nothing more to spill. Then he's still. The pool of black spreads my way, and I reach out a hand and touch it. It's sticky, warm. Only then do I know this is real.

"Urgh." Cass sighs. "I thought that would feel good. But it was just a little depressing." She crouches in front of Seb. "What's wrong with me?"

I roll onto my back, hands covering my face. *Can't deal, can't...*

Cass grasps my hand and presses it to the trigger of the crossbow, before I can react.

"Fingerprints." She breezes. "Now get up, Maggie. Final act. Don't fail me."

I'm close to the wall, where the candles are, the heat off them is threatening to singe my hair—*like poor Lawrence, don't think about it*. Flames, can I use them on Cass, somehow?

"Come on, Mags!" She's at the boarded wall now, pulling at the planks that have been loosened. "Time to fly!"

I wasn't the one asking for divine inspiration, but I think I got it. I hold my wrists to the flames and grit my teeth as the plastic ties heat up, melt, and snap. Quickly as I can, I bring my feet around and steady a flame under my ankles.

I'm free.

I don't remember how I stand up, or how I make it across the cave, but I'm running down the tunnel, madly, no light, just keep running. I'll get out somehow. Cass shrieks, and I can only assume she's after me, and that she'll have the crossbow.

Headlamp, it's in your jacket.

I fumble for the light, can't find it. *Maybe she emptied my pockets, maybe I did, can't remember*—and I slam into a wall.

Gulping like a fish, the wind knocked out of me, I steady myself. Nose hurts. Maybe it's broken, like Steph's. *I am not ending up like Steph!* I feel my way around a corner, *got to keep going*, and suddenly, there's a passage. My eyes are getting used to the dark. Don't dare sprint. I crouch low, hands out in front of me, creeping, fast. I strain to hear Cass behind me.

And then I see it, close to the ground. The light at the end of the tunnel.

I drop to my knees, stare into the hole. I swear I can see sky, just a patch of stars, the glow from the full moon, on the other side of the rocks.

It hits me. This is where I came before. The gap in the rocks where my friends abandoned me. The gap they all fit through, and I didn't. I was too big, I was caught tight, and he cornered me and pulled me out.

I pause, heart thumping, looking back the way I came. There is another option, the branch of the tunnel I didn't take, the entrance Cass must have dragged me in by. But that means retracing my steps, running toward the killer with the crossbow. I bend low, look through the gap again.

The authorities cleared the rockfalls because of us, and then those same authorities changed their minds and piled new rocks to discourage pesky tourists. Time passes, rocks crumble, land slides. I am much bigger now, but so is the gap. Maybe big enough to squeeze through.

I throw my jacket off, get on my belly, and edge backward into the hole. Don't want to go in headfirst, going to wait until the last second to feel that rock surround me. I shimmy on my front, pushing with my arms, reversing my body through that gap, and it's good, it's all clear, I have room to breathe, I can fit!

And then I see the light, strobing, looking for me.

Cass is still some way off, but she's coming this way, as if she knows I'm here. Of course she knows. Because Saint Margaret didn't die by taking her own life and jumping off a ledge. Saint Margaret was *pressed* to death.

Cass guessed that I would run. She'd know I had a fifty-fifty chance of picking the wrong tunnel. She'd be sure that if God was on her side, He'd send me this way. To fulfill my destiny, meet my end, crushed between these rocks.

Well, fuck that, I can still beat my fate.

I push and wriggle with all my might. She's getting closer. She's running now, and the light is bobbing up and down, and I can hear the footfall, and I stop myself from crying out. Because I'm nearly through, and so very scared, sweat slicking my neck, the rocks compressing my ribs, cracking my pelvis, there's no room to turn, no air to breathe. I'm stuck.

The light stops. Maybe, just maybe, she won't see the gap at the bottom. I might have been wrong. Perhaps she doesn't know about it?

But I'm not wrong.

"Maggie, you've got huge balls, I'll give you that." Cass titters. "Can't have been easy to weasel your way into that hole after what you went through before. Ben and Steph told me the whole, sorry tale. You're brave." She hunkers down. "Praise God, that He gave you the guts to come here. Sebastian altered the assignments on the school's computer system, but it was by the grace of God you all actually came. Doesn't He say to Trust in Him? But now I'm tired, aren't you?" She scratches her head. "It's been a lot. You must be exhausted! And you're stuck." She points the crossbow at me. "So be a saint, and come out of there, yeah?"

"You can't shoot me. It's not what happened to Margaret in

The Book of Saints." I gasp. She groans and rubs her face with one hand, the crossbow dipping in the other.

"I know that. But I think God would be just fine with you sacrificing yourself the same way you killed my dad. And it's certainly a lot easier for both of us."

"But I'll run! And you can't shoot me, because how could I shoot myself with a crossbow!" I pant at her. "It doesn't work with your grand plan!"

"Nope." Cass stands up. "A flaw, I'll give you that. But I think you'll come voluntarily." She begins to walk back down the tunnel. "Because Ben isn't dead yet. In fact, he's conscious, and in pain. But I'm not done. Saint Benjamin was tortured until he died, remember? I have bolts, I have knives, he'll be begging me to end him. I'll make sure he suffers worse than you can imagine, while you run down the hill like a coward!" Her voice is getting fainter. "And by the time anyone comes to rescue him, he'll be dead. You will have saved your precious skin. But your soul will be lost forever."

In the dark, I follow the sounds. Ben's hoarse, labored moans pull me in. A snatch of Cass speaking in sharp, quick whispers. And then the screaming starts, and I break into a run. I cannot do what he did to me, all those years ago. I won't abandon him.

In the main chamber of the cave, Ben is propped up against the wall, barely conscious, but he sees me, and the look of futility in his eyes nearly makes me turn and flee.

The arrow in his shoulder is broken off, half of it lying on the floor. Cass is standing over him, blood on her hands, that sly smile playing on her lips when she sees me. Silently, she rises, hands me *The Book of Saints*, and points to the way out to the ledge.

"No," Ben mouths, but no sound comes out, his head lolling against his shoulder. I ignore him, make my way to the break in the boards, and step outside, feeling the breeze cut through me, the relief of freezing air on my skin. I look up to the bloodred moon as I shuffle to the edge of the cliff, tears running down my face, my legs don't feel like they belong to me, but it doesn't matter anymore.

Cass is behind.

"Send a prayer up to Him. And then do it."

I pause at the edge. Don't look down. The mountain skyline is exquisite, layer on layer of shadow. No more mist now. It will be over quickly. I grip *The Book of Saints* tightly, bringing it up to my chest, and take a breath.

She gives me a few seconds. And then she gets impatient.

"Now! Jump!"

I can't.

"Do it, or I swear, I'll make him pay! I'll pluck out his eyeballs, I'll kick his teeth in, I'll slice him up!"

"No."

I lean back, only slightly, but enough for her to notice. That's the invitation. And she takes it, like they always do. She pushes into my back, and at the right second, I pivot, just like Dad taught me, and draw the foul. *The Book of Saints* connects with her jaw, and Cass steps out into nothingness.

There's a grab and a slam, both of us hitting the ledge hard. Cass dangles over the side, and my upper body slides because she's got me by a tight grip and she's not letting go. I'm slipping, digging toes into dirt, both hands trying to pry her fingers from me. I see the fear in her eyes, like the driver's eyes, but it's different, because there's hate, and I never saw hate in his eyes.

Gravity is winning. We're both going over, and suddenly there's a rib-breaking thud on top of me, and someone grasps a strong, wiry arm around my shoulders.

"I've got you, Mags," Ant cries in my ear.

"She's coming with me!" Cass screams, and just like I'd shown her to rappel, she bends her legs and pushes out from the rock face, hands linked around me, hauling me with her.

"No!" Ant reaches out and brings something down hard on Cass's face. Cass's cries out in pain, instinctively releasing a hand to clutch at the pen that is buried in her soft cheek. Her eyes flash with shock as her grip around me fails, and she falls, screaming.

Ant drags me up to the ledge. We lie in each other's arms, clinging for dear life, panting.

"Gotta check she definitely fell."

"She fell."

"Gotta check anyway. Because. You know."

Been there, done that. I nod, let them go. After a few seconds,

Ant comes back to me. We hug again, on the cold stone floor. I thank them incessantly, and then we cry, because we can.

"She said she'd poisoned you with the chocolate drink." I squeeze her tight. "I thought I'd lost you, you were passed out in the car, she said you were dead."

"Like anyone can hold me down for long." Ant grunts. "I puked that gross shit up."

"And … the pen?"

"The only weapon I could find." Ant sniffs. "Just as well I forgot to give it back to Cass after I left that note on the cairn."

I remember something.

"Oh my god, in the book. Saint Cassian. He was stabbed to death by his students. They used their pens."

"Overkill." Ant holds me, whispers in my ear, "Only takes one."

We cry some more, and when we're through, we dry our eyes, help each other up, and rescue the hell out of Ben.

CHAPTER 26

The lights are dim here. I can sense movement nearby, but my luck's held out so far. I run back into the shadows.

Quickly, think!

I shiver, pull my clothes around me. You'd think I'd be used to the cold after everything, but I cannot stop shaking. Maybe it's the adrenaline? It's not like I haven't had a truckload of that, either.

Get it together!

Got to find my way. I'm on my own.

And I know he's out there.

Okay. I steady my breathing. Timing is everything. Ahead, my way is blocked. There's a diversion I can take, but it's risky, a climb, and I don't know if my legs can make it. *Come on!* The longer I linger, the more in danger I am of being discovered.

Have to make a break for it. Run, and don't look back! Never look back!

I take a breath. A hand comes down on my shoulder.

"Maggie Atkins! What d'ye think you're doing out your bed, child?"

I turn, to see the eyes glaring at me. Big, brown eyes, brow furrowed. I'm doomed.

"So, are you going to hurry yourself back? Or do I have to carry you there?" The duty nurse—Janet—looks up at me, hand on hip. "Because Lord have mercy, I may be half your size, but don't you go thinking I can't scoop you up in these arms!"

"I need to see my dad!" I plead with her. "He's on Ward Twelve. You have to help me get up there!"

"I have to do no such thing." Nurse Janet's accent is the weirdest mix of Glasgow-meets-Jamaica, and she has double the fierce to match.

"Don't you want me to see him?"

"Now, did I say that?" She tuts, turns on her heel, and beckons me to follow. "You need to trust me, young lady." She glances over her shoulder and her eyes give the game away, with a fleeting twinkle. "Because that's not Santa Claus sitting at your bedside, waiting."

I run.

"No running on the ward!" Nurse Janet bellows after me.

They gave me my own room at the children's ward here at the hospital. Ben's down the hall somewhere. Ant was too, but they were discharged yesterday. And Dad is on the floor above. Although we've video called on my mum's phone, I want to see him I-R-frickin'-L, so badly, and we haven't been allowed.

Until now.

I spy him, through the wee window in my door. He's sitting, head in hands, foot tapping. He'll be turning stir crazy here. Same old Dad. Thinner, older, maybe. He has one of those cannulas in the back of his hand, like me. Sweats. White hospital slippers. He'll hate them.

I open the door, he looks up, and we rush to each other, hug.

"I'm so, so sorry," he says into my hair, his arms squeezing the breath out of me. "What you've been through…"

"I'm fine." I inhale his smell, like I did when I hugged Mum, drink it in, and feel home and safe. "I'm sorry too. I thought I'd abandoned you. But it's okay now. We've got each other back."

And we stay like that, for the longest time. There are tears, and words, from both of us, and they're almost all good.

Turns out, Dad's story is not so different from what we'd guessed. Cass was telling the truth when she said she'd spiked his tea with sleeping pills. He'd felt off halfway through the hike, but put it down to the early morning and the stress. When the boat escaped, he'd barreled down the river a mile or so past where Ant fell in before he was able to land, and he'd begun the hike back, but by that time, the water bottle pills were kicking in, big style. He basically passed out in a ditch.

They tested some of his water for sleepers, too. Yeah, Cass lied about that. She didn't put a couple of pills in his bottle. They're waiting for the results to come back, but they think it was more like a handful.

Dad doesn't remember much, but he's been told he probably

threw up a bunch of times, slept for who knows how long, and when he finally woke, he'd found himself in his sleeping bag. He tripped and hallucinated, and damn near died of exposure, but somewhere through all of his delirium, he'd managed to send a Save Our Souls message on his GPS navigator.

As soon as he could walk again, he came looking for us. Reached the shepherd's hut at the same time as Mountain Rescue.

They found Stephanie.

Word went out fast, the rescuers jumped on my note in the hut, which sent them on the wrong track—but then some eagle-eye spotted one of Ant's arrows, scrawled on the torn-out pages.

They discovered Lawrence in the ravine: conscious, burned and broken, but actually trying to crawl out. Apparently, it took three paramedics to strong-arm him onto the stretcher, because he thought his brother was hurt somewhere nearby and didn't want to leave him.

And lastly, they found us. My mother had got that text message after all, and the brave responders who were already out there, looking for us on the mountain, zeroed in on a new location. As Ant and I were coming out of the cave, dragging Ben on the sleeping mat and wondering how to hot-wire a car stuck halfway up a hill, we saw the lights. I think that's how it happened when I was six, too. It felt familiar, almost like I was expecting it.

I only stay in the hospital a couple more days. At home, my parents won't leave me alone, and for once, I like that. Mum has let Dad crash round at ours for a while. It's not going to be the Big Happy Ending for them or anything, but it's kind of nice to be all under the same roof again, even if it is temporary.

Ant hangs out a lot, and it helps in every way. If any other member of our group had woken in that vehicle and seen the cave up ahead, they'd have turned tail and run away. But not Ant. *I left you once*, they said. *I wasn't going to do it again.*

And we're going to be there for Lawrence, when he's back. His parents have taken him to some fancy clinic in Switzerland to get his face fixed. I'd be more worried about the inside of his head, but at least his folks have the money for all that. I have no idea how Lawrence will come to terms with what his brother did to him. Seb was led by Cass, there's no doubt of that, but there had to be so much hate inside of him already. Cass was merely the spark.

She was not everything she said she was. English, yes. An orphan brought up by her Italian grandparents in London, that was all true. They kicked her out, last year—shunted her north to a great-aunt. But she was not Maximilian Del Vento's long-lost daughter. Her mother died when she was very young, and it was true she never knew her father, but Del Vento wasn't him. Ant reckons Cass became obsessed, learned that this strange tale of a deluded, religious zealot who Pied Piper-ed a bunch of kids away to a mountain happened near where one of her distant relatives lived, and decided, for whatever screwed up reason, that he must be her dad. Ant says there are rumors that Strother High found a bunch of stuff on a school computer, a blog, searches, and timestamps for when Seb altered the assignments. I guess it will all come out, in time. To be honest, right now, I don't care. Don't want to give either of them oxygen. Don't want to be a bit-part player in someone else's twisted legacy.

And, I'm going back to school, next week. Me and Dad both. It might be too soon, but it's not like I'm going to process all this for a solid month or three at home and emerge fixed, brand new, and shiny. Might as well get back in the fight. But I'm going to take things one step at a time. And one of the first steps is Ben. He's had a longer spell in hospital than Ant and me, but eventually they discharged him. This I'll do alone.

When I arrive at his house, I let myself in, like I always used to, eager to get out of the cold night air, hurriedly turning my key in the lock, as I call out and kick my shoes off in the hallway. Getting dark in here. I flick the light on.

He's lying on the sofa in the lounge, surrounded by dirty plates and cups, crutches on the floor, console on his lap. His dad's at work, as usual. His mother stayed for a few days, but now she's gone back down south. Ben and I have messaged a bunch, but I kind of waited for her to go before I showed up in person.

"Hey." I smile brightly. "How's the leg?"

"Hey." He glances at me briefly, then returns to staring at the blank screen of the TV.

"Won't be long until you're on your feet again," I say awkwardly. Ben nods again, doesn't look at me.

"Been playing anything good?" I clear the armchair of car

magazines, sitting down, racking my brains for something normal to talk about that doesn't sound too desperate.

"Gone off gaming. And don't want phone or TV, because of the news."

"Yeah. I hear you."

"Been reduced to reading actual books."

"Good god, that it should come to this!" I laugh, shaking my head. "So, do you want a cup of tea?" I get up, go to swipe his used mug, but he grasps my hand.

"I'm so sorry I left you with him. I was six years old, Maggie. I was terrified."

My breathing stops, I start to pull back…but, *no*.

There's more than one kind of running away.

He looks so guilty; I hate that I have that effect on him, but it's not my fault, I know that now. I squeeze his hand before I release it, and sit down again.

"We were tiny kids, Ben. Anyone would have run."

"Not you! You came back for me!"

"But maybe only because I remembered how it felt." I search his eyes, wishing there was some way I could erase all the fear and grief and desperation I can see there. "*I know you*. You would have done the same for me if it had happened like that. Because, is it harder to live with being left, or being the one who does the leaving? We've both suffered. But that stops now." I reach out to touch his arm. "Thank you for saying sorry, tho'. I've wanted to hear that for years. And I absolutely forgive you, if that's what you need to hear. Of course I do."

"Thanks." Ben sniffs. "And for coming back. I'll never, ever be able to repay you, and Ant—"

"You did already." I lean forward. "You led us up that mountain when your heart was breaking. You found the weather station, and the parking lot, you made all the right decisions when everyone else was coming unglued. And you damn well very nearly drove us home."

"Yeah, bummed I didn't get to do that." He chuckles quietly. "Knight in shining, mud-splattered armor."

I take his hand again. "Ant and me, we'll tell Steph's folks everything you did. They should know how amazing you were, how much you cared."

He nods. We hold hands again for a few seconds, and then stop before it gets too awkward, or it feels like we should kiss or something. Because that's not what I want anymore. I let go and look at the palms of my hands. They're so scarred, but the marks will fade in time.

I make the tea. And afterward, I make an excuse that I have to leave, and it's true, I do.

"Friends forever, yeah?" I say, half mocking, as I stand in the doorway. He gets up from the sofa, kind of limps over and crosses his arms, in case I'm going to try and hug him or something. But I'm not.

"Friends…if you'll put up with me."

"I'd have to be a saint to do that."

He shakes his head, laughing softly. "Can't believe you went there."

"No filter." I smile at him. "Not anymore. Been way too careful for way too long. Let's see how that goes."

I leave him, begin the journey home. It's dark outside, but the streetlamps light my way as I walk tall, and far, far above, in the ink-black sky, a new moon is rising.

DON'T MISS ANOTHER
TWISTY THRILLER FROM
KIRSTY MCKAY IN
HAVE YOU SEEN MY SISTER?

CHAPTER 1

I didn't realize it at the time, but the first clue in my sister's disappearance was the shoes.

Running shoes, in oxblood red, Gaia's favorite color. She's always moaned about her ridiculously massive feet. She's tall, so that's the payoff for the endless legs, I guess. But then she'd scored these gorgeous blood red sneaks, and she loved them.

They were memorable shoes. So you would have thought I'd remember them that chilly morning on the day of her disappearance. I even tripped over the stupid things, nearly broke my neck. You might assume that later, I'd put two and two together. If her blood red sneakers were on our bedroom floor here at the holiday lodge, Gaia couldn't be out running.

But you'd be wrong to assume anything about me.

"Did Gaia stay at her place last night, or here?" Dad had asked, happily frying breakfast leftovers.

I frowned, thinking back to leaving the party. It was at

Gaia's friends' house, a last-night get-together for all the kids who work here at the ski resort, and I'd tagged along. When the party ended, I'd lingered by the open door awkwardly, trying to ignore a couple making out noisily on the deck while I waited. Gaia was inside on the stairs, deep in conversation with one of her work friends, her black, curly hair bouncing as she talked, brown eyes wide and expressive. I'd felt bad for interrupting, but also very ready to ditch and head home.

"Hey, Es, go. I'll be right behind you, okay?" Gaia eventually turned, gave me an encouraging—or possibly snarky—thumbs-up.

"It's snowing again. Didn't this place get the memo about spring?" I remember I shivered, glanced at my watch. It said 10:35 p.m., but the second hand wasn't moving. Dead. I had no idea how long we'd stayed at the party—that's one of my things, time is totally meaningless—but I suppose it must have been well into the early morning.

"Seriously, I'll be fine, Es," Gaia shouted. "I can cope with a lil' snow, ya know!"

True enough. She's been working the ski season at Moon Mountain Resort since last November. It's her gap year, before she goes to college here in America, and me and the folks are visiting from England. Gaia's majorly smart, a scholarship kid. I had to hope she'd be able to find her way back to the holiday lodge.

"I'll walk Gaia home." Craig appeared, blocking the view of my sister with his tall, muscled frame. He's American, a ski instructor, one of Gaia's friends. And, lucky fella, he'd been my teacher on the slopes this past week. I'm so horrible at skiing I think I nearly broke him. Not that I feel guilty about it; he's kind of the worst.

"Skedaddle, Esme. I'm gonna close this door, we're freezing in here." The door shut in my face. *Yep, the worst.*

So earlier today at breakfast, when Dad asked me if Gaia had slept here at the lodge last night, I assumed yes. I'd gone straight to sleep, didn't see her come in. But she said she would follow me home, so that's what must have happened.

"Gaia came back a bit after me." I glanced at Dad over my mug of black tea. "Must be out now, running off her hangover."

Dad grunted, and like that, any nagging doubt about her not being here was gone. If I'd only thought about the running shoes...

But I didn't. I sat shoveling Dad's vegan lentil surprise into my mouth at the breakfast table, taking in the views of Moon Mountain for the last time. It's stunning; the remains of patchy snow glistening on the slopes, framed by the dark, jagged silhouette of pine tree woods on either side. We've never had a holiday like this before. Big stretch for the parents, money-wise, but we wangled the luxury lodge for free and it's been worth it to see Gaia. Not that we've seen as much of her as I would have liked—she's been working, after all.

"Esme, did I hear you say you walked back on your own last night?" Ma swooped into the kitchen, her arms full of clothes. I was tempted to wind her up, but didn't have the energy.

"Addy walked me. She was staying over at her parents' lodge."

That placated her. My sister and Addy Addison have been friends since forever, and Addy's a sweetheart. She's also the reason we got the fancy accommodation free; her uncle owns the resort. She and Gaia scored jobs together—my sis can work here legally because her birth dad was American—and Addy's family is mega rich, so nobody ever tells them no.

"As long as you weren't wandering around alone." Ma's voice had an edge; she's way overprotective of me. That's one thing Addy and I have in common. In my case, it might be justified, but Addy's eighteen and sensible and her dad's *still* all up in her business. God knows what he'll be like when she starts college and he can't keep tabs on her. I think one of the reasons I like Addy is that she doesn't seem tainted by the parental interference. Wish I could pull that off.

"Aw, cut Es some slack," Dad stuffed the rest of his breakfast into his mouth before Ma could whip the plate away. "She's sixteen, after all."

"Not yet she isn't." Ever the stickler for accuracy; my birthday's in a few days' time. "And she's not a *normal* sixteen."

"Julia!" Dad almost spat his sausage out.

"She knows I don't mean it like that, don't you, Es?" Ma bent in for the forehead kiss.

I do know. What she meant was: I'm not super-together like she is, like my sister is. What Dad thought she meant was: I have dyspraxia.

If you haven't heard of dyspraxia, fair. Neither had I until I got diagnosed four years ago. Sounds way worse than it is. Officially, it means I have problems "placing myself within time and space." That sounds kind of sci-fi, but what it boils down to is that I get extra time on tests because I have zero sense of how many minutes have passed. And there's the clumsy: I drop things, bump into stuff. Don't know left from right, can't do directions. Sometimes I talk inappropriately loudly, sometimes I mumble; that's one of Ma's particular faves. Dad makes out he's chill about the dyspraxia, but Ma gets on my case.

"Pack your things when you've finished. And Gaia's too. I don't want us having a last-minute rush, okay?"

I didn't answer her, but it wasn't really a question. Ma runs a tight ship. She'd planned for us to all leave Moon Mountain together and drive to Boston for a final night with Gaia, before we leave my sis and take the sad flight back to London.

So I packed, right after breakfast, to keep Ma sweet. Maybe I didn't realize about Gaia's shoes—even as I stuffed them into a gym bag—because my brain works different than other people's. Or maybe anyone would have done the same. Outside, the sun was bright and the day dripped away like the snow off the roof of our lodge as I packed. All done, I reclined in the big armchair by the fire, finishing the final pages of a book. Dad appeared, fresh from cramming luggage into the car.

"Wasn't Gaia supposed to be saying goodbye to her friends today? At a brunch?"

"Think someone mentioned that last night, yeah."

"Should be over by now." Dad frowned. "She can't still be running around the resort. Text her, will you?"

"No phone."

Dad sighs, remembering how I'd killed my latest phone. Death by ski lift on the third day of the vacation. He should be grateful it wasn't me plunging from the chair, could have totally happened.

"Use mine." He reached into his back pocket, knew I wouldn't make the catch, and carefully placed the phone in my hands. "Ask her when she's coming back. Your mother's gone to check out; she wants to leave on time."

So I texted.

———

Gaia never answered that text I sent from Dad's phone, and she didn't come back. We ate a sandwich, I finished my book and wandered out to the deck. It was still cold, but the sun is so much stronger here than at home. Dad was sitting in an Adirondack chair, head back and eyes closed like it was summer.

"Almost 3:00 p.m.," he croaked at me. "Your mother is not going to be pleased."

Ma was striding quickly up the lane, her mouth set, cheeks flushed with the effort. Even for her, it was quite a pace, walking as fast as possible without actually running.

"Jim!" she called as she got closer. "Jim!" There was a catch to her voice that made Dad open his eyes. "Gaia wasn't at the brunch."

"No?" Dad stood up and walked slowly down the steps. "Couldn't face the pancakes, eh?"

"Jim," Ma grabbed Dad's arm. "Her friends haven't seen her since last night. Nobody knows where she is." Her face flickered. "Gaia *is gone*."

ACKNOWLEDGMENTS

Thank you to all at Sourcebooks who have helped me deliver this story, which, although entirely fictional, has led me on a very personal journey through the mountains. All thanks to my editors, Gabbi Calabrese and Annie Berger, for their clarity, inspiration, and patience. And also for their bravery, because bravery is so very important these days.

To my lovely, wise agent, Veronique Baxter, and all at David Higham Associates for believing in me, then and now. You're the best.

All my love to my rock, John, for tireless support and provision of sustenance for body and soul; to Didi, for the soccer therapy; to my idols, Xanthe and Louie, for the playlists; and to Tilly, for keeping me in the moment.

Finally, to my readers. Thank you with all my heart. Please keep strong, keep reading, and keep being the good in the world.

ABOUT THE AUTHOR

Kirsty McKay is a former actor who was born in the UK but spent many wicked awesome years in Boston, MA. She now lives in the hills of Northumberland, England, with her family, beloved muckhound, and a lot of bad weather. She is the author of *The Assassin Game* and *Have You Seen My Sister?*

Follow @kirkybean.bsky.social, Instagram @thekirstymckay, and TikTok @kirkybean.

sourcebooks
fire

Home of the hottest trends in YA!

Visit us online and
sign up for our newsletter at
FIREreads.com

....

Follow
@sourcebooksfire
online